Dark Network
James McCrone

This is a work of fiction. All characters, organizations and
events portrayed here are either products of the author's
imagination or used fictitiously. Anyone seeing a resemblance
to actual persons, living or dead, is paying the author an
extravagant compliment.

Library of Congress Control Number: 2017909728

ISBN—978-0-692-79784-6 (paperback)
ISBN—978-0-999-13770-3 (ebook)

Cover Art Design, Daniela Medina

DARK NETWORK

James McCrone

An Imogen Trager Novel

As always, for Lisa

I am deeply grateful to the following people during the preparation of this book for their support, insight, and good sense: Jim McCue, editor; my family—Lisa, Fiona, Annie and Jake, Don & Carole, Elmer & Lois; Judy Aks, Maura Mahoney, Marga Rose Hancock & Debra A McClane

To all of you, thank you.

"Virtue is more to be feared than vice, because its excesses are not subject to the regulation of conscience."

— Adam Smith

1

It was daytime. She knew that much. Pale light filtered in from the high arrow-slit windows on the wall behind her, scattered and reflected about the room by the two-way mirror on the wall facing her, a cold yellow light in a cold yellow room. Agent Imogen Trager sat quietly at a metal table facing her interrogator.

Though she tried to appear alert and sharp, she was tired. Tired of the questions, the repetition, the obvious way they tried to get her to implicate herself or betray herself through contradiction. What had she known, when had she known it; what did she do with the information, whom had she told? Her fears about Duncan Calder and Doug Pollack threatened to undermine her brave exterior.

"Well, what does Pollack say?" she had asked in exasperation.

"At the moment, Agent Trager, Assistant Director Pollack is in a medically induced coma. We may never hear from him. I need to hear it from you."

Imogen wondered if it was true, wondered if Doug was being subjected to the same kind interrogation as she was.

"You say you suspected Agent Kurtz. When did you begin to suspect him? What were your clues?" Agent Neil Brody flipped to a new page on his yellow pad and sat back.

Imogen had grown to hate Brody in the short time they had spent together. Sporting fashionable lace-up shoes, a well-tailored, expensive midnight blue suit, he asked questions not like an investigator following information, but like an HR manager entering responses into printed boxes. He sat urbanely at an angle to the table, legs crossed, hands folded in his lap. Occasionally, he would reach languidly for the pen and jot something down, the notepad at arm's length.

"As I believe I said before," Imogen began with elaborate patience, "we did not suspect Kurtz at all—until he started shooting at us."

"And why do you think that was?"

"He was terminating the only people who really knew what was going on—me, Calder and Pollack."

"I mean, why didn't you suspect him? You say the whole department was dirty."

"I believe I said that I worried about who to trust. The operation to turn the Electors was operating at a national level, my phone at the Bureau had been bugged."

"Yes, but why trust him? Was your judgment impaired by your past relationship with Kurtz?"

Imogen sighed as she thought, "So, we're on to that now." It had taken long enough.

* * *

Springfield, Illinois

In the broad hallway in front of the Governor's office inside the Capitol building, the US Attorney, the Illinois Governor and the Illinois Attorney General were trying to hold a joint press conference. Their responses to questions—and the questions themselves—were difficult to hear, because as each spoke, a crowd of protesters, convinced the election results in the state had been sabotaged, booed and jeered from the far end.

"At our behest," the Governor began amid shouts of derision and whistling, "and working with our own Illinois Attorney General's office, the Public Integrity office at the Justice Department has thoroughly reviewed the results. And after extensive . . ." As the jeering grew louder, he repeated, "after extensive review and re-review . . ."

2

A chorus of booing from the crowd gathered in the hallway and along the stairs gave way to chants of "Fix! Fix! Fix!" The governor, no stranger to potent politics, nevertheless blinked into the cameras. He exchanged an amazed look with his Attorney General, who looked at the US Attorney.

* * *

Chicago, Illinois

Two hundred miles to the north, on Chicago's South Side, a twelve-year-old boy was accompanying his small twin brothers as they walked home from school. One of the twins pointed to something sprawled in among the ivy at the back of a fenced-in vacant lot at Justine and West 59th. "Is that a man?" he asked.

The elder brother told them to wait. He would check. In the fading December light, he scaled the six-foot chain link fence quickly and dropped down on the other side. "Stay there," he said again to the twins from his side of the fence.

He pulled out his phone and switched on the flashlight as he walked cautiously toward where vines had grown over and through the fence at the back. Next to the lot was another empty lot, and next to that, an abandoned building; behind, an alley and another abandoned building. Nothing moved. There was no sound but the small twins in their big coats kicking at the dirt covering a depression in the pavement. As he moved closer, he could see what looked like an arm, reaching out imploringly across the grass. He stopped and crouched down a few feet from the outstretched fingertips and aimed the light into the underbrush. "Mister?" he said.

He looked over his shoulder to check again on his brothers. "Is he dead?" one of them called out. The boy shone his light on the hand, then traveled along the arm until it reached the man's face, which was spattered in freshly coagulated blood. "Mister?" he called again, staring into the corpse's open eyes. He pushed aside some of the vines for a better look.

3

The dead man had been shot through the neck and in the head. The boy stood up abruptly. He dialed 911.

"There's a dead man at the back of the fenced lot at 59th and Justine," he said to the dispatcher. "Me and my brothers found the body. He's been shot."

He hung up, crouched down again and took a picture for Instagram, then ran back to his brothers. He scaled the fence again and dropped to the ground in front of them. He knelt down, zipped up the coat of one twin a bit tighter and helped the other get one of his mittens back on. He looked toward the back of the lot, now shrouded in darkness. "All right," he said to them, "let's get home."

* * *

Salem, Oregon

The reporters gathered in the Governor's wood-paneled Ceremonial Office to hear her official reassurances were distracted by a large crowd outside. The crowd was protesting her defense of the Democratic party's process for replacing Don Meadows as an Elector, following his death in mysterious circumstances earlier in the month.

"Shame, shame!" they shouted, until through the magic of social media, the Salem chorus harmonized with their brothers and sisters in Illinois. "Fix! Fix! Fix!"

The Governor looked past the reporters. The passion outside had caught her off guard.

* * *

Wichita, Kansas

The man on the couch had been watching a mute discussion. He turned on the sound.

". . . contentious, unpredictable presidential election in American history continues to astonish," the anchor was

4

saying. "Where does the country go from here? Our correspondent, Hugh Salter, begins with some background."

"It's been an unprecedented election, one that has raised Constitutional questions that will endure for either party's new administration," Salter began.

"An unpredictable and acrimonious primary season was only a hint of the rancor that was to come. James Christopher ran what some called a dismayingly incoherent campaign. But his acceptance of the establishment's choice as his running mate—former Massachusetts Governor, Bob Moore—gave a vital boost to his campaign bid by calming key donors and party stalwarts.

"Revelations, mere weeks ahead of the vote, about possible donor misdeeds and leaked medical documents indicating that Diane Redmond may have suffered a Transient Ischemic Attack in the past clearly hurt her numbers, giving a boost to Christopher's campaign.

"Polls indicated the nation was evenly split on the eve of the election, but it was the Democratic challenger, Diane Redmond, who was declared the winner late the following day, having secured a slim lead and the requisite absolute majority of Electoral College votes—271 to 267," he said over visuals of the victory rally and its obligatory balloon drop, Redmond behaving spontaneously at last as she congratulated the crowds on their congratulations.

"But immediately there were charges of voting fraud in Illinois. Then, on December 19, came the switched votes in Minnesota, New Hampshire and Colorado, with the Faithless Electors in those three states throwing the election to Christopher," the reporter intoned over pictures of Faithless Electors hiding their faces as they climbed into cars amid lightning storms of press photographers.

"Most shocking of all, an alleged rogue FBI agent, Thomas Kurtz, was shot dead in a gun battle involving Secret Service agents in the parking garage of the Eisenhower Executive Building, next to the White House. FBI Assistant Director Douglas Pollack and a witness, Professor Duncan Calder, were also wounded.

"Following those events, FBI Agent Imogen Trager revealed that the switched votes themselves may have been tainted, bought or coerced as part of a nationwide scheme— allegations that appeared to be proved true when the three Faithless Electors were murdered the same day by as-yet unknown assailants.

"The nation is in its third day of a kind of limbo; and everything remains undecided at the very least until January sixth, when the new 115th Congress convenes. Protests just today, in Illinois and Oregon, underscore how fractured and contentious the mood is. The FBI, stung by revelations that one of their own may have been a conspirator, has yet to make public what, if anything, they know. Already, both campaigns are digging in—"

The man on the couch muted the television again and picked up his phone. He dialed. "Are you watching CNN?" he asked. "This is perfect for us. Keep up the media drip about Illinois; maybe even start with this guy Salter," he gestured at the television. "How you do it is your call, but keep it alive." He listened for a moment. "Right. Destroy that agent . . . the girl . . . her credibility, her reputation. Then kill her."

He listened again, nodding. "You have our full support." He listened again. "You're welcome. Not easy, but if we hold our nerve and do what's necessary, it'll happen." Another pause to listen. "Yes, the House vote is key, too. Anything else? This is the last time you and I will speak before Inauguration Day. You've got one month." He hung up.

* * *

Imogen stared at the two-way glass across from her. She wondered who was behind it—if anyone. Who had been watching the interrogation? What was happening?

The gun battle had only been three days ago, but already the events of the past week felt like a different lifetime. How was Duncan doing? Was Brody telling the truth about Pollack being in a coma? She shuddered inwardly as she saw again the

6

grisly scene—Tom Kurtz dead, Duncan fading, Pollack sinking against the doorframe. As the Secret Service agents ushered her through the door that led to the White House, she had tried to look back, but the men shielding her had blocked the sightline.

She wondered if that would be the last memory she'd have of them—not of their faces, not who they were, but thick, sticky blood pooling on the rough concrete floor, the splatters along the wall and on the stairs, the gunfire still reverberating—a high-pitched tinnitus ring muffling all other sound.

"You and Agent Kurtz were intimate," said Brody, breaking into her reverie.

"Yes," said Imogen, looping a strand of red hair behind her ear, glad no one had brought up her relationship with Calder yet.

"When and for how long?"

"About two years ago, for about six weeks."

"Did you know then about Kurtz's alleged involvement with this electoral conspiracy?" he asked.

"No."

"Was that the reason for your separation? Was knowing that you would be reprimanded for fraternization the reason you didn't come forward?"

"No," she said. "it just ended. I ended it." If the investigation into who was behind the plot was progressing, Imogen felt certain it wasn't being done by Brody, a time-serving idiot with only pre-approved opinions.

"There's something you're not telling me."

"Agent Brody, after two days in here together I don't think there's anything I haven't told you." Had he thought this was where he could begin breaking her down, she wondered. Did he expect her to erupt in tears?

Brody scooted his chair forward and leaned on the table, his face close to hers. "Then tell me again." He stared at her flatly, impassive, his menacing witlessness looming at her.

Imogen stared back. She had never got the hang of that interrogation technique in training, she thought. Maybe as a result she would never be a proper field agent. But if Brody's job was just dutifully checking boxes, Imogen had questions of her own.

"One," she began, "Haven't you had enough time? After 48 hours you've had ample time to check my story against the facts as they are now known.

"Two, if there's a trail to follow, it's getting colder by the hour—all of our leads are dead. What, if anything, is the Bureau doing? We have the three dead Faithless Electors, killed by the conspirators—presumably to keep them from talking. We have the seven other dead Electors prior to that who were killed presumably because they refused to switch their votes, two assassins dead in the stairwell at Doug Novaczeck's building. How many more corpses do you need?

"Three, this must be bigger than Tom Kurtz, because he was dead before the three Faithless Electors were killed, so he couldn't have given the order. How were they getting their instructions? Who's pulling the strings? How do they get paid? Is there a known-associates file begun on anyone?"

Brody stared at her coolly, content to let her tirade exhaust itself.

"Four," she continued, her anger growing, "what groundwork has been done to ascertain the movements of the dead conspirators? Can you place any of them at any of the places where one of the murders occurred?

"And Five: until you establish a better understanding of the conspiracy network, you could still have dirty agents, so that even if you're doing some of the things I've outlined, you may not be able to trust the intelligence you're getting. In all of this, I'm the only one who is obviously—demonstrably—not involved. The nation is being ripped apart, but I have to sit here and answer questions about who I fucked?"

Brody continued to sit across from her, his bland expression betraying nothing. The door to the interrogation room opened. Brody stood up. Imogen looked at him, wondered if she should stand up, too.

A compact, powerfully built man, slightly shorter than Imogen, at five foot, six inches, walked in; Brody, long and lean in his elegant suit, towered over him. The newcomer held out his hand and Brody dutifully handed over the yellow pad.

"Thank you, Agent Brody." He turned to Imogen.

"I'm Don Weir," he said, holding his hand out now to her. Brody walked quietly out of the room and pulled the door closed. "I'm the acting executive assistant director until—as we all hope he will be—Doug Pollack is back on the job."

Imogen stood up and shook his hand. "How is he?" she asked.

"Not good. He's in a medically induced coma. It's amazing he's still alive, and he may well lose his left arm."

"My God."

"Half an inch to his right, or a slightly different trajectory for the bullet and we would not be here right now. Pollack would be dead. You and Professor Calder would be dead and Kurtz would be lauded as some kind of hero."

"But they think Pollack will pull through?"

"The doctors say they're hopeful, but that's all they'll give us." He paused. "You understand why we needed to do all this." He gestured with the notepad at the room.

"Of course," said Imogen. "And Duncan . . .? Professor Calder? How is he?"

"He's not out of the woods yet, either, but they think he'll make it."

Imogen smiled, relieved.

"Sit down, please," said Weir. He drew up the chair Brody had been using and sat down. In the room's cold light, his scalp shone through his fair hair and tight crew cut making him appear almost bald. His neck and torso were strong, bull-like. The seams in his jacket puckered with the effort of containing his beefy arms.

"You are correct," he began, "you are someone I know I can trust. Brody's been thorough. That's why we're letting you out of here a little later today. Do you know the name Frank Trebor?"

"No. Should I?"

"Allen Covington?"

"No. Who are they?"

"I was hoping, given your relationship with Kurtz that he might have mentioned them, or that you saw them?"

"No, I'm sorry."

"Have you ever heard of the Jefferson Tigers?"

"That club he was in at Princeton?"

"You know about it?" asked Weir, brightening.

"Only that much. There was a picture in his apartment of him and some of the guys—twelve, maybe fifteen years ago," said Imogen. "They looked pretty drunk."

"Two of the men in that photo were Frank Trebor and Allen Covington—the two who killed Novaczeck and tried to kill Calder. I know you're eager to get out there, but we need to understand one another. After what you've been through, it would be understandable for you to have strong emotions about what's happened. The FBI—and your efforts particularly—foiled a plot to steal the presidency. The danger to the nation is over. Things are still a hell of a mess out there, but that's the political side. It's not our business or our job. Our imperative now is to find out who killed those Electors and tie this thing off."

"Very good," said Imogen, feeling that maybe she should show she could knuckle down when necessary.

"Whoever committed these murders has everything sewn up tight, and the investigation is going to take time and patience. Justice is putting every resource it has behind our efforts, and somewhere we'll find a loose thread we can start pulling at. I have a team of forensic accountants from Treasury working on untangling Kurtz, Trebor and Covington's payment network, and we have field agents spread out across the country going through the police files on the seven dead Electors and the three Faithless Electors. We'll find something," he asserted confidently, though perhaps more for his own benefit than hers.

The FBI had been caught in the scornful, wide-eyed gaze of the public. Don Weir was feeling the pressure. He did not misspeak when he said he hoped Pollack would soon be back on the job, and he could return to the relative obscurity of organized crime investigations, where he had made his reputation. Nor was he the only one stunned by the events of the past month. The Attorney General, as a political appointee, had been contemplating what was possibly her final month on the job, depending on which candidate ultimately won. She was now no longer considering what she would do or where she would go next, but how she would survive.

The Bureau's former institutional and bureaucratic allies were suddenly reticent to offer assistance, and public hearings with the Judicial Oversight Committee were scheduled. Worse than the recalcitrance of supporters was the sharp chill that revelations of Kurtz's treachery had sent through the whole department. Internal squabbles, turf wars and minor ideological differences within the Bureau, while regrettable, were normal, and by their very nature were limited in scope.

In the new normal, though, FBI agents found themselves obliged to question the trustworthiness of their colleagues. In turn, this new institutional reality was ossifying the ideological camps both outside and within. For that reason, Weir brought much of his own team, people he hoped he could trust, when he was made acting executive assistant director. Adding Trager, and her analyst background, as he said to the Director, would round out the skill sets of his core team.

"In many ways you're the face of this investigation, Trager. You exposed the Faithless Elector plot—on TV, standing next to the president and the AG. You've been cautious and had good instincts from the beginning. We need that now. I want you to begin by analyzing Kurtz's files and movements—see if we missed anything. Then I want you to focus on his university days at Princeton and work chronologically, closing the circle . . . I hope."

"Okay," said Imogen. "So, I'll get to work on establishing connections to pursue? I was thinking that overall we could do a network analysis of who's talking to whom, overlay it with—"

Weir held up his hand. "Unfortunately, Kurtz knew a lot about FBI link analysis, and we can't even establish a hub. No emails, at least none we can find. If they were using dead drops or face-to-face, we didn't know to be watching them.

11

No obvious regularity, either. Frankly, there's more pattern in a Jackson Pollock. The fact that it's all been very low-tech is probably how they stayed off our radar in the first place. And it's why finding them now is turning out to be so difficult— particularly since they've all probably gone into hiding."

"That's interesting," she said. "Because good research training helps you distinguish real patterns from seeming patterns."

"Training such as you've had." He looked at her flatly.

Imogen stared back, wondering, is he asking a question?

"Yes," she said. "It teaches you how to uncover patterns that are hard to see, and to subject patterns you do see to scrutiny so you don't make spurious connections."

Weir stared a little longer. Finally, he said: "You will be working alongside Special Agent-in-Charge, Amanda Vega. She's walking point on all this, overseeing the field agents and you. The Treasury agent reports directly to me. All your information goes through Agent Vega. Understood?"

"Yes, sir."

"I need you focused, Agent Trager. And I need to know you're working to the task. I've got agents all over the country," he said again, "following clues, going over police reports, establishing leads. Something from one of those spheres of inquiry—or multiple ones—will lead us to the conspirators." He sounded as though he was reassuring himself, as much as briefing her, and his jargon was beginning to irritate her. "The job of the group you've been detailed to is to go over Kurtz's movements, his connections to see if you can tease out anything there.

"As far as patterns and connections are concerned, everyone who works here has received pretty much the same training Tom had. He seems to have anticipated everything we're going to do and covered his tracks well. We're getting nowhere with that line of investigation."

Weir paused. Imogen was about to say something, but he cut her off: "Agent Trager, you're not properly a field agent, you're not ex-military. You're a wonk who gets things done. I'm going out on a limb here bringing you in at all after your affair with Kurtz and going to the press the way you did. But I requested you specifically because I'm betting on you to think of something Tom wouldn't have, to find the back door he left unlocked. Frankly, I'm hoping your past relationship—inappropriate though it was—will be a help in that endeavor. And," he added, "we know there's no way you're involved in any of this."

"Understood."

"Amanda Vega will be collating and examining the field notes and evidence from all of you, looking for matches and opening new lines of inquiry—anything that might lead us to these killers."

"So we're not even going to look for the conspirators?" Imogen asked. She could hear the annoyance in her own voice despite efforts to disguise it.

"The killers are the conspirators, Agent Trager. We're scouring the country. If we can find the triggermen, we can charge them and show something for our efforts. Then, we go up the food chain and find out who gave the order. Despite your recent experience, that is how investigations are conducted. Is that clear?"

"Yes, sir. Of course."

"Fine. You've done a good job, Agent Trager, under difficult circumstances, and now I need to see your best."

"I understand, sir," she said. And there's no need to patronize me, she thought.

Weir paused, staring intently at Brody's yellow pad. Between the jotted sentences were a series of doodles. Imogen could see them, and almost smirked as she noted that Brody had drawn a series of boxes.

When Weir looked up, he fixed his gaze on Imogen, his face betraying some inner working or turmoil. "One last thing," he began. "Something more. There is one area where I would like you to tread very carefully." He paused and glanced toward the door.

"As you pointed out, we can't be entirely sure whom to trust. I'm confident that Kurtz was the only agent betraying us. But I don't want to be stupid. I'm using field agents from

13

all over the country to chase down leads, but I don't know everyone, so we're keeping the big picture close.

"It's unlikely—but possible—that there's a Kurtz-mole in every field office, and I don't want the bad guys to know how much, or how little, we really know. Kurtz's mentor here at the Bureau was an agent named Andrew Colls, now retired. He's also a Princeton alum, one of the founding members of the Jefferson Tigers. He's been interviewed, of course, and we've looked into his background and recent activities— everyone with ties to Kurtz has. He's clean. But I'm not entirely satisfied Colls is in the clear.

"I don't have enough to open an investigation on him," Weir continued, "but as far as I'm concerned—and I may be alone in this—Colls remains a question mark. Let's be frank, Kurtz was his guy. However: until and unless we have something more to go on, we won't question a respected, retired FBI Agent."

"I know who he is," said Imogen, nodding. "If he's involved, talking to him again would risk alerting him before you had good data or evidence."

"Exactly. And . . ." Weir looked down at the pad again. "And, Agent Vega is also something of a Colls protégé. She's worked for me for years, and I've never had reason to question her judgment or loyalty. But we can't afford to be foolish. She knows nothing about the line of inquiry we are currently discussing, and she should not become aware of it. If you begin to see things pointing to Colls, you are to bring them directly to me."

"Very good, sir," said Imogen. As Weir had spoken about the investigation and its various facets, she had shaken off her frustration at being given such menial work. She found herself looking forward to being mission-focused, working with the good guys against the bad guys, whatever and however small the role. But now, the mixture of uncertainty and dread she thought she had left behind her in that blood-soaked parking garage began rising within her. She didn't feel like an investigator but like a spy herself. To her colleagues, her perspective would be valuable though probably unwelcome. And as a relative outsider, she knew, she was also someone who could be hung out to dry.

"We understand each other?"

"Completely," said Imogen, looking him in the eyes. Except you don't understand the first thing about me, she thought.

"Excellent. This is important work. You're perfectly placed to do it, and I know your skills will be invaluable."

"Thank you."

"And, Agent Trager: if you go to the papers like you did with the Faithless Elector plot or talk to anyone but me about what you find, I will find a way to put you in jail for as long as the law allows."

* * *

New York City

At a rally outside her re-opened campaign headquarters in New York City, Diane Redmond's new campaign manager was holding forth: "This plot clearly points back to the Christopher campaign. We call on the Justice Department to do their job. The will of the people is in jeopardy. This is not politics, it's murder. My predecessor, my friend, Jim Novaczeck, was murdered as part of this Faithless Elector plot.

"The FBI has been investigating for more than a week and it still won't—or can't—definitively say who these killers were, whether they were acting alone, or as part of a larger conspiracy. People will say this is personal to me; and it is, obviously. But it's also personal to every voter in this country. Someone was prepared to kill to steal this election from the American people. And all evidence points to Christopher."

* * *

Bethesda, Maryland

Back in the DC area, at a downtown bar, it was like a meeting of two old friends. Special Agent Andrew Colls, Rtd., navigated the after-work crowd and deposited the drinks on the table. "This ought to help," he said with a smile of encouragement.

"Thanks very much," said his drinking companion, FBI Agent Phil Jezek, as he reached carefully for his glass. "I'll get the next round."

Colls was at ease, dignified, as befitted his status. His head of iron grey hair, strong chin and chiseled, hawk features gave him a patrician bearing. He had the comfortable air of a man accustomed to people doing things for him without his asking. There was also something about the grim set of his mouth—a latent, sullen streak, quick to anger, belying the marble façade.

Jezek, very much the junior, tried to look as if he was relaxed, enjoying himself, but being in this presence clearly had him awed. Colls, after all, had been briefed by secretaries of defense, spoken personally to presidents.

Jezek sat straight up, smiling eagerly and too much. He kept his suit jacket on, though Colls had shrugged off his North Face winter coat before going to the bar. Jezek touched his tie knot whenever he was about to speak, as though worried that it might have come loose—or that he was about to be garroted.

Though 38 years old, Jezek looked much younger. His build was slight, and his boyish face was framed by short, curly dark hair. He was affable, friendly and generally well liked, despite what seemed an innate ability to ingratiate himself with superiors. Perhaps because of his youthful appearance, superiors were inclined to wink at or forgive his blunders and striving, as they might have a younger man. His ability to curry favor drew him into the orbit of great and important investigations, but left him picking up lesser assignments within them. Never Special Agent in Charge, his career was cyclically poised to take off, but never quite did so.

"I'm wondering how you are," said Colls. "Things must be crazy at the Bureau."

"That's for sure. But I'm fine. Thank you for asking."

"I'm worried about the divisiveness I see there. Too much self-examination, not enough good casework. You know they actually called me in for a debrief." He leaned back in his chair and took a drink, letting that statement sink in.

"You?" asked Jezek, incredulous.

"I'm guessing it was anyone who had been close with Kurtz."

"Yes, but you of all people."

"Makes sense," Colls allowed. "Dot all the i's, cross all the t's. It was voluntary, of course. I may be retired, but I care deeply about the mission and reputation of the Bureau."

"No one knows more about it than you."

"Thank you," said Colls. "I went, of course. Seemed like my duty to respond. The least I could do. If I'm honest, it was kind of nice to be back at Headquarters."

"I'll bet."

"But being there also made me worry a bit. I wonder, are they still navel-gazing, looking for sleeper cells?"

"Well, after Kurtz, you can hardly blame them."

"Are we sure about what Kurtz allegedly did? I mean, where's Pollack?"

"Pollack's in the hospital. Coma."

"Terrible," said Colls. "But they have hope he'll recover?"

"I'm not part of the Faithless Elector Task Group, but what I hear is that it could go either way."

Colls shook his head sadly. "So we may never know what really happened there."

"As much as I hate to believe something like this about a friend—about Kurtz—I was talking with a buddy of mine, Agent Fitzwater, who knows someone on Secret Service detail. We don't have the full picture as to why yet, but Kurtz did it: he tried to kill Pollack and Agent Trager and that professor. And Pollack killed Kurtz."

"The Faithless Elector Task Group?" Colls asked. "Who's staffing that?"

17

"I don't know a lot about it, but it's being headed by Don Weir."

"Good man," said Colls as he sipped at his drink.

"And his lieutenant is our old pal Amanda Vega."

"That's great. Those two will do a fine job."

"Let's hope," said Jezek. "Amanda seemed pretty depressed about the lack of progress or leads when I saw her yesterday."

"That's a worry. What did she say?"

"It's not what she said so much as her manner. You know, when she's on to something, she's a tornado . . . or a hurricane: Hurricane Amanda. Didn't you call her that, sir?" It had just slipped out, the "sir." He felt stupid.

Colls nodded, smiling distantly.

"She just seemed kind of subdued," Jezek continued. "She did say she was pissed off about Trager being brought back into the fold after she blabbed to the press. She understands why Weir wants her, I guess, but she doesn't like it."

"Why does he want her? I'd've thought she was damaged goods."

"More than you may know," said Jezek, conspiratorially.

"What do you mean?" asked Colls.

"Did you know that she and Kurtz were an item?"

Colls looked at his hands and nodded solemnly. "I did. Tom told me, and I told him to break it off. Implored him. It could ruin his career . . . could have."

Jezek nodded sadly. "In any case, I guess they're hoping she has some kind of inside info."

"She's not a field agent, is she?"

"No," said Jezek. "An analyst, I think."

Colls looked at his empty glass. Jezek, suddenly noticing it was empty, leapt up. "Same again?" he asked and hurried for the bar.

When he got back, Colls was on the phone. "I'll call you back in two minutes," he said into the phone. "Phil, I'm sorry. My daughter."

"Is everything all right?"

18

"Yes, yes. Thank you. Minor parenting emergency with my granddaughter, but I need to go. I do apologize." He stood up and pulled on his jacket. "I really thought we'd have more time. But listen, I'd like to meet again. It's so nice to catch up. Maybe we could make it something regular?"

"That'd be great," said Jezek, still holding a drink in each hand.

"Let's just plan on next Thursday, then. Here? Same time?"

"Sure," said Jezek.

"Great. See you then!" Seeing that Jezek had no hands available, Colls clapped him on the shoulder as he walked past.

Outside, he picked up speed. As soon as he'd rounded the corner, he took out the phone and dialed.

"It's me," he said. "I think it'll work. I've set up regular weekly meets. Not perfect intel, but we won't be totally blind. I'll see Mr. Cooper and get him up to speed. But so far it looks like clear sailing: they're in damage-control mode, mopping up. They think it's over."

* * *

Fayetteville, Arkansas

Outside his home, on a hastily erected platform, James Christopher began with a prepared statement, but he quickly moved to issues and ideas closer to his heart. Standing next to him were his wife and their teenaged daughters, and his running mate Bob Moore.

"Friends," Christopher began, "we said it during the campaign, and it's coming true now: the fix was in!" The crowd roared its approval. "We're hearing nothing about the vote-rigging in Illinois and elsewhere that stole the election from us." He paused for emphasis, let his remark sink in. "The Justice Department seems to want to let that one go, I guess. But we won't let them, will we?" The crowd roared again. Christopher's family clapped happily in the

19

background. Moore moved to the front of the improvised stage and pumped his fists.

"The government—" the crowd booed "—the crooked, deceitful government is doing all the things we said they'd do," Christopher continued. "We're seeing it. They want to keep themselves and their friends in power—at any cost: At. Any. Cost!" he enunciated to wild cheers.

Bob Moore leaned into the microphone and exclaimed: "It's gonna cost them the White House!" Still more wild cheering. "We will not allow them to continue to ignore you any longer. We will not allow them to steal this election from you!"

Moore stepped to the edge of the stage in front of the microphone, exhorting the crowd further. Christopher and his family stepped off the stage to wild applause and even louder chants of "Fix! Fix! Fix!"

2

Weir and Imogen met Agent Amanda Vega in the parking garage of the building where Imogen had been detained. It was old, possibly disused. Though empty, it felt cramped and oppressive. To Imogen this garage appeared potentially more dangerous than the one she'd been in only three days ago. She felt unsteady at the memory as she walked toward Agent Vega. In the bewildering silence, her ears seemed to resonate as they had before with gunfire. She found herself glancing at the stair doors, assessing entrances and exits. Every instinct told her get out, get free, get into the open air.

With great difficulty, she mastered herself, as Vega opened her car door and walked toward her, hand outstretched. There was no warmth in Vega's expression, nor was there malice, just more of the standard-issue FBI flat stare.

"Agent Trager," she said blankly.

"Agent Vega," said Imogen.

"Well, you've had a helluva time."

"I'm ready to get to work," said Imogen. She wondered if that sounded as hollow to Vega and Weir as it sounded to her.

Vega was the same height as Weir, and, like him, stocky. The shoulder holster and utility belt under her FBI raid jacket contributed to the bulk. Her thick black, neck-length hair was cropped short at the sides but swept back dramatically on top.

"I've briefed Trager," said Weir, handing Vega a file folder. "As you and I discussed, she'll start with Kurtz and begin looking for any connections we might have missed."

"Good," said Vega.

"I suppose I could start with Kurtz's apartment," said Imogen.

Agent Vega smiled. She touched Imogen on the shoulder. "Not today." She glanced at her watch. "We'll make a clean start in the morning." She turned and began walking back toward her car, the door still open. "I need you sharp," she said over her shoulder. Vega reached into the front seat and brought out Imogen's purse. "We have all your effects here: ID, phone, keys to your apartment and the Philadelphia house. Your car is . . . ?"

"Still in Philadelphia."

"You'll use a Bureau car for the time being," said Weir.

"Very good," said Imogen.

Vega drove Imogen home. "I'll have someone pick you up in the morning, and we'll get you fitted out and fully briefed," she said as she dropped Imogen off in front of her apartment building in Arlington. "My office, seven a.m.," she said and drove off.

Imogen stared at the front of her building for some time before moving mechanically toward the front door. She fumbled with her keys and let herself into the lobby. She paused again at her front door, dreading what lay in store for her behind it. Presumably, the apartment had been searched thoroughly. As she opened the door, it was no comfort to find it exactly as it had been four days earlier, the untidiness meticulously restored. She put her keys and purse down on a table by the door and looked around, taking it all in.

She was numb. Standing just inside the door, she looked toward the kitchen—did she want a glass of water? Was there any wine left in the fridge? Should she make a sandwich? Was she hungry? Automatically, she walked to the bedroom, where she collapsed sideways across the bed. It was good to lie on her own bed.

Staring at the familiar floral pattern of her duvet, she wondered briefly how she could ever have wanted to change it. When she awoke, it was dark outside, and she was cold. She rolled herself into the duvet, plumped a pillow and briefly struggled for the energy to get up and turn out the light. But before she could, she fell back to sleep.

Halfway down the block, in a row of parked cars, the passenger seat of a dark grey Buick Lacrosse was occupied. The observer had watched Imogen go inside and saw the light go on in her bedroom. Two hours later, when a new scout took his place, the light was still burning.

* * *

Highland Park, Illinois

Traffic along the southbound lanes of the Skokie Valley highway just outside Highland Park crawled in single file past a squad of police and emergency vehicles massed at the shoulder, lights flashing brightly against the snow. A portable generator and searchlight had been set up, illuminating a horrific one-car crash.

The car had bounced off the concrete median, back across two lanes of traffic, flipped over and rammed through the wooden fence separating the train tracks and the highway. The driver of the coroner's van walked up to the window of the sergeant's patrol car and knocked. The sergeant cracked his window, not wanting to let the heat out.

"Can we get the body?" the coroner driver asked the sergeant through the crack. The sergeant peered down toward the wreckage for a moment and nodded.

* * *

Fort Belvoir, Virginia

That same night, Weir dropped in at Fort Belvoir Hospital to check on Pollack. He found him still in a coma. In the room next door, Calder lay stupefied with painkillers. Their rooms were surreal.

In the darkness, Weir's eyes could just make out shapes that seemed to hover and shift in the dim, pale green light emitted by the banks of machines attached to each body. As he moved into Pollack's room and his eyes adjusted, he noticed how Pollack's skin had drawn taut across the skull and at the knuckles. Smooth and luminous, like hardened wax, it seemed to shine with a dull luster in that ghostly light. Weir wished he hadn't come.

He walked down the hall to where a guard sat at a folding table, watching television on a propped iPad.

"Anyone been by?" he asked as he picked up the log sheet to sign his time out.

"No sir," he said. "No one."

Weir looked at the screen, tuned to a 24-hour news channel, as he wrote in his own name on the log. He checked the time. 1:20 a.m. He held out the log for the guard to initial.

"So what's next for the nation?" one of the anchors was intoning. "Earlier today, I asked Professor Bellamy, of Rutgers University, what the options are."

"Of course," said the professor, enlighteningly, "nothing in future is certain. But we can speak in probabilities. The Constitution provides for the possibility that no one would achieve a majority win in the Electoral College. We won't know for more than two weeks what will happen—not until January sixth—when the 115th Congress is sworn in and they meet to certify the votes."

Across the bottom third of the screen a title was looping: "Constitutional Crisis: Presidency in the Balance."

"Yes," said the anchor, "but what is likely to happen?"

"More than likely, the three so-called Faithless Elector ballots will be challenged and refused," said the professor. "And that means, the House will vote for the president."

"Why can't we say for certain, and why is nothing happening now? Is it exaggerating to say that the nation is coming apart?"

"Well," Professor Bellamy began.

"Today alone," the journalist interrupted, "two armed men staged a protest outside Redmond's headquarters in North Carolina. There have been more allegations of fraudulent voting—as yet unverified. Demonstrations have led to gun violence in Oregon and upstate New York. Reporters have received death threats. This is unprecedented."

24

"As bad as all that is—and it is bad . . . actually, it's not without precedent," said Bellamy. "The nation's first contested election in 1800 was a tie—as this one is likely to be—and the House didn't agree on a president—Jefferson in that case—until there had been thirty-six rounds of balloting."

"Yes, professor, but—"

"—The election of 1876 was a disputed election, and it was particularly virulent. It was also one of the four elections where the popular vote winner did not win the Electoral College. The Compromise of 1877 brought it to a close, of sorts; and the Compromise effectively ended Reconstruction.

"In the 2000 election Gore lost in the Electoral College despite winning the popular vote," Bellamy continued. "These were all great upheavals with plenty of rancor and bitterness, but there is a process. For whichever candidate prevails, it is vital that this process be observed if the government is to have any hope of legitimacy, and not just for the nation at-large, but internationally. It would be folly—not to mention unconstitutional—to intervene in the process. So: it's the incoming Congress that will have to grapple with this issue, and they have to be sworn in first."

"What happens then?"

"Assuming the three votes are refused, which seems the most likely scenario, there will be no clear 270-electoral-votes-majority for either candidate. And if that is the case, the vote for president goes to the House and the vote for vice president goes to the Senate, as is provided for in Article Two, Section One of the Constitution, and clarified by the Twelfth Amendment."

"Don't they vote for both at the same time?"

"No. And we could very well have a situation where the president and vice president are from different parties."

The guard turned to Weir. "Is that true?" he asked, incredulously.

"Yes," said Weir. He looked back down the hall toward Pollack's and Calder's rooms and almost envied their oblivion.

As he stepped through the elevator doors, he could still hear the professor on the newscast: "And it's even odder because it is the president of the Senate—but of course that is generally the outgoing vice president, who . . ." The closing doors cut him off.

* * *

Imogen awoke with a start just after 5:30 a.m. Her heart beat frantically, and for a moment she was unsure where she was. She calmed down just long enough to get her bearings and worry that she was late for work. The clock beside the bed showed it was December 23rd and she had ample time. She slowly extracted herself from the duvet cover and sat up at the side of the bed.

She rubbed her eyes and ran a hand through her hair, which felt rough and tangled. She pulled a lock of red hair in front of her eyes and examined it. A shower was needed. She had been in the same clothes for days now. Imogen stood up and peeled them off her body. She let them drop to the floor, kicked the pile into a corner with some others, previously discarded, and went to the shower.

The phone pinged as she was finishing twisting her hair into a quick "bun." The agent picking her up had texted that she should be prepared for the reporters hanging around the front of her building. She walked over to the living room window and looked out. She could see a news truck with a camera crew and at least two reporters. Quickly, she drew the curtain shut and sat back on the arm of the sofa. Her heart knocked.

The phone pinged again. It was Vega: "*just got a text from Davies in front yr bldg*," the text read. "*Press waiting. Don't sweat. Walk purposefully. Don't run, don't cover your face. You say no comment, that any and all questions re FBI biz should be referred to David Lewisham in the pub info office. See you at work!*"

26

Imogen drew a deep breath. Vega made it sound so simple. Maybe it was simple, she thought, brightening. Though in the next instant she deflated again, realizing it probably wasn't.

She checked her hair one last time in the hallway mirror, looping a stray strand behind her ear, did a teeth check—it wouldn't do to have bad hair, or a bit of oatmeal bar stuck in her teeth for the cameras—grabbed her keys and headed out.

Indeed, it was not simple. As she walked across the lobby she could see through the front door window that there were five reporters and two cameramen on the pavement between her and the waiting car. She took a deep breath and opened the front door. She feigned a smile as she walked out, as though surprised at this attention. Then, she fixed her eyes on the car, past the knot of reporters. Cameras clicked and the crowd bunched toward her: "Agent Trager!" two reporters yelled, demanding her attention. "Imogen!" yelled another.

"What can you tell us about the investigation?"

A young woman from one of the networks elbowed her way in front and came to a stop right in front her: "Agent Trager," she began "how much closer are you—"

"—The FBI does not discuss current cases," said Imogen, trying to hold a pleasant expression on her face. "Any and all questions need to be directed to David Lewisham in the Public Information Office. I have no comment."

"Can you just tell us—"

"Please," said Imogen as she pushed past them. She was six feet from the car. A reporter followed her and pressed his card toward her. "Maybe there's something you need to say off the record," he said, pushing the card into her jacket pocket. She opened the car door and sat down, glancing at her driver.

She did not allow the pleasant expression on her face to fade until they had rounded the corner at the end of the block. She felt shaken, not because the reporters had had questions, but because, naively, she hadn't foreseen that reporters would be involved.

Feeling much more herself, Agent Imogen Trager met Agent Amanda Vega in Vega's office—Tom Kurtz's former

27

office—at 6:58 a.m. Imogen had debated with herself about what to wear for this first day, but had decided, since she would be doing field work, that she should turn up in standard-issue FBI windbreaker jacket, dark blue polo shirt, khaki trousers and sensible cross-trainers. Vega was dressed almost exactly the same Imogen noted with satisfaction. Vega handed her three thin files.

"Weir wants you to get to work on Kurtz and then follow up on Covington and Trebor before moving on to their Princeton days. He seems to think you can find something we can't."

"He said my small part was this group. He said that since Tom had trained as a field agent; since he had in fact supervised the training of field agents, he would know what and how to hide things from other field agents. He's hoping I can find something different by looking at it differently."

Vega shrugged.

"Do these files tell me what you've found and where you are so far?"

"Yes."

Imogen looked dubiously at the thin files in her hand.

"And, yes," Vega continued, "we've found nothing beyond making the connection between Trebor and Covington, which, for all we know, could just be a coincidence. See Sharon across the hall. She has the car requisition forms and all that. I want a standard end-of-day report each day."

"Understood," said Imogen and left, dissatisfied with Vega and with herself.

As she walked across the hallway, she thought about how different it had been working for Pollack. She missed him. She had liked the way he took her into his confidence, asked her opinion, gave her as much of the big picture as he could. This was evidently going to be very different. Weir was nowhere to be found and Vega didn't feel the need to discuss her thinking. Maybe because she was too busy coordinating so many other agents. Maybe she didn't know anything. As she walked across the hall, it occurred to Imogen that it was possible Vega didn't trust her enough to take her into confidence. Since there were things Imogen couldn't share with her either, perhaps, she thought, it was all for the best.

Pollack's assistant, Sharon Voth, now Weir's assistant, turned ashen as she looked up at Imogen. As she'd crossed the hall, Imogen had glimpsed Sharon in the outer office, and noted how composed and professional she was as she went about her business. If Sharon could stay professional, keep her focus without becoming unmoored under these extremely difficult circumstances, then she, Imogen, should emulate her.

"Genny," said Sharon, standing a little unsteadily.

"How are you, Sharon?"

Imogen moved to the side of the desk. They hugged one another tightly just out of sight of the open door.

When both had regained their composure, Sharon stood back, still holding both of Imogen's hands. "It's good to see you. It's been awful," she said.

"I'm sure," said Imogen.

"They tossed Doug's office. *Doug's,*" she repeated in disbelief. "They tossed Tom's—obviously. Yours. The debriefing they gave me was nothing of the kind. More like an interrogation."

"I'm sorry."

"I don't think they have anything to go on," she said quietly. She seemed a bit dismayed. "It's nothing they've said, but after twenty-two years I can read these guys. Normally, there's a swagger about them. It isn't entirely unattractive," she added with a grin. "They're used to being the ones who know exactly what's going on and what to do next. But I don't think they have a clue right now."

"That's the sense I'm getting, too. I don't think anyone really wants me involved in this investigation."

"No. They need you, Gen."

"Thank you. That's one person who thinks so. Any news about Doug?"

Sharon shook her head sadly. "Nothing new." She walked behind her desk and picked up three small cardboard evidence boxes. "I have this for you," she said, putting the boxes down on the corner of her desk. "The top one is Tom's, the other two belong to the other . . . killers. Stuff to get you started—phones, keys, date books, wallets." She paused, then pointed at the top box, Kurtz's. "He still had a picture of you, you know."

Imogen stared at the boxes. "He tried to kill me."

"I just wanted you prepared," said Sharon.

"Thank you," said Imogen distantly.

"Just sign here for the evidence boxes," said Sharon, pointing at three blank lines on a log, "and here," she said, producing a second log, "for the car. You can see Gino in the garage, first level. He'll tell you where the car's parked. I made sure he gave you a nice one."

Imogen smiled.

Sharon handed Imogen the keys. "Also," she said handing Imogen one of Weir's business cards, "that's my direct line on the back. Call me if you need anything, or if you learn anything more about Doug. I'll do the same. I already have your number."

Imogen put the keys and card in the pocket of her jacket and picked up the boxes. They were much lighter than she had anticipated. "Thank you," she said.

Sharon put a comforting hand on Imogen's shoulder. "The whole election. There's never been anything like it. They need you. You're the one who's going to find out how to get these bastards," she said. "And you're going to do it for Doug."

*　*　*

Imogen felt ghosts all around her. No sooner had she shaken the quiet terror of having to walk deep to level four of the parking garage to retrieve her car than she was at Tom Kurtz's apartment in Bethesda. She rummaged through the box holding Kurtz's effects and pulled out the remote control for the garage door. She eased the car in slowly and parked it in Tom's assigned space.

How many times had she traveled that precise route with him from Pennsylvania Avenue to Bethesda, and come to rest right in this spot? she wondered. Was he part of a conspiracy even then, two years ago? He must have been, she thought. This hadn't happened overnight.

The log noted that the set of keys she had in the evidence box was a spare set, and that Weir had the others. As she slowly got out of the car, she shook them lightly, feeling their weight in her hand. She wondered if these were the ones Tom had made for her.

Her phone pinged. Imogen frowned: to reach it, she had to shift the boxes in her hands. It was Vega: *"make sure chk w me when you go into the field"*

She set the boxes down. *"At Kurtzs apt now. Then to Wheaton to check Trebor and Cov."*

Imogen felt annoyed. Going over the evidence in each of their apartments was something that had been discussed. Did Vega think she was just out for a coffee? She stuffed the phone into the back pocket of her trousers and picked up the boxes.

In the elevator, she leaned heavily on the back wall as the doors closed, only to be reminded of the times she and Kurtz, alone in the elevator, had torn passionately into each other, groping, kissing hungrily, devouring each other ferociously. She was inside the apartment door now, seeing with her mind's eye the clothes they had stripped off lying along the hall, a trail leading to the bedroom.

She closed the door gently behind her. As she continued to see what had once been, she wondered how anything that had happened could have been true, could have been real. Had the thought ever crossed his mind, as they lay naked on a lazy Sunday morning that he might have to order her killed? Was there an endgame to their relationship? How, she wondered, does someone bury his own nature so deep that it never betrays him? Was it a kind of insanity, a psychopathy?

Still standing just inside the door, she felt the weight of Matthew's death, the Electors' deaths. Glimpses of remembered images of Kurtz bombarded her: Kurtz as lover, dismal boyfriend, assassin. She focused on the thought of

Calder and Pollack, hanging onto life; thought of what failure would mean. Could she really find a way in?

Her phone pinged again. *"OK make sure keep me in the loop next time,"* was Vega's reply.

Imogen wanted to type: "What loop?" but thought better of it. This was not the way she was accustomed to working. She began composing a defiantly long reply in her head, detailing why she had chosen this course of action. It was precisely what had been approved and suggested by Weir. She wondered how Vega would react, felt her mind wandering to notions regarding the limitations of texts, their tone-deafness, their propensity to be misunderstood. 140 characters was enough to launch a war. Finally, she typed *"OK"* and put the phone away in her back pocket.

She closed her eyes and shook the annoyance and memories from her head. She opened her eyes, trying to see the apartment fresh, ready to make a start. She put the boxes down on a little table in the hall, dropped her jacket in a corner at the front door and took a few steps in. She had always left her coat in that corner when she came over.

* * *

In the newsroom at CNN, Hugh Salter was staring at an email he had just received. The sender was "Patriot76." Salter's phone rang.

"Yes?" said Salter absently. "This is Hugh Salter."

"Mr. Salter, I sent you an email."

"Patriot Seventy-six?"

"Yes."

"I'm looking at it now." His eyes scanned the attachments. "I heard from Senator Eliot's staffer that this stuff was bouncing around. Has the senator seen it? How did you get it?"

"Yes, he has, and he's pretty upset. You can see there: the Justice Department relied on flawed information for their Illinois vote tampering investigation. That, or it was a deliberate attempt to mislead."

"I'm still trying to—"

"—You can see, they didn't come near bothering to count every precinct. The whole report is riddled with assumptions."

"It looks like a statistical model. I'd like to get it to—"

"Model or not, wouldn't you assume they'd count everything to be accurate? Isn't a prediction model better the more people you count for your base? Why didn't they?"

"Is there a number I can get back to you on?" Salter asked.

"I'm moving around a lot. Email is best."

"Are you going to tell me who you are?"

"I'm a concerned patriot." And he hung up.

Salter stared at the screen for a moment, then dialed the number of Senator Eliot's staffer.

"This is Hugh Salter, calling for Casey Hague." After a moment, Hague came on the line. "It's Salter. I've seen the spreadsheet, and I've talked with Patriot Seventy-six, as he calls himself."

"Pretty damning, don't you think?" said Hague.

"From what I can make out, it's a sampling."

"Exactly. Not a count. A sampling."

"Would you or the senator speak on the record?"

"I'll tell you what: you run with your story, and the senator will give you an exclusive first interview confirming the details. We had thought to go with the Spectator or The Hill first, but I persuaded him you were the guy—non-partisan, solid political chops, nose for news, all that. It's an important story, and in order to protect the source, it can't be seen to come from Eliot first. He will confirm the findings once they're public. For now, say: 'a source close to the Justice Department' or something."

"It'll run tonight, probably. I'll be in touch." Salter hung up. He hadn't had a scoop in months, he reflected. This could be really good. Not only was the Illinois count unsound, the investigation into voter fraud there was unsound too—and with the presidency in the balance. He dialed the news director and asked if he could come by right away.

33

At a little after three that afternoon, Imogen was back at her office. She dropped the boxes on her desk and sat down heavily in her chair. She had scoured Tom Kurtz's apartment, his storage unit at the building and his car in the impound lot, as well as the apartment Trebor and Covington had shared in Wheaton, out in Maryland, but had turned up nothing new. After a moment, she sat forward and opened each box again, taking stock, hoping that seeing it all together in front of her might suggest something. It didn't. She put her face into her hands and leaned on her desk.

There were keys, their wallets, phones, a receipt for a huge tub of whey protein bought at GNC the day before they were killed. She made a note to the file that she could not find a lock to one of the keys on Kurtz's chain. The size and shape of the key suggested a padlock, but she hadn't found it. Imogen examined the key again. What could this unlock? Absently, she put the set in her jacket pocket.

The FBI had retrieved two phones from the bodies of each of the dead men: a newish top-line smartphone and a cheap, disposable flip phone, a "burner" to be ditched. She reviewed the data other agents had collected. No calls had gone between any of the three personal phones in the last year, so there was no connection there.

Her own phone pinged in her back pocket. Imogen stared toward the ceiling and groaned, anticipating more shit from Vega. She shifted on her chair to free the phone. *"Don't forget end-of-day report each day."*

"OK" Imogen replied. She opened a low drawer in her desk and tossed her phone into it. She slammed the drawer shut. Weren't these things supposed to make our lives simpler? she wondered. Everyone expects you to be connected—available right away, all the time. To turn these damn things off would be like an act of treason. She considered locking the desk drawer. Perhaps she should get a burner herself.

Imogen stared at the dead suspects' phones in front of her. "Or," she thought, "if you were committing treason, would you turn it off?" There had been calls between all three burners, as well as to a fourth number, identity unknown, which had ceased functioning. It seemed they were changing the burners (or at least the SIM cards) frequently. There was only a month's data on the disposables. There had been no calls or texts between any of them on their personal smart phones, but maybe there was more these could tell her.

Imogen picked up her desk phone and dialed Kurtz's old extension. "Agent Vega?" she said. "It's Imogen. Will you counter-sign a phone warrant for me, or do I need Weir? I want to track these phones, dates, times, locations."

"We checked," said Vega. "There was nothing we could work with for any of them."

"Yes, I see that," said Imogen. "Now, I'd like to see if I can figure out any patterns in their movements. I'll get the forms from Sharon."

"Bring them by," said Vega and hung up.

* * *

Don Weir's phone pinged. It was a text from the Deputy Attorney General. *"youre going to want to check out cnn"* it read.

Weir stood and turned on the television in his office. Vega, who must have been on the same text chain, knocked as she entered. Weir waved her in. Together, they faced the screen.

". . . Hugh Salter is at the Capitol with more," said the anchor.

Salter came on screen. "Today, evidence has come to light which calls into question the FBI's findings in the Illinois voter fraud investigation in Illinois. Earlier, Senator Drew Eliot, chair of the Judicial Oversight Committee, had this to say."

The news story cut to Senator Eliot, standing in the Senate corridor behind a battery of microphones. "Time and again," he said, "we see bias and distortion from this administration.

At a time when the nation needs unity, this administration—and now the FBI itself—seem to be allowing politics to drive their investigations."

The news cut back to Salter, who held a sheaf of papers in his hand. "These documents," he said, "which I received from a high-ranking source near the Justice Department, demonstrate—at the very least—that Agent Imogen Trager's analysis of the final Illinois report was flawed."

Don Weir clasped his hands to his balding head and shut his eyes tightly.

"Viewers may recall that it was Agent Trager's work that brought the Faithless Elector Plot to the nation's attention—"

Weir turned off the television. "I'll go see the Deputy." He walked slowly out the door, like a teenager who has to tell his father he has just wrecked the family car.

Vice presidential candidate Bob Moore had been deputized to speak at a news roundup: "No, I don't think it's reckless," he was saying in answer to a question about his running mate's rhetoric. "And I take issue with your assertion that it's inflammatory. Three electors switched their votes, as is their right. This check is part of the design of our great Constitution. Each Elector said they did so mindful of righting the wrong perpetrated in Illinois."

"Yes, and candidate Christopher said 'elsewhere,' too," said one of the anchors. "There has been no hint of tampering anywhere else."

"But there has been in Illinois, and the Justice Department and the Attorney General seem unwilling to take that on," Moore rejoined. "People are wondering what this admin-istration is hiding."

"Yes, but—"

"We have a system for electing the president: the Electoral College. The system carried out its function—let me finish," he added, though no one had interrupted him—"and that system gave us a winner: Governor James Christopher. Those brave men . . . and woman—the Electors, were then murdered. What does that say about government complicity?

Particularly as we have yet to know who these assassins were. Wouldn't the Justice Department be putting everything they had into finding them? Let me finish," he added again. "I think we have to ask who this indecision serves, who benefits from the fog and confusion created by this made-up dilemma?"

"Governor Moore . . ." another pundit began imploringly.

"This fog of indecision makes our enemies stronger. We have terror at home, terror abroad; jobs leaving. And we are the only ones who have legitimately won."

Getting the data from the various cellphone carriers was complicated and time-consuming, but Sharon's assistance had sped up the process. By six o'clock that evening, Imogen had the data, and she was fully immersed in her work, plotting signal coordinates and times, when Weir arrived.

"How's it coming?" he asked.

"It's coming," said Imogen without turning around.

"Explain it to me."

Imogen pushed back her chair and turned to face Weir. "We only have about a month's worth of data on the disposable phones, but we can go back years on their personal phones. I thought I might be able to glean something by determining when they shut off their regular phones—or put them into 'airplane mode.' Where were they when the phone signal went dark? Where were they when the signal reappeared? Does the data hole tell us anything? I'd also like to compare the location data between that last month on their burners with what we can get for their personal phones. Where and how much overlap was there?"

"Anything yet?"

"No. I just got the full data sets about an hour ago and I'm looking into how best to plot their movements. Just putting the data into something I can use and begin to query will take some time." She hoped her tone did not betray the impatience she felt. That she felt she might finally be able to get back on the conspirators' trail was urgent in her, as was the need to show something for her efforts.

"What do you think you'll find?"

"I'm not sure. If we can put them at the scene of one or more deaths, that would be something. If other leads develop and we can place one of those as-yet-unknown people in close proximity to something we've flagged through this effort, establish a new connection, that would be something. If we narrow down an area and time and then sort through the messages that were occurring during that time at that place, and the numbers of those who were sending them, that, too, would be something."

"Is this your normal process?"

"There's no normal to FBI work, is there? But insofar as I amass data and look for links, yes. I often try to let the data suggest the next step; and often it isn't until it's all out in front of me that new things occur to me."

"Tell me about your process with the Illinois tampering findings?"

"Sure, but it should all be in the report. Doug has it."

"I'd like to hear it from you," said Weir.

Imogen smiled inwardly. "I'd like to hear it from you" was supervisor code for, "I don't understand what I'm looking at."

"So," she began. "Christopher's people were claiming there was tampering in Illinois. The Illinois USAO's office asked us to look into it."

"Right."

"So, in order to ascertain whether or not a series of late returns has been engineered in some way, you go back to earlier voting contests. It's possible, of course, that a few given precincts are just chaotic and incompetent and that's the reason they report late, but that will usually be borne out by history. History will establish the norm. If a given precinct's returns or their reporting of them varies from the norm, you scrutinize that precinct."

"How many precincts did you study?"

"All of them, but I focused on those with late returns."

Weir laid a sheaf of papers on her desk. "Is this it?"

Imogen drew herself closer to the desk and examined the papers. "No," she said after a moment.

"No? Your name is on these. We're still confirming, but they came from an email from you to Doug Pollack. I need you to think, and I need you to explain it to me so I can understand, because the shit-storm is approaching hurricane force."

"And I'm in the eye of the shit?" said Imogen.

"We all are!"

Imogen looked again at the papers. "What's the date of all this?"

"November eighteen," said Weir.

"Right. I see. This is not my report. This is data backing up a memo I sent to Doug just after the election." She pushed her chair back.

"You're sure?"

"Yes. The USAO in Illinois requested that we look into allegations of voter fraud. This was my preliminary look-in at whether there was anything substantive to the tampering claims, whether it merited a full field investigation."

"And was there?"

"My memo stated the data were inconclusive and would require further investigation. These papers were the back-up. They were a sampling."

"And did you follow up?"

"Yes. My full analysis formed the basis for the report the Office of Voter Fraud issued. I analyzed the data from all precincts, with an emphasis on those with late returns, for the final report."

"So what's this?" he asked.

"Back-up for why I thought we should look a little deeper, even though it was inconclusive. After I sent the memo, nothing happened for three weeks or so. I later learned, at a meeting I had with Doug and Tom Kurtz in early December, that the Public Integrity Office had asked us to hold off doing anything until the recount had been concluded. It was something about not wanting to interfere in a state matter while the Illinois AG's office was still conducting its own investigation. Didn't want to have a 'chilling effect,' were their words, I think. Frankly, I also think they were a little gun-shy after some of what happened in the lead up to the general election."

"Thank God," said Weir.

"What's this about?"

"CNN is running this," he tapped the pages on her desk, "as a story about how Justice hasn't done its job, and that there might be a political cover-up. Now Senator Eliot on the Judicial Oversight Committee is clamoring for a full investigation, and he sounds like he wants heads. On platters."

"And the AG wants to give them mine?"

"We protect our own," Weir said forcefully. "When we can," he added. "But this is good. We're in the clear: somebody leaked a preliminary document, not the data we made our decision on. They'll probably want to scour the real report now. Any problems there?"

"No. I stand by my data. In the end, it was pretty standard stuff."

"Great," said Weir, visibly relieved. "How did you get the data? I just want to see this from all angles."

"Doug directed Tom . . ."

"Tom Kurtz?"

Imogen nodded.

"Fuck!"

"You can't fudge a data set that big," she said, hoping to sound reassuring. "It would leave fingerprints that someone like me could easily see. In fact, I remember Tom being particularly upset that I had found shenanigans on both sides. To be clear—although there were irregularities, none of the irregularities rose to a level that would have changed the outcome." Imogen looked at the cellphone data on the table behind her. "I could go over the Illinois findings again, if you'd like."

"No," said Weir. "I'm sure it's fine, but obviously we can't have you investigate your own work."

"Of course."

"Stay on what you were doing. Keep Vega in the loop."

"I will," said Imogen, letting the thought of a noose pass as soon as it appeared.

"And keep your head down," said Weir as he turned to leave. "The press will be all over you. You still have no comment."

"I understand."

After Weir left, Imogen returned to her data sets for the three personal phones. She was at a loss for how to plot their movements. It would need to be a clear, simple representation if she was to tackle 18 months' worth of data. The more she stared at it, the fuzzier it all became, the more distant seemed any clue.

Needing a break, she stretched, stood up and walked out into the hall. It was past 10 p.m. and the place was deserted. Her trainers made a soft crunch with each step along the pale, high-gloss stone floor. The door to Vega's office—Kurtz's office, as she could not help thinking of it—was closed; so was the door to Weir's. She walked the length of the hallway to the ladies' restroom, the crunch-squeak of her shoes echoing faintly. She threw some water on her face and the back of her neck and then went on to the break room.

As she sat there at one of the break tables, sipping cold water from a paper cone, her mind wandered to Calder, recuperating somewhere. Not knowing where he was being held or how he was doing made her fears for him the more menacing. While in interrogation, she had spent three days thinking he was probably dead. With the knowledge that he was alive, she found herself almost frantic about needing to see him.

She wanted desperately to be with him again; wanted desperately out of this silence, beyond this impasse. Earlier in the day, the phone data had seemed a promising line of inquiry, but now she felt defeated before she'd made anything of it all.

After three cones of water she walked slowly back to her office. "Maybe," she thought as she walked along, "I should take another look at the burner phone data. It's a much smaller set, after all—more manageable."

Coming fresh to the data on the disposable phones, her eye fell immediately on a series of calls from the fourth number, whom she had nicknamed "Benny," short for "Benedict Arnold." She didn't have his physical phone, but she had the number, and that, plus a warrant, had been enough. Benny seemed to be the ringleader. Communication went mostly between him and Kurtz, with Kurtz directing Trebor and Covington. All three had called Benny on November 21.

As she scrolled through the data on her screen, there were, as one would expect, calls—always calls, never texts—between Benny and Kurtz, between Kurtz and Trebor and Covington, between Benny and two other numbers. It was possible that these were Benny's superiors. There weren't enough calls, however, to make a real guess as to how precisely they fit together.

There was a lot of chatter throughout early December. Trebor and Covington's activity continued until December 16, the day Calder killed them. Kurtz's burner phone activity stopped on December 19, the day he was killed.

On December 19, the Faithless Elector plot was revealed. But Benny was still communicating with his seniors (if that's what they were) the following day. Indeed, his level of chatter remained unchanged right up to 4:11 p.m. on December 21, when all the signals stopped.

Imogen scrolled back through the spreadsheet on her screen hoping she could find something helpful in the frequency or intervals between their calls back and forth. She also wanted to see if she could cross-reference the calls with known movements or activity.

As she looked back through the month, all four burner phones—Kurtz, Trebor, Covington and Benny's—had leapt to life on November 21. If they were changing phones once a month, it was probably on or about the 21st. The reason the FBI couldn't find any chatter after December 21 was not because it had stopped but because they had changed phones.

Why risk exposure when there was nothing to gain? she wondered. What did Benny and his co-conspirators still have to talk about?

3

Bleary-eyed from her late night, Imogen stopped in to see Vega first thing the next morning. "Agent Vega," she said, knocking on the door as she entered. "Could you authorize some computation time on the big main frame at IT Services for the cellphone data, please?" She passed the form to Vega, who took it and signed it without looking.

"You really think this will help?" asked Vega, pushing the paper back toward Imogen. "We've looked into Trebor and Covington's backgrounds. They were nothings. Both got their gentleman's 'C' at Princeton—that's a C-minus or expulsion to you or me—both tried to get into the FBI, and couldn't, even with Kurtz's help. They each failed to make military careers, one of them in the Army, the other in the Navy. They were bartenders and gym rats. They had kind of a creepy rep with some of the female staff. Nothing horrible, just standard bullshit guy stuff. They just don't add up to anything. Until they became killers there was nothing interesting about them one way or another."

"Right," said Imogen. "This link analysis I'm working on isn't a variable-based approach, but—if it works—a social network analysis." Imogen considered telling Vega about her intuition the previous night that there was something still going on; that Benny was probably still active. Given Weir's stated misgivings about her, however, not to mention Imogen's own tenuous position, she thought it made sense to hold back until she had harder facts.

"You mean like Facebook?" asked Vega.

"I suppose that might be helpful, too, but—"

"—We've looked at that, too. They were pretty right-wing, plenty of 'Thanks Obama' kinds of satirical posts, but again, nothing that would suggest any of this."

"Variable-based approaches," Imogen began, hoping to get Agent Vega focused, "look at people's attributes: race, gender, socio-economic class; that kind of thing. Social network analysis—the thing I'm looking to do—looks at who they are interacting with, irrespective of all that. As I got going on all this, I looked back at a Naval Intelligence guide to Social Network Analysis and Disrupting Dark Networks, and—"

"—Dark networks? Like terrorist organizations, drug cartels?"

"Exactly."

"A little melodramatic for a few phone calls, don't you think?"

"Do you have a better term for a murderous conspiratorial group bent on upending a presidential election? Look," Imogen continued, "both you and Weir said there was minimal communication and no cross-chat beyond themselves, no evidence on their computers or in their cars or apartments. I've reconfirmed all that. So: how were they getting instructions? Maybe the fact that one of their phones was turned off just as—or while—they were demonstrably in transit toward one of the killings . . . that could tell us something. Maybe we can demonstrate that as well as killing Novaczeck, either Trebor or Covington was present at one of the other deaths—that would mean something."

"I see."

"We're not just looking for a needle in a haystack. We're trying to figure out who put it there."

*　*　*

Weir sat with the Deputy Director, Bill Dyer and Public Information Officer, David Lewisham, in Dyer's office on the third floor, all three focused on the television, which was playing a forum debate saved from the previous night. Five politicians, along with representatives from the Pliny and

Creeks Institutes were joined by former and current White House press corps reporters, all arrayed around a heavy oak table.

"This can't be merely about politics," said one of the press corps journalists, "the nation expects its leaders to do what's right."

"Yes," said the Pliny Institute spokesman, "but what is the right thing?"

"And how," said a senator, "are we to do the right thing without someone claiming we're playing politics?"

"The route is clear," said a Democratic senator, who had been re-elected in the November general election. "The preponderance of evidence is that the three Faithless Elector votes are tainted," he said, "and must be rejected."

"Agreed," said the Pliny man.

"Agreed," said another senator. There was vigorous nodding from around the table.

"And since those votes would have gone to Redmond, it is equally clear that the states, voting in the House, must vote to elect her president."

"Well—" began the spokesman.

"—she would have won the Electoral College vote except for the Faithless Elector mischief, and she did win the popular vote."

"That route is not clear at all," said the spokesman.

"The people—to the degree that they are represented in the election of the president—have made their choice clear."

"We have these checks and balances for a reason," another senator began. "The Electoral College is supposed to be a deliberative body."

"And they failed."

"Redmond . . . and Christopher," he corrected, "each failed to get the requisite majority of Electoral College votes."

"And that is not a failure of the system," the spokesman purred.

"Are you saying we shouldn't listen to the people?"

"My state of South Carolina voted heavily for Christopher: he won all of our nine votes in the Electoral College," said

Senator Eliot. "If I vote for Redmond, what am I telling the people of South Carolina?"

"That you're a statesman? That when the chips are down you have the best interests of the nation at heart. You know Burke's speech: 'I am your representative, not your delegate.'"

"Edmund Burke? I will not be lectured by you sir, of all people!"

"We are also forgetting that the Illinois contest was not straightforward."

"I think that was pretty well put to bed, senator."

"The senator makes an important point, however," said the Pliny spokesman. "If—since each state has one vote—if the state delegations voting in the House cast their one vote for whoever won their state, it would be very close, but Christopher would win. More states voted for him, even though fewer Electors and fewer people did."

The deputy switched off the television. "It goes on like that," he said, "and it'll keep going on unless we can find something specific, something definitive that these politicians can hold on to."

"And the Bureau will continue to take the heat," said Lewisham.

Dyer turned to Weir. "You seem to have dealt with the Illinois questions. I don't expect that to come up again. Where are we in the investigation, Don? Anything new?"

"I'm sorry, Bill," Weir said. "Nothing as yet. Kurtz knew us better than we know ourselves. We've created a trace of events. We're checking all the police files on the dead Electors, but so far nothing. Most of them were as dull as a day in Minneapolis. We're delving deeper into known associates, but again, we don't seem to be getting anywhere. But I'm confident something will break. It's only been four days." Weir stood up, taking that as his cue to get back to work.

For the most part Weir was glad he was outside of politics. He was happy to let Lewisham and Dyer have that aspect. He liked things clear. He hadn't liked the deputy's dismissive tone when he said "these politicians." Their concerns and deliberations sounded valid—exactly the kind of questions they should be considering. That was their job. And his Bureau had a job.

Imogen called to ask Computing Division to plot the whereabouts of Trebor, Covington and Kurtz and to create an animated timeline of their movements based on cell-tower triangulation data. She asked that these movement traces be created so that they could be superimposed to look for similarities and rendezvous. "When you come to lost signals, don't just skip over them," she directed. "Note them. As well as tracking where they go when their phones are on, I want to understand particularly when they dropped off the grid, and where they popped up again."

"Cool," said the man on the phone, Trey Kelly. "Yeah. I'll get right on it. It's gonna take two, maybe three days to get the data in the shape you want."

"Hmm," said Imogen. "That long?"

"Well, with the holidays, we're kind of a skeleton crew, but we'll get it done."

"Thank you," said Imogen as she hung up. "Holidays?" she thought. She looked at her computer calendar. "Christmas? Already?"

She tried to collect her thoughts; tried to surmount a growing anxiety. When she wasn't still hearing the ringing aftermath of gunfire, she sensed—could have sworn she heard—the inexorable ticking of time running out.

Why had there been no breaks in the case, she wondered. What other leads were being followed up? What was she not being told? What the hell did Vega do all day? What, for that matter, was Weir doing? She thought back to her original conversation with Weir in the interrogation room. She had to be careful—to keep her thoughts and actions as much to herself as she could.

She picked up the phone again, and dialed IT Services. Trey picked up.

"Hi, it's Agent Trager again. Sorry to bother you. I had a thought. Will you be working on the data yourself?"

"Yeah. Me, and whoever else. I was just about to check to see who else had drawn the short straw down here."

"I could come there . . . if you think it would be helpful. I can definitely do the lower-level coding and sorting. The involved, esoteric stuff, I'd leave to you, obviously. I have 'TS' clearance. There's no issue there. Would that help?" Imogen was aglow with the idea of some hands-on work. That she could get a first look at the data without the prying eyes and interference of her new bosses was a particularly satisfying thought.

"Yeah. That could really help."

"I could come by in an hour or so."

"That'd be great."

"Just one thing," she said. "Where are you?"

Amanda Vega nodded to Sharon as she walked past and popped her head into Don Weir's office.

"I'm heading out unless you need something," she said.

"No, that's fine," he said. "Oh wait: where's Trager?"

"Not in her office?"

"No. I just looked in."

"I've got Gino in the garage paying attention to the car. It hasn't moved all day.

"Well, she isn't Christmas shopping for Kurtz," said Weir.

"If she's not in her office, she must've run out for a sandwich or something. Probably going to work all through Christmas, poor wonk. I kept her on a short leash for the first few days, but she clearly wasn't used to working that way, and she seems for real."

"Do you think she's onto anything?"

"I don't know, Don. I doubt it. At least she's not in anybody's way."

Sharon appeared at the doorway. "Unless you need anything else, I'm going to head home," she said to Weir.

"No, Sharon. Thanks."

"Merry Christmas," she said.

"Merry Christmas," Vega and Weir replied in unison.

*   *   *

Boston, Massachusetts

In Boston, in a boardroom with a commanding view of the skyline, a man put down his teacup and scowled at his ringing phone. He made an apologetic gesture as he ducked out of the meeting.

"She's back at work," said the voice at the other end.

"I've seen that. On TV."

"And that's making it difficult to keep an eye on her. There are reporters outside her apartment building; there were some milling around in front of the Bureau building, too."

"You have your source inside." He walked into an empty meeting room that looked out over Boston Harbor. "Her movements are less important than making sure we know whether they're making any progress."

"Agreed. But later, we'll—"

"—She's not going anywhere. When the time comes, she won't be hard to find. Is that the only reason you called?" the man asked, his voice edged with annoyance. "What are you hearing about their progress?"

"They're nowhere. They're focusing on the small fry."

"Good," he said, as walked out of the empty room and back toward his meeting. "When there are new developments or new information, contact me at the prearranged times. But not before." He snapped his flip phone shut and reached for the boardroom door.

*   *   *

Imogen was grateful she didn't have to go down into the garage for her car, but she rather wished she had it with her as stepped out of the DC Metro at the Stadium Armory station. It was only 7p.m., but already the area was deserted at that time of night on Christmas Eve, putting her in mind of T. S. Eliot's "half-deserted streets."

"Walk straight back from the station, past the youth correctional facility on your right," Kelly had said. "If you've reached the sewer treatment facility, you've gone too far. Our door's in the back of the old DC General Hospital. It says 'Bus Rentals.' Buzz number three, and I'll come let you in."

It was very cold, and dark. Immediately upon leaving the main street, everything changed. Though 19th Street was deserted, it was bright. The streetlights as Imogen turned off 19th were the old amber sodium-vapor lamps. She could hear them hum as she walked down the street that led past the Youth Correctional Facility. The yellow-brown light they cast seemed to pulse as though each streetlamp were beating its last.

> Every street lamp that I pass
> Beats like a fatalistic drum

she quoted under her breath. Eliot always had the words for what she was feeling—but how the hell had he known?

> Midnight shakes the memory
> As a madman shakes a dead geranium.

She turned her collar up against the wind coming off the Anacostia River and stuffed her hands deep into her pockets. She scanned the street and side streets for any other people. None. Nothing moved. Hulking public works equipment huddled at the edges of the darkness, like hungry animals held at bay just beyond the illumination of a campfire. Imogen stepped quickly in and out of the diffuse pools of light.

She found the Bus Rentals sign and buzzed #3. She stamped her feet to keep the circulation going and blew into her hands to warm them. After a few moments, Trey Kelly opened the door.

"Good evening," said Imogen. "I'm Imogen Trager; I'm here to rent a bus."

Kelly smiled and opened the door for her. They stepped into the vestibule and she showed her ID. He looked at it, nodded, gave a thumbs-up to the security guard through the glass. "Nice to meet you, Agent Trager," he said as he handed her back her badge and shook her hand. "Trey Kelly."

He must have noticed the quizzical look on her face as she looked at his identity card, held on a lanyard around his neck: "David Douglas Kelly III," it read. "Yeah," he said, holding it up. "I wasn't about to be 'Little Davy' my whole life. My cousin took to calling me Trey." He shrugged. "And it's better than 'Trip'."

The guard buzzed them back in. He waved as they walked past.

"Merry Christmas," the guard said.

"Merry Christmas to you," said Imogen.

Trey forced himself not to stare at Imogen as they began walking down the passage. He had not had any expectations regarding her from their phone conversations. He'd assumed she would be another of the Bureau's faceless, interchangeable agents. So nothing prepared him for her as she arrived, shaking her bright red hair from under a woolen cap, unzipping her jacket, a vision of bright elegance in an otherwise dismal part of the world. Trey had the vague sense that he should maybe run ahead and clean up a bit.

Trey Kelly was 31—only about five years younger than Imogen—and tall and lanky. His face was open and frank. Around his eyes and mouth there seemed a readiness to smile, not to ingratiate, but because he was prepared to find things funny. This quality was in such stark contrast to the stony, practiced inscrutability of most of her FBI colleagues that Imogen found him instantly appealing.

Though not unkempt, he had the air of a man who paid sporadic, non-specific attention to his appearance. His black hair was closely cropped and sculpted, in contrast to a four-day beard. His glasses were expensive, fashionable, oversized black frames, but the lenses looked as though they had been dropped in a puddle and hastily wiped on a shirttail.

He wore a Lacoste polo shirt that was stretched and stained, the short sleeves revealing the "sleeve" tattoos running down each of his arms. The blue ink set against his dark skin looked almost like intricate jailhouse tattoos. Imogen was intrigued, but like Kelly, felt perhaps she shouldn't be seen to stare. His trousers barely covered his narrow backside, she noticed, as he raced a bit ahead of her.

In his office hung a blue blazer, pressed white shirt and tie for the unlikely event he had to attend a meeting with his superiors. The clothes were all still covered in plastic sheeting from the cleaners, which was fortunate, since they had hung there, at the ready, for the better part of two years.

Though he was comparatively young, it was already generally assumed that he would soon be head of the whole group. He was talented and focused. His work on cyber-warfare, data security and information retrieval had helped increase and extend the FBI's grasp.

"So what is this place?" asked Imogen as they walked on, "and why the secrecy?"

"It isn't secrecy, really. It's just not talking about ourselves much. We're sort of hiding in plain sight. This is listed as the IT department for the Bureau, if you look it up, which we kind of are. And we do projects like yours that need a lot of computing power. Mostly, though, we exist to store and back up everything the Bureau needs. I created an algorithm that cycles which sites at any time are backing up which other sites through which servers, so that no one can hit us and destroy our records. I guess if they hit every site at the same time, that would be bad, but that kind of coordination and planning—I hope—would be hard to keep quiet. Folks like you would be bound to know about it . . ."

"Let's hope." Imogen presented her bag to show Kelly. "I brought some food. There's enough for three or four of us. One veggie option, too. I hope it's enough. I didn't know how many people were on a skeleton crew."

The room was empty.

"Two, it turns out," said Kelly as he took the bag and looked inside.

The place felt a bit like a bunker. There were no windows. A series of small offices surrounded three sides of a central room. A wide arc of desks dominated the fourth side, facing a glass wall. Behind the glass wall were rows of servers, dark, black, here and there spotted with a diode glow of blue or red.

The lighting in the main office area was poor, not much brighter than the amber of the streetlamps outside, but each workstation had its own reading light.

"The boss only left one person in charge?"

"Well, see, I'm the boss of this area."

"And you're working on Christmas Eve?"

"Well, my folks have been gone a long time . . . girlfriend's out of town. Everybody else has somewhere to go, someone to see. I figured, why not? Besides, one day I'm gonna need time off and I'm gonna get to bring down the hammer, or at least some deep guilt." He smiled.

Imogen smiled. As she looked into his face, she couldn't for the life of her imagine him ever bringing down the hammer.

"Food looks good," he added. "But let's get to work." He put the bag down on a desk.

Imogen's phone interrupted almost immediately. She didn't recognize the number, but quickly realized the text was from Sharon: "*not sure why but W and V are keeping tabs on you. watching the cars movements. watch your ass, girl. Merry Xmas!*"

Imogen texted back unmerrily: "merry X. thanks!"

"Yeah," she said to Kelly. "Let's get to work."

Kelly sat down at a workstation facing the glass wall. He turned on a reading light and logged back onto his computer. "I've looked at a couple models for this kind of data representation," he said, "and I think this one is the best, most elegant." He pointed to the example on screen.

Imogen wheeled her chair closer.

The days were represented as mini-timelines within each month, above which a scalable map displayed the phone's geographic movement in an animated display. "You can pause it any moment and know exactly where the phone is at that time, and you can zoom in and out." He showed her the data she had sent over. "Can you start plotting this?" he asked.

It all looked straightforward to Imogen. "Sure, no problem."

"Great," he said, as she shoved a pile of papers to one side of a desk. "You can work here. Log on with your regular PIN, et cetera."

"Okay."

"If you would, first do like a three-month batch for each carrier and then let's run a bullshit check on it. I want to make sure those guys sent us good data."

"Makes sense," she said.

"While you're doing that, I already took a sampling, and I'm going to run a program on it to make it a bit more precise. When a phone's just pinging—as opposed to when it's actually being used—cell tower triangulation data is accurate to within, like, five meters, which is pretty amazing. But that might not be good enough for us. I wrote a predictor program that can shave it down to more like one-and-a-half meters when pinging and pretty much dead-on when in use. But I still have to do a bullshit test on it, too. When I'm sure it works like we want it to, we'll use it on your data."

They worked in silence for the better part of an hour, when Imogen rose to stretch and grab some dinner from the bag lunch she had brought. She gulped a few bites of turkey sandwich and then sat back down. When they were finally finished and ready to run the data, it was almost five hours later, just after one in the morning, Christmas Day.

They sat munching the welcome but not entirely festive sandwiches as the final batch compiled the final bullshit test. Imogen offered Kelly some potato chips from her bag. He shook his head, no, his eyes focused on the computer.

"No wonder he stays so skinny," thought Imogen as she looked at him. "I've had two sandwiches and a bag of chips, and he's barely through his first sandwich."

"Here we go," said Kelly, and he clicked "run." He could have been clicking "play": it ran like a video.

Each of the personal phones was color-coded: Kurtz, red; Covington, green; and Trebor, purple. The disposable phones each had carried would figure on the timeline only during the last month or so, along with that of Benny. Each disposable was represented by their personal color-code but in a darker hue. Dates and times ran below the map of each man's route over the past year. Imogen and Kelly stared for a moment.

"Okay," said Kelly, "let's sync the timelines."

Imogen paused the program and synced the timelines to begin at the earliest common date and time available to them, 11:59.00 p.m., June 30, 2015. Then they overlaid each timeline and aligned them on a geographic grid. As the lines representing the three dead men's lives wandered across the map, there was constant overlap between Trebor and Covington, as expected, but none with Tom Kurtz. Nonetheless, watching Tom's movements, Imogen was grateful that by this time she was no longer with him, and so wouldn't have to explain her own movements.

Now and then as the timelines continued playing out, Trey would pause the program and they would register landmarks on the map that Imogen had from the files—Trebor and Covington's apartment, the bar where they worked, the gym where they worked out; Kurtz's apartment, the FBI building. The data was extremely good, and it was surprising how little down time was showing up for their regular phones—except late at night, which, again, was to be expected.

Kelly increased the speed of the playback. "We've got like a year and a half to cover, and we can't be doing it in real time," he said, smiling.

Suddenly, on July 19, all three lines converged. Both Imogen and Kelly straightened up. They looked at each other as if to say, did you see that?

Imogen flagged the encounter, and then reversed the playback a little.

"That looks like the very northern part of Rock Creek Park," said Kelly. "What the hell?" He peered closely at the screen as if hoping to see their faces. "Are they having a picnic?"

Imogen ran July 19 back more slowly. "They definitely all go there, but they're not there at the same time. It's Kurtz at 3:21, then Covington and Trebor at 3:45." Imogen marked the spot and flagged the date and times.

She started the program running again. As the trails scrolled forward once more, patterns began to appear in Covington and Trebor's movements. They traveled in a fairly proscribed orbit, generally, though not always, together from apartment, to gym, to a Subway restaurant near their apartment for lunch, a GNC store for whey protein, to work at the bar and then home.

All their movements so far confirmed Vega's team's investigation. "Amanda's right," thought Imogen. "These guys aren't remarkable at all." She had hoped to find something, but except for their sojourn in the park, there was nothing new. She wondered idly if they were gay.

Kurtz's movements were more random. While his route mostly circulated between his apartment in Bethesda and his Bureau office on Pennsylvania Avenue, there were notable detours, and "dark" spots. Imogen began checking these forays against Kurtz's known case files. He had been to Boston on FBI business in late July, and had flown out to Springfield, Illinois and then Chicago, also on verified FBI business, in early August. It was almost comical to watch how quickly the line would move whenever one of the three got into a car or on a train.

On August 19, at a little before 3p.m. Imogen saw Kurtz's trace zip south, stopping along Delaware Ave Southwest between K and L Streets.

"What's that?" said Kelly, "Lansburgh Park?" He quickly called up the coordinates on another computer next to him on the desk. "Yeah," he confirmed. "Lansburgh Park." Half an hour later, Covington's line crossed the spot in Lansburgh Park where Kurtz had gone. Trebor, it appeared had had to go into work early that day.

Kelly stared at his screen. "Wait. Isn't there a—?"—he interrupted himself—"Yeah, police station, right next to a fire station, right next to the DMV. If that's a meeting spot, your boy's got some balls."

This second intersection—or drop-off, most probably—had happened a month to the day after the first. A very curious choice of venue, yes, but here at last was a pattern. The 19th of the month, each month, was the day to watch.

They skipped ahead.

On September 19 there was no activity at Rock Creek or Lansburgh Park. Imogen and Kelly exchanged glances. Imogen had been keen to see the pattern play itself out, so she was frustrated when it didn't. But at 3:17 p.m. on Monday the 21st, Kurtz was back at Rock Creek Park. Trebor and Covington passed by half an hour later.

"Why the deviation?" Imogen wondered. She pulled up her calendar and looked backward through 2015. The 19th was a Saturday. Maybe, she thought, a Saturday in the park risked being seen too much.

On Monday, October 19, they were all back on schedule, and each timeline moved through and stopped in Lansburgh Park. The pattern held throughout the eighteen months for which they had data, always on the 19th between 3 and 4p.m. unless it was a weekend, one month in Rock Creek, the next in Lansburgh.

The traces for the four disposable phones all appeared abruptly on the screen on November 21, and in each case the three known numbers made one call to "Benny" while still near to the Rock Creek drop site.

"So that's where they were picking up their new phones— or more probably the new SIM chips. Those would be easy to conceal."

"I agree. I'm sure that's what's happening," said Kelly. "This part bugs me, though," he said, tapping the screen and pointing at the fourth number. "I've isolated his movements, but it's no good. It's clear he's driving around. The phone seems to be one-way only. He doesn't call back. And look, the moment all three have checked in, it goes dark."

"You know," said Imogen, "there was no pick-up on December nineteenth. These two," she pointed at Covington's green and Trebor's purple line, "were dead. With everything going on, Kurtz probably couldn't get there. There were no new SIM cards on him. Maybe he wasn't the one delivering them. Maybe he was picking up, too."

Kelly was busy triangulating the most recent sets of signals at Lansburgh Park. He called up Google Streetview and twisted his screen to show Imogen. "Whatever they were picking up," he said, pointing at the screen, "it's either under that garbage can there, or somewhere around that shed next to the community garden. You want to borrow my car keys?" He flashed her a winning smile.

Imogen nodded, tried to smile back. She was eager to get out for fresh air. Just before the playback ended, she had noticed that on December 15 all three of the personal phone traces went dark, just after the lines associated with the burner phones for Trebor, Covington and Kurtz showed calls from Benny. Their three lines quickly converged, but not at Rock Creek or Lansburgh Park. On December 15 all three converged and sat for hours in Arlington, Virginia—just outside her own apartment.

It was now a little before 8:30 in the morning. Christmas Day. The sun rose dully into a sky the color of dirty snow. Imogen was distracted as she rolled along deserted streets toward Southwest DC. They'd been right outside her bedroom window, she thought. Jesus. So Kurtz had been onto her from the moment she had picked up Calder at the airport when he had flown out to tip her off about the whole conspiracy. What if she had gone back to her apartment, as she had thought to do, before going to see Calder at the hotel? Would Kurtz have tortured her to find our where Calder was? Based on what she had seen back on December 19, he was prepared to kill anyone and everyone. And he would have killed her but for Pollack and Calder, still recuperating in hospital somewhere. She almost missed the turn onto Delaware Avenue SW.

She stopped in front of a parked police squad car and walked into Lansburgh Park. A high fence separated the police department parking lot from the park. As she walked up the path, there was a dog-run to her left, the community garden directly in front. She walked up to the garbage can she had seen on Kelly's computer screen—amazing technology, she thought—and shook it gently. It moved a bit on its base, and she was able to tip it slightly away from her. But there was nothing there. She tipped it most of the way over, but still she saw nothing. She took the lid off and examined it, but again, nothing.

She walked to the shed at the corner of the community garden. It was locked, the robust padlock holding firm. She reached into her pocket and pulled out Kurtz's spare keys. The padlock key fit. She thought back to Trebor and Covington's personal effects, but couldn't remember a matching padlock key. They would have needed one.

Inside the shed, just tools, bags of dirt, potting equipment—nothing of any use to her. In the low light, she scanned the plywood floor, looked at the roof, and still found nothing. Then, finally, behind the door, she noticed a faded green folder tucked between the framing and the plywood siding. Before touching it, she put on her gloves. She took it down. Inside was a plastic zip-lock bag.

With the folder under her arm, she locked the shed and walked back to the car to examine the envelope. There were three SIM cards and a new phone number to call.

4

On her way back to Bus Rentals, Imogen stopped by a diner standing forlornly open. She couldn't wait to show Kelly what she'd found, but since this meant hours' more work, she felt some breakfast was deserved. As the smell of the bacon, sausage and egg sandwiches filled the car, she made a note to herself that she should eat some greens or fruit soon.

As Kelly let her in, she waved the green folder at him through the window with a thumbs up and big smile. For his part, Trey looked subdued.

"So there was something there?" he asked.

"Yes, SIM cards and a number. We know the SIMs weren't used, but we should definitely get going on the number listed here. This could be a break."

"Good," he said. They sat down at a table in the computer lab and Imogen laid out the envelope and the food. "Before we start," he said, "I think you need to tell me what's going on."

"What do you mean?"

"I kept working on the cellphone trail, and I noticed that all three of them were stopped outside an apartment building in Arlington for a long time a few days ago. Your apartment building."

"Yes."

"One of the trails we're following is an FBI agent named Tom Kurtz. What's an FBI agent doing spying on another agent? And why is that agent now spying on him?"

"You know about the Faithless Elector plot," she began.

"Yeah, of course."

"This plot has been going on for some time before the general election on November eighth," she began. "You and I are just beginning to see how long it's been going on. But back on December tenth, a young grad student at the University of Washington, in Seattle—Matthew Yamashita—who happened to be polling Electors for his dissertation, noticed that there were a series of deaths—seven total—among the contact names he had: seven out of one thousand seventy-six."

"There're only five hundred thirty-eight Electors," said Kelly.

"Right," said Imogen, showing by her expression that she wasn't used to people knowing the precise number.

Trey smiled. "When you grow up in DC *without* representation, you tend to focus on the one time you can have an impact and to know a lot about it."

"Yes, of course," she said. "Well, Matthew was polling Electors from both parties," she explained. "Each party chooses its slate of Electors in each state. Whichever party's candidate wins a plurality in the state sends its Electors to the state capitol, as they just did last week, on December nineteen. The Electors for the other parties stay home . . . though in fact the other parties, like the Green Party, Independents and any others all choose a slate, as well.

"Anyway, Matthew focused on the two main parties—so five thirty-eight times two . . . one thousand seventy-six."

"Right. Got it."

"Matthew looked into the deaths and found they were all recorded as accidents. He was a stats guy, and he pretty quickly demonstrated that there was no way that so many Electors dying could be random. If it had been one, or even two, you could say it was random. But this many accidents isn't accidental."

"So how come no one else noticed it?"

"Electors are only tracked within their own states. There's no national coordination until the very end, when the votes are tallied in Congress, and they're going off of a final list. Matthew's was the only list of all the Electors, so he's the only one who saw it all. And no more than one Elector had died in any one state.

"Matthew's grad advisor was my mentor, the chair of my committee back when I was at grad school, Duncan Calder. He was skeptical at first. Apparently Matthew had had conspiracy theories before. But Matthew contacted a Washington Post reporter, and within the day they were both dead."

"Shit! How did that happen?"

"We're still not sure. The reporter's name was Jerry Ingram. He probably called the wrong person looking for a quote or confirmation."

Imogen looked at the display on the screen. "In fact," she said, pointing at the screen "I need to pull up the files on Matthew and Jerry's deaths. The reporter died somewhere here in DC. I wonder if we can show that it was Kurtz and his crew that did it."

"Then what happened?" asked Trey.

"So, now the conspirators are after Duncan. He's frightened, doesn't know what to do. At which point he contacts me, but on his way to the airport, they tried to run him off the road. From the moment Duncan touched down, Kurtz and his people were onto us, I think. I finished up my part of the Illinois investigation, and then I reviewed the data."

"The Illinois investigation that's blowing up right now?"

"Yeah. It's strange. There's really nothing to it. Both sides were trying to change the result for their candidate, but the ballot stuffing on each side wouldn't have changed the result. I proved it. My analysis was the meat of the Public Integrity Office of Voter Fraud report."

"So why is it still an issue?"

Imogen shook her head helplessly. "You tell me. I don't get it. I mean I guess with everything so politicized and polarized these days it was naïve to think . . ." As the thought trailed off she stared past the banks of computers into the server room.

"But I'm getting ahead of myself. It turns out that the most damning piece of evidence that these deaths are not accidents—which Duncan uncovered after rescuing Matthew's data—is that only Democratic Electors had died, and only in states with a Democratic plurality.

"Why didn't you go to your boss, or his boss?"

"We didn't know about Kurtz being a turncoat at the time, but Duncan was wary—and rightly, it turned out—of involving the FBI. This conspiracy was operating at a national level: Matthew had called someone and now he and the reporter were both dead. So I broke channels and got Duncan a meeting with Redmond's campaign manager, Jim Novaczeck. We figured that as the one who would lose if the plot succeeded, there was no way he could be involved.

"But Kurtz and whoever else he had working on the inside tapped my phone and they were already there, waiting for us. When Duncan showed up, Novaczeck was already dead. Duncan barely got out of there alive, and he killed Trebor and Covington in the process." She tapped their two trace lines, showing where they stopped on December 16.

"A professor killed them?" Trey asked incredulously.

"You might be surprised."

"So were the seven replacements all plants?"

"That was our thought, but it proved to be completely wrong. The replacements were just that—replacements, legitimate alternates. But, there were three Electors, one in New Hampshire, one in Minnesota and one in Colorado, who switched their votes, giving the Electoral College vote and the election to Christopher.

"I don't know if we'll ever know what really happened, I guess, but those seven dead should be regarded as heroes. I expect the conspirators tried to bribe them to get them to switch their votes; then when that didn't work, they threatened them, and each of those seven still said 'no,' so they were killed. I'll bet the bosses hadn't bargained on that—on so many not caving in."

"Yeah," Trey agreed.

"I don't know if you remember, Christopher's running mate Bob Moore called those switched votes a 'historic zenith the Founding Fathers would've been proud to witness.' I wonder what he thinks now."

"Probably thinks the same thing."

"Yeah. . .jerk," said Imogen. "So, after Duncan was almost killed, we ran to a place I know in Philadelphia and holed up for a few days while Duncan recovered and we figured out our next move. When the Electors met and the Faithless Electors switched their votes, I contacted my boss, Doug Pollack, telling him we had the goods."

"Wait, so now you trusted the Bureau?"

"I had always trusted Pollack. It was Calder who persuaded me to be suspicious. But after what happened with Novaczeck, there really was no alternative. Pollack had us meet him in the parking garage of the Old Executive Building, where I would give him the evidence we had, and we would both deliver it to the Attorney General. And you know what happened then. We met there because she was preparing to go to a joint press conference with the President, Redmond and Christopher—all three of them—to talk about what was really happening. It was while we were still in the parking garage that Kurtz—one of the hit men—shot Pollack and Calder, and tried to shoot me. Pollack finished Kurtz off."

"Shit," he said.

"It gets weirder," she said. "Tom Kurtz and I were—we dated briefly a couple of years ago."

"The guy who tried to kill you?"

Imogen stared at the far wall. In her mind's eye, she saw Kurtz wheel and fire, saw Pollack spin and drop with the force of the bullet, heard the second shot, catching Calder in the back, saw the pain and terror in his face. "Yes," she said.

She wondered how much more she could tell Kelly; wondered how much more she should tell him. Should she go into her feelings for Calder? she wondered. Should she talk about their love? And was that what it was, love? Had there been enough time? Where would they—where could they— pick up again? The feeling of emptiness and solitude she had mostly kept at bay came back in a deluge. She was right where she had been for so long now, alone.

Professionally, she had always felt like an outsider at the Bureau, but she had had Pollack to talk with, and, for a time, Tom. Being able to bounce things off others had made her outsider status bearable, even invigorating. She could be seen as someone distant, above it all, who followed the truth of the data and cut through the distractions others allowed to pile up around questions and problems.

In contrast, her feeling in the days since the plot had been exposed was of almost total isolation, as though traveling in a country where she didn't speak the language. With the revelation from Sharon that Vega and Weir were keeping tabs on her now, she was losing hope of having anywhere to turn.

She looked at Trey Kelly, sizing him up, his amiable, warm non-FBI goofiness, crumbs from his sandwich accumulating on the front of his shirt. His lack of personal fastidiousness aside, he was like her, in many ways: like her, a bit of an outsider, and while not properly an agent, yet someone offering an expertise useful to the Bureau's needed work. She stared at him a little longer. With so many people dead she worried what it would mean to bring Trey inside it all.

"I'm not sure how to say this," she began, "so I'll just say it. I'm pretty sure my bosses don't want me on this case. It may be that everything is as it seems, but experience tells me not to trust that it is. Despite what they've said, and despite Tom Kurtz's clear involvement, I don't think they're taking the conspiracy angle as seriously as they should.

"Frankly, there's this . . ." she searched for the word, ". . . this institutional smugness about the investigation; like they feel they've already done the heavy lifting and now they're just tracking down a murderer. To be honest, I worry that there are people who don't want to find any other FBI sleepers; and those very people, while not conspirators themselves, are unwittingly abetting the bad guys by making sure dirty operatives aren't exposed."

How much of this was Trey taking in? He seemed to be following it all closely. A mind was working on what she told him.

"Also," she continued, "I know they're keeping tabs on where I go. I doubt they know I'm here because I didn't use the company car. I'd like to say to you, 'you should know what you're up against,' but I don't know what you're up against—or me, for that matter. All I know his how fucking dangerous it is, because bodies keep turning up, and I don't want to add mine or yours to the list."

Trey was serious too. "Well," he said finally, "since it's Christmas, it looks like we've got the rest of today before you need to let them know what you've found. And I've got more to show you."

* * *

In Fort Belvoir Hospital, across the Potomac in Virginia, Duncan Calder was stirring. He blinked deliberately and slowly, willing the room into focus. In the low light, he could discern the outlines of a hospital room and tubes rising out of his left arm toward an IV bag. Machines hummed. There was a very low beeping which seemed to indicate that his heartbeat was regular and steady.

"Not dead," he thought distantly. For a moment or two as his eyes roamed the room he could feel nothing of his body and couldn't seem to turn his head. Slowly, he pivoted his head to the right. There was a door, which he must have come in through, but he had no recollection. Leading where? He stared at it for a time, blank. And now to the left he saw windows, with the blinds closed almost flat. He had been with Imogen, he remembered. Something had happened. It was warm and quiet, peaceful. "Imogen," he thought and fell back to sleep.

At the nurse's station, a security guard and the nurse who had alerted him to Calder's movement watched the closed-circuit screen, saw Calder turn his head gingerly from side-to-side and fall back to sleep. The guard checked his watch, walked to his table and noted that Calder was coming around. The nurse texted the doctor on call.

"Check this out," said Trey, grabbing one of the egg and cheese breakfast sandwiches. "This is November nineteen in Rock Creek Park." He took a huge bite of the sandwich. "Here's Kurtz," he said through his food, "and he calls a number. Here's the other two, and they call the same number. They're letting Benny—their handler, or whatever you call him—know they're up on the new numbers."

"And we have the numbers they were going to switch to on December nineteen." She spread out the contents of the envelope. "This is the handler's number," she said, pointing to a handwritten note. "I'm hoping he's still using this phone."

"Ya think?" said Trey through another mouthful of egg and cheese. He swallowed. "Wouldn't he throw the phone away?"

"I don't know. I'm guessing, but maybe in a way he can't," said Imogen. "It could be their Achilles' heel. If they're all interconnected, and they don't communicate unless it's absolutely necessary, then changing even one number outside of the schedule risks them all. A change in the system might invite scrutiny, or at the very least involve extra messaging—maybe even having to go higher up the food chain for authorization, which, again, risks drawing attention. We need to get the same data we have for these three on this new number." She tapped the paper.

"What if we did have more?" said Trey coyly. "What if we could go back eighteen months like we did with these guys? What if we knew the numbers they called all those other times when they picked up the new SIMs."

"Sure. That would be great, but how would we do that?"
Trey smiled, pleased with himself. "I called my man Mike at NSA—we were hacker-geeks together at school. He's working today too. I asked if he could get me a list of phone numbers calling from our two spots in Rock Creek and Lansburgh Parks on the dates we identified, at the time we're sure they were there. And I told him it would be best if the

search could be narrowed right down to numbers broadcasting from those spots for the first time ever."

"We can do all that?" asked Imogen, incredulous.

"No. We can't. But NSA can." He flashed her a mischievous grin.

"Don't we need signed warrants and all that?"

"Yeah," he said, popping the last bite of egg sandwich in his mouth, "we will. We'll need a search warrant and an inter-departmental request for NSA data sharing. We'll just need it backdated. You can do that, right?"

Imogen was stunned. She wasn't sure anymore what was possible, wasn't sure she liked what lay behind the door she and Trey were opening. It still didn't get them names, but if it worked, it could show them one of the cells inside the network. Added to other agents' data, it might expose the whole conspiracy.

Even so, she was uncomfortable with Trey's cavalier attitude toward NSA's snooping. He was acting like it was all just another tech-head toy for him and his nerd buddy to play with, and they could sort out what was legal and appropriate later; as if it weren't a potential abuse of power. Did it compromise her values, she wondered—her belief in accountability? She stared off for a moment longer. How far, she speculated, could she go in defense of principles before she had abandoned them all?

Well, she had seen some adept finessing during her time at the Bureau—and in the name of much less important causes than the Presidency of the United States.

"Yeah," she said finally, "no problem . . . I'm sure."

"And frankly," Trey said, "if there are bad guys in the FBI, doing this all the right way might give us away too early."

"True," said Imogen. "We definitely need to add this new handler number to the mix. Let's ask your buddy to go back another month, in case it came on earlier than the others."

Trey grabbed his phone and sent the text. "Done," he said. "It'll take Mike a few hours. You look exhausted. There's a couch back there I sometimes use."

Imogen realized just how tired she felt.

Kelly's phone pinged. He smiled. "He's on the job. Why don't you have a rest? I'll just bunk here," he said, indicating a sofa by the tables.

Just as he was lapsing into sleep, Imogen wondered if she owed Vega a Daily Report.

*   *   *

In Georgetown, at the home of a prominent "K" Street law firm, two men took a break from the festivities at a Christmas Day drinks party to slip into an empty library, away from the other guests.

"I really do need to get back to Boston," said one as the second man helped him into his overcoat. "But tell me, how is the coalition-building going?"

"Not so well," said Senator Eliot's Chief of Staff, Casey Hague. "There's a willingness to be helpful, I think, but they need some encouragement, some reason they can point to; and maybe an incentive."

"The Illinois scandal isn't enough?" He pulled a plaid scarf from his coat pocket and put it around his neck.

"No," said Hague. "A lot of them don't like the look of it, but they feel like the results and the report were legitimate. And those who don't feel that way are telling me they think they need to show some faith in the rule of law after everything that's been happening."

"Stay calm. We're working on that. I can send you more for them to worry about through our mutual friend. You understand that the slow drip works better than the all-out assault, don't you?"

"I guess," said Hague.

"The slow drip is very disturbing to the party bosses and the nation. They don't know whether there's ever an end to it. And as long as we're involved, there won't be. Our mutual friend has some more awkward findings, which he'll be passing on to you and that reporter shortly. It's up to you exactly who you share them with on your end."

"Okay," said Hague.

"The public doesn't like it either when bad reports just keep coming," he said. "Innuendo here; some disturbing statistics there; stories about how close the vote was in some states. All these opinions about the Illinois result—it doesn't really matter now whether there was tampering or not, there will always be doubt, however many reports say it's in the clear."

"And there's more to come?"

"Much more; we've hardly started with some of this stuff."

"You barely have thirteen days. January sixth is right around the corner," said Hague.

"We're doing our part. You do yours. And don't fixate on the sixth. There's no way any of this goes through on the first day's balloting. We're in this for the long haul. We had a plan and we built in contingencies." He buttoned the navy overcoat.

"The FBI is focused on trying to find out who's behind the killings," he continued, "and failing." He smiled more broadly. "But that was just the beginning. You know it is," he said, patting Hague good-naturedly on the shoulder, "post-haste, post facto, post-truth. I'll see you next week. Bring me some good news."

* * *

Trey shook Imogen awake. "My man Mike's come through. You ready? I could use some help," he said. He turned and walked away.

Imogen blinked, confused. "Right," she said. "Coming." She felt awful, disoriented after working virtually 24 hours at a stretch. She was dizzy as she swung her feet to the floor. Her eyes refused to focus on her watch. Propelling herself out of the back and down into the main computer room, she walked directly to the table and rummaged through the bag of food she'd brought god knows how many hours ago. A small carton of orange juice was welcome, if warm. The taste and sugars brought her around quickly, though her stomach still felt uneasy.

Trey smiled, and gestured to where he wanted her to sit. She wondered what she looked like. She checked her watch again: just before four in the afternoon. "Is it still Christmas?" she asked through a yawn.

"Yeah, and I have a present for you. Lots of work ahead of us. There's coffee," he added, pushing a Styrofoam cup at her.

Going through the numbers of the callers Mike had identified was daunting, but they quickly hit on a formula for testing them and the work went swiftly. By 6 p.m., they had sent Mike a tracking request for a series of specific numbers. By 8:30, they had a data dump back from him, and a little after 10:00 they had a working timeline of the movements and activities for their four targets.

Imogen and Trey ran quick bullshit tests on their data to make sure they were on the right track. The movements shown by the new data matched those of their three known targets from their personal phones. It was them alright.

"I think that's about all we can do today," said Trey.

"It's much more than I had hoped. We've got a part of at least one cell of the network," said Imogen. "Thank you. This could be a big break. We can see that they were directed by Benny to watch my apartment. Here's the call," she said, indicating a moment on the timeline. "And here's the call directing them to Novaczeck's building. Here they are at the building. And, as I thought, we have evidence that something's still going on."

She pointed at the screen again. "I need to check with the files in my office, but I'll bet this is them killing the Post reporter. And here's a call from Benny to someone in Boston, and two from Mr. Boston to someone in Newton, New Jersey."

"I don't like calling him 'Mister'," said Trey. "Too much respect."

"Beanie?" Imogen offered.

"Too close to Bennie." He laughed. "Wicked pissah!" he said in a poorly executed New England accent.

Imogen smiled. "Fine, he's 'wicked.' We'll designate the unknown guy from Newton as 'Fig' then?"

"Hmm," said Trey ruefully. "I love Fig Newtons."

"I'm going to need to get this back to the Bureau in the morning," said Imogen, "where I have full notes on the dead electors and Kurtz and others; and I want to confirm that they killed that reporter. I guess I'm going to need to show it to Vega and Weir. I hope there are usable prints on the baggy with the SIMs in it." She paused. "You can send this data to me, can't you?" Imogen asked.

Trey shook his head. "It's too big. What I'll do is give you a link and a password. The show will run right off of here."

"Great, but—"

"—I already thought of that. Here's a back-up drive." He smiled as he wrapped the cord around it and handed her the drive. "Keep it somewhere safe. It's all the data. I compressed it. But it'll take a really powerful system to run it—what we have here, or what a university might have."

"Are you going to take a break?" she asked.

"Yeah. I'm spent. I could run you home too, if you'd like. We've got Benny's new number, plus Wicked and Figgy," said Trey. "They're flagged now. If any one of them turns on that phone, we'll know about it. No problem getting full wiretaps now, is there?"

As Imogen stepped out of Trey's car in front of her building, the man in the parked Buick took pictures of her, of Trey, of the license plate. He put down the camera and pretended to be rummaging in his glove compartment as Trey drove blithely by again.

* * *

Imogen took her own portable drive to the office and deposited it in a low drawer of her desk when she arrived, barely rested, at 6 a.m. The portable drive that Trey had given her was in a bag with her laptop at home. Even if the FBI was still monitoring her, she hoped it was a detail they weren't likely to notice. She texted Weir and Vega that she had some new developments to show them immediately. Both responded that they would be in before 7:00, and were as good

72

as their word. She gave them a quick summary, turning her computer screen around and clicking play.

"Pause it a second," said Weir after a few moments.

Imogen froze it.

"How did you get this?" asked Weir.

"I thought you were just looking for chatter," said Vega.

Imogen explained it in full: how she had followed up the phones because she thought doing so might show that the network was still actively talking; and it was.

Her first step, she told them—following their regular phones—had led to the drop areas. She and Trey, the director of the IT group, had been able to confirm that they were getting their new SIMs from these drops because she had found the last one, uncollected. She pointed to the green folder from the potting shed. And more, she told them, trying not to seem like she was gloating: there was a fourth person of interest who was clearly the handler, not Kurtz. From the fact that they called when they had the new SIMs, and usually from the area where they picked them up, she had been able to go back and trace the other numbers they'd been using over the past eighteen months.

"And I'll need a backdated warrant for all this, I think," said Imogen. "And a memo request, also backdated for NSA file sharing."

"Done," said Weir distractedly, still staring at the screen. "What else do you need?"

"Going forward, we need to be able to listen in, too," said Imogen. "Agent Vega," she said, "I'm hopeful there's a usable fingerprint on the baggie on this envelope."

"I'll get it down to the lab myself," said Amanda Vega as she stood up. She had to involve herself; she was being outpaced by an agent she was supposed to be commanding. She had never been very keen, she found herself thinking, on redheads.

"Also," said Imogen, "can we check again whether Trebor or Covington had a padlock key like this?" She showed her the one she had from Kurtz's belongings. Vega looked closely at the key. Her eyes narrowed.

"Do you think it's the handler?" Weir asked as Vega walked out.

"It could well be. I'm afraid I haven't done much more than compile this, so I want to spend some time noting movements, calls, cross-referencing with any other activities and see what comes of that. There are more numbers to follow up, too. And those might be productive. This might be a good time to bring in some other agents," she added.

Weir was texting. "Hang on a minute. I want the Director down here before you start again." He sent the text and looked up at her. "This is a really big break. Excellent work. But I'm not going to bring in more agents just yet. I want to contain the information for now. I told you when we met that I worried that Agent Colls, retired, might somehow be involved." He looked toward the door: "Or one of his disciples. Judas, maybe. Let's keep this close for a few days."

* * *

Squinting in the hospital's unhospitable light Duncan Calder blinked to focus on the doctor. His shoulder throbbed.

"Good morning, professor," the doctor began, a little too jovially in Calder's opinion.

Calder opened his mouth but no sound came. His mouth tasted foul.

The doctor passed him what looked like a child's "sippy cup" with a straw. Duncan tasted the water gratefully, letting it fill his mouth. It was sweet and cool. He swallowed and the coolness turned to burning. He took another pull from the straw, which eased the burning in his throat.

"Better?" asked another, much taller man, standing behind the doctor. His tone was less friendly than the doctor's: flat, impatient.

"Yes," Calder rasped.

"Do you know where you are?" asked the doctor.

"Hospital?" said Calder. Was it a trick question? he wondered.

"What can you remember?" asked the tall man with the impatient tone.

5

Imogen picked up her Washington Post in the hallway outside her apartment. She was rested and eager. "Illinois Questions Unanswered," a headline declared.

She felt a jolt as she saw her picture, and then her name in the first sentence: "In the continuing struggle over the Presidency, FBI Agent Imogen Trager's analysis of the Illinois results has raised more questions than it answers," the story began. It went on to rehash the conjecture and rumor surrounding her work, citing the official statements and findings only late on the continuation page.

She arrived at work later than she would have liked, her excitement diminished, and dreading Weir. Sharon met her just outside her office. Imogen hoped she'd come to bolster her spirits.

"Holy shit, Gen!" whispered Sharon, smiling. "Vega trotted in two guys from the evidence team. They'd forgotten to note a padlock key that Trebor or Covington had—something about it being vital to the investigation; that it matched one Tom carried."

"So they had it?" she asked as they walked to Imogen's office. Imogen threw her bag carelessly in a corner and shrugged off her coat as she sat down.

"They did. Monroe kept it to see what it fit but hadn't properly noted it. I've never seen Weir so angry. Or Vega. Those guys are lucky to still be alive. They're gonna be working the carpool til they retire." She smiled and shook her head. "What's happened?"

"Our first real break, I think," said Imogen.

"I knew it!" said Sharon.

"We don't have anything yet," Imogen cautioned. "We've found something, but we don't know what it means."

"You got the break. Good work, girl!"

Just then, Agent Vega stepped in to Imogen's office.

"Agent Trager, it is not appropriate for you to be discussing current investigations no matter what your personal history—"

"—Yes, thank you. I was merely making sure Ms. Voth knew how important and vital her work had been, and how much we all appreciated it."

"Uh huh," said Vega. "We've got a line on the fingerprint. Wanna take a ride?"

Imogen jumped up and followed Vega into the passage, pulling on her coat as she walked. Vega was talking rapidly, and walking almost at a jog. "We found him here in DC," she said. "James Allen May. We'll get him. You don't have armor or a sidearm, do you?" she asked as they coursed through the hallway.

"No, neither."

"Then you'll stay in the van. This guy's got a long history with the DC Police, drug-dealing, weapons charges. Don't even open the door. Understood?"

In the parking garage, Imogen sat on the front seat of Vega's truck. Agents swirled around her, getting last-minute instructions, checking weapons. Her heart raced. She was glad of the activity, happy that things were moving, pleased to see first-hand what all her work could bring about. But as she looked at the swarming agents in their black attack armor, she kept seeing the agents streaming into the garage ten days earlier, her head spinning with fear; Calder, Pollack and Kurtz covered in blood.

Vega tore out of the garage. She barked orders into a headset as she drove, leading a menacing group of four identical black SUVs weaving in and out of sparse traffic southwest toward Congress Heights. She was calling for status updates and telling agents which street corners she wanted controlled. Imogen held on, mesmerized.

As Vega's SUV sped deeper into Congress Heights, the passing homes changed from modest to dilapidated. Imogen's excitement gave way to misgivings. It was difficult to imagine a mastermind launching a nationwide conspiracy while scratching out an existence on these litter-strewn streets, where even some of the freestanding houses had iron bars on the windows and doors.

Vega pulled up just short of a squat beige house about midblock. Two of the trucks behind her surged past and slammed to a halt, one at the curb, the other on the lawn of the house. Agents in full armor swarmed out. Imogen looked back for the fourth truck, but it had turned down the alleyway and was storming the house from the rear.

She saw agents break through the door with a battering ram and surge inside, machine guns aimed high and low. She wondered what it must be like to be invaded like this. Did their target live alone? Was he with his family? Were they sitting around the breakfast table when their front door caved in?

She didn't wonder long. What seemed seconds later, a man was dragged from the house and thrown onto the frozen lawn. An agent pushed a knee into his back and handcuffed him, then hoisted him by the handcuffs and propelled him to a waiting SUV. Another agent came out onto the front step and signaled all clear to Vega and Imogen.

"Let's check it out," said Vega opening the door of the SUV.

Imogen followed Vega into the house. It was dim and bleak. And cold. She could see her breath. It was almost as cold inside as outside. Imogen walked carefully over beer cans, sports-drink bottles and other trash.

"Electricity's been shut off," said one of the other agents scanning the house. "No running water either."

Imogen walked through the wreckage. Open food resting on a stove that didn't work. Futon mattress on the floor. Flashlights, crushed juice boxes, a candle melted onto the kitchen counter. Her heart sank. This wasn't a lead. It was a human tragedy.

"What about the basement?" Vega asked the agent.

"Clear," he said.

"Anyone else?"

"No one," he said.

Vega frowned. "Papers? Cellphone?"

"No papers."

"Check his phone right now. Make sure there's been no communication in the past twenty minutes or so. Then tag it. Let's clear out and get the evidence team in. Every inch."

The ride back to headquarters was less dramatic. Vega updated Weir over her headset as she drove.

"Yes, we've got May. No. Nothing else. Evidence will go over the house, but first impressions are we won't find much." Vega listened for a moment, and her face turned sour. "Are you sure that's necessary? Yes, of course, sir." She hung up.

"Weir wants you in as part of the interrogation," she said.

"Have you ever done an interrogation?"

"I've been interrogated," Imogen offered.

Vega shook her head.

Imogen and Vega hurried to their respective offices to collect information for the interrogation. Imogen printed a picture of the recently retired agent Andrew Colls. She made a quick check of the hallway and then dialed Weir's number.

"It's Imogen. I'd like to bring along a picture of Andrew Colls to the interrogation."

"I don't want you tipping off Vega, if she's involved."

"So, should I not bring it?" she asked.

"No," he said, "bring it. I'll show up about ten minutes into the interview and ask to confer with her. Hold your fire until then."

"Understood."

* * *

Hugh Salter stopped putting dishes into the dishwasher to take a call. It was Patriot76.

"Oh, it's you," he said. "Thanks, but I'm not looking for any more career-damaging scoops."

"It's Christmas, Salter. I'm offering you a gift."

"No. Christmas is over, and I look stupid. The company looks stupid. I thought it looked like a preliminary model; I said it looked preliminary, but then I went with your assessment."

"You only have the government's assurance that's what it was," said Patriot76.

"Come on." Salter's thumb hovered over the disconnect button.

"They're covering up fast. They have to. I'm going to send you over something. That agent, Trager? She and Kurtz were involved. You don't think they want to keep that hushed up? He, Kurtz, was point-man on the Illinois investigation. He got her the data, and now he's dead."

"What?"

"I think we need to know: did she massage the figures to suit her boyfriend? Was she in on something else and had to kill him? Did she corrupt him—lead him astray—and then kill him? Have you seen her? She's gorgeous!"

"The FBI has been frank about what hap—"

"—I don't think we can buy their version of events about what happened in that parking garage."

"What are you talking about?"

"The professor with her, Calder? He was a suspect in the Novaczeck murder, but he somehow gets a pass into the parking garage next to the White House?"

Salter had walked quickly to his home office, where he was now scribbling furiously. "What was Calder's first name again?"

"Duncan. Duncan Calder. Professor of Political Science at the University of Washington in Seattle, a specialist in voting and electoral politics."

"And where is he now?"

"No one knows. We don't know where Doug Pollack, the Executive Assistant Director, is either. Are they alive? Are they being questioned?"

"My God," said Salter. It was beginning to feel like Christmas after all.

"I'll get you those pictures of Trager and Kurtz together."
Patriot76 hung up, and Salter sat down at his computer.

"Well," Vega said to James May as she walked into the
interrogation room, followed by Imogen. "You're certainly
moving up in the world." She dropped the folder containing
his prior offenses record on the table.

"I was about to say the same for you all," said May. He
was handsome and animated, 19 years old, according to his
file. His hair was razored on the sides and twisted into the
beginnings of dreadlocks on top. "This is nice," he added,
looking around approvingly at his surroundings. He glanced
approvingly at Imogen, too. "Real nice."

His eyes roved over the room, and Imogen. The gaze was
not furtive or jumpy. He would fix on something, take it in,
then move to the next thing.

Vega paused. "Where do you think you are?" she asked.

"Well, not that shithole Seventh District station, that's for
sure."

"I'm Special Agent Amanda Vega of the FBI. This is
Special Agent Trager."

"FBI?" He shifted uncomfortably in his chair and looked
around again.

"Do I have your attention now?"

"What the fuck's FBI doing breaking into my house? I
ain't done shit."

"Well," said Vega, "that's what we're here to find out."
She resettled her chair.

"You got the wrong guy. There's nothing I ever done the
FBI would care about."

"You know what Jimmy, I hope that's true. But let's talk.
Because right now, I'm looking at you as an accessory to
murder." Vega looked over at Imogen.

"Accessory to—?"

"—Tell us about your day on December sixteenth," said
Imogen, "Last Friday. Where were you? Where did you go?
What did you do?" Imogen tried to keep her expression flat,

dispassionate.   She hoped her face didn't betray her own amazement that it had been less than two weeks since the whole plot had been revealed.

Vega had been paging through May's priors record. "We know you're a runner . . . that you do things for people. We can't quite tell if you're attached to one gang.   Are you freelance?   Tell us about your movements on December sixteen."

"Here's the thing," May began, "I do a lot of little things for people. Some of them wouldn't like me talking about it."

"We're FBI, Jimmy, I don't give a fuck about dope right now. I need to hear everything, and if you're cooperative, I don't need to pass on anything I hear to the DC Police."

"Tell us: was there anything out of the ordinary?" asked Imogen.

"The old white guy, you mean?"

"Maybe," said Vega. "Why don't you tell us everything?"

"Ok, I shape up along MLK, anywhere I can find a spot between Lebaum and Mellon. People roll up—"

"—Wait," said Vega. "Shape up? Like longshoremen? Like migrant workers?"

"I gotta work, don't I?"

"Go on."

"People roll up. They say 'Jimmy take this here, see this guy there; Jimmy, deliver this; bring back a message.' I've got a pretty good rep for not looking at what I carry, not saying anything if I get scooped."

"Do they ever text you?"

"Nah. They know where I'm gonna be."

"Never?" Vega prodded.

"Not serious people."

"Ever deliver a green folder?" asked Imogen.

"The old white guy . . ." he said, nodding as though many things were becoming clear. "Look," he said, fixing his eyes on Vega, "if that's what y'all want to talk about, I can cooperate. Anything else, you need to charge me, and I need a lawyer." He turned his head and scratched his ear, but his eyes never left Vega's.

"Fair enough," agreed Vega. "We stick to the old white guy."

Imogen opened her folder and laid out a picture of Kurtz.

"Was this him?"

"Nah."

She laid out a picture of Trebor, then Covington.

"No," he said to both. "Old," he said. "I told you he was old."

"Did the old white guy ever text you?"

"No."

There was a knock at the door, and Director Weir walked in, followed by a uniformed agent. "Agent Vega, there may have been some new developments. Could I speak with you a moment?"

"Of course," said Vega, and she got up from the table. She accompanied Weir outside. The uniformed agent stayed.

When the door closed, Imogen turned back to May. "Have you ever seen that man before?"

"The boss just now?"

"Yes."

"No."

Imogen took out the picture of Colls. "What about this man?"

May looked closely. He smiled and nodded. "Yeah, the old white guy—that's him." He tapped the photo with a finger.

"What kind of car did he drive?" she asked, glancing at a sheet containing Colls' details.

"Our deal's still on? We talk only about this guy . . . and then you're gonna let me go?"

"I guess it depends on what we hear, how cooperative you are. So, what kind of car did he drive?"

"Dark, dark blue Lincoln. Like an MK-Z."

It matched. That was Colls' car. She was simultaneously happy to have caught a break and apprehensive about what that break could mean. She steadied herself, took a deep breath. "Did he ever text you?" she asked.

"No. He'd just roll up same as everyone else."

"Then what? What were your instructions? How many times did you make deliveries?"

"I've been doing it about two years . . . maybe not quite."

"How often?"

"Pretty much every month. Regular. I should've figured he was into some deep, ugly government bullshit." He paused. "What murder? Who's been killed?"

"Let me ask the questions. How often?"

"Believe me, I didn't know anything. I do my job. I keep my head down, don't ask questions. Did the old white guy kill someone?"

"You ask a lot of questions for someone who doesn't ask questions," Imogen observed. "What else can you tell us?"

"I stick with local shit mostly, but he was regular, once a month and he always paid up front."

The door opened again and Weir and Vega walked back in. Imogen looked over her shoulder at Weir. She nodded. "Confirmed," she said. "It's him."

Weir looked at the ground. "Dammit," he whispered.

Imogen turned away as Vega looked between both her and Weir. Weir opened the door again. "Miller," he called down the hallway. "Will you come here please?"

Miller appeared at the doorway. "You and I will escort Agent Vega to interrogation room four. Agent Vega, will you voluntarily allow me to examine your phone?"

Agent Vega stiffened. She stared straight ahead. She did not blush, but her face became red. "Sir?" she said, "may I ask—?"

"—I am hopeful that we can resolve any issues or conflicts by a brief discussion."

"I am pleased to assist you in any way possible, sir," said Vega tightly. She handed her phone to Weir. "And this is my personal phone," she added, handing it to him.

"Thank you," said Weir. "Interrogation four," he repeated to Miller. Vega and Miller left for the other room. "Everything goes on the two-o-nine form," he said to Imogen. "Be clear." He closed the door behind him.

The guard in the room sighed his relief as the door closed.

"What the fuck is going on here?" asked May.

"Walk me through how each encounter would work," said Imogen, searching through her papers.

"I think there's some weird shit goin' down, and I—"

"—They have a job, and we have a job. If you'd like to get out of here and go home, let's stay focused." Imogen cast her mind back to May's house, and suddenly felt that perhaps 'home' wasn't much of an enticement to him. She refocused.

"Tell me, how would each encounter work?"

"I'd see his car, and I'd walk to the curb. I'd get in, and we'd drive a block or two. He'd hand me the bag, give me some money, and I'd get out."

"Where did you take it?"

"It was two places."

"Each time?"

"No. One month it was Rock Creek Park. The next month, Lansburgh Park. Then back to Rock Creek the following month."

"How did you get there?"

"Taxi. He'd give me a hundred dollars for the job, plus twenty for Lansburgh, or plus sixty to Rock Creek. For Rock Creek, I figured out that I could take DC Metro to Silver Spring or Forest Glen and then take a taxi and pocket the extra thirty-five or forty dollars."

"Very entrepreneurial," said Imogen.

Outside interrogation room four, Acting Assistant Director, Don Weir dialed the Deputy Director, Bill Dyer. "It's Don," he said. "Can you tell me what channels we've used to disseminate the intel regarding the network data Agent Trager presented?"

"None. Only I and the people on your team know any details. I told the AG we finally had a good line of inquiry, and that I would report back as soon as we knew more. I probably mentioned the network analysis to her, but only in general terms. What's happened?"

"It's paid off, Bill, but not as we might have liked. It looks like the bleeding isn't localized."

"Fuck. Who?"

"Colls. The courier ID'ed him."

"How do you want to proceed?"

"I'm about to put Colls under surveillance. I think I'd like to leave him out there thinking everything's fine while we institute a full field investigation. I want his phones tapped, not just monitored. I want to understand more about the whole network before we commit. I want this contained."

"Yes, right. Of course, there's a risk he might find out and cut off all ties. He might even run." Dyer paused. "No. I want you to pick him up today, Don. Do it yourself. Hand-pick your team, and do it quietly. Minimal scope."

"Understood, sir. I've detained Agent Vega, and I need to debrief her. Like Kurtz, she's a bit of a Colls protégé. I'd like to trust her, she's a damn good cop, but this business with the padlock key has me worried. I'm going to scrutinize her office and her phone before we move on Colls. About two hours."

"Fine. Let me know how it goes. You'll have the warrant before you move on Colls."

"Thank you, sir." Weir hung up. He peeked through a small window on the door into interrogation room four. Agent Vega was sitting up straight, her forearms resting on the tabletop. She looked straight ahead.

Still outside, he dialed a number. "Guthrie? It's Weir. Time to set up shop. Colls. Like we discussed. Top secret, even within the Bureau. Set up immediately. We move to arrest in about two hours. Once you're established, stay on site until you hear from me."

Weir signaled to an agent waiting down the hall. "Bishop," he beckoned.

Bishop walked up swiftly. Weir gave him the two phones. "Scrutinize the calls made from these; the past two years. Particularly this one," he said, pointing at Vega's personal phone. "These are Agent Vega's company and personal phones. I realize scrutinizing a fellow agent is awkward, but it's vital. You are not to communicate anything about this investigation to anyone. Not even your teddy bear.

"Either I or Agent Trager will forward you a list of numbers you'll need to cross-reference and scrutinize. I want to know who everyone is; and make damn sure you don't just rely on the name on the contact info in the phone. I want texts, too. See Sharon in my office. She'll expedite it all."

"Understood," said Bishop.

"Fast, please. I need to see your first results in about an hour."

Bishop nodded and went. When he was out of sight of Weir, he broke into a run.

Sharon Voth was just hanging up from talking to Weir when Bishop strode into her office, his face flushed from running.

"Did you ever see anyone hanging around?" Imogen asked May.

"Nah. Nothing. Look, people are gonna know I got picked up. If you just let me go, my friends are gonna think I gave something up about them."

"I'll talk with my boss. We'll make sure you're safe."

"Safe? Why wouldn't I be safe? I'd just tell them it was FBI; that they didn't give a shit about nothin' else. They were looking for the old dude who used to come by."

"Yes, I see," said Imogen.

Weir was seated across from Vega in room four. "Okay, he said, "we have an ID from your fingerprint subject over there, who says that Andrew Colls was orchestrating the drops for Kurtz and his team. Colls may even turn out to be Benny from the telephone surveillance that Trager put together."

"What? Colls is Benny? How do you figure?"

"Your man in there just ID'ed him as the guy who would give him the SIM cards to drop off."

"Colls?" Her eyes stared blankly into the middle distance.

"Do you have anything to add to that?"

"No, sir."

"When was the last time you saw Colls?"

"At his retirement party back in September," she said.

"You're sure?"

"Any other contact? A phone call, text, email?"

"Nothing, sir. I mean, I saw a Facebook post here and there—'retirement is sweet,' 'thinking about you all in the trenches'—that kind of thing. I'd hit 'like' because that's what you do. Some people talked about missing him . . ." She trailed off. "May I speak freely, sir?"

"I would encourage you do so," said Weir.

"I thought he was an arrogant prick, sir, but I know you can't choose your bosses. I was grateful, I guess, for the little attention he gave me and for what it had probably done for my career. But, sir, not much liking him is very different from suspecting him of being capable of anything like this. I don't see it."

"We're searching your office and your contacts for the past two years," said Weir. "Is there anything further you want to disclose at this time?"

"Should I have an FBIAA rep present for this, sir?"

"That is certainly your right."

"There's no damn way I'm getting bounced out," she asserted. "Are you arresting me?"

"No. And I hope we won't have to."

Vega took a deep breath, seemed to push the rising anger down. "I have had minimal association with Agent Colls," she began. "Let's be honest, I'm not one of his real protégés."

"Who is, for instance?"

"Here at HQ it was mostly Kurtz and Jezek and maybe a few others."

"Phil Jezek?" asked Weir.

"Yes. Or in the case of Jezek, maybe I should say 'acolyte.' At any rate, there was clearly an affinity among them, and Colls helped them along professionally."

"And you . . . no?"

"Not really. I was the odd one out. I wasn't chummy-clubby like them. I don't drink, except for the occasional beer, don't go in for politics; and since my father died last year, I don't go out much because I'm home with my mother. Frankly, I didn't go out much before then. Colls, Kurtz and Jezek were all about promotion—of themselves, mostly. I think I was—certainly, I always felt—like window-dressing for them. A female, and an Hispanic as part of their group kind of threw people off the scent."

"The scent," Weir repeated. "And what did it smell of?" he asked.

"Musky cologne, bourbon and crisp privilege. I don't think I'd have put this together before. But, that group of guys was pretty conservative."

"Politically? That's hardly very damning."

"Yes, sir. I guess I mean more than conservative, then: reactionary, maybe. And there was something more to it. Nothing—prior to Kurtz's involvement in this plot with the Electors—nothing that I could put a finger on. But in hindsight, thinking about it all in terms of what you're telling me, it was like a barely secret agenda."

"Like what?" he asked.

"Like they were looking for certain kinds of people, and not necessarily the most competent agents; just ones who were . . . I don't know, angry and frustrated about the same kinds of things; about how maybe the right sort of people weren't running things anymore? They were hardly collecting the smartest as friends. I mean, Jezek's an idiot." She paused.

"You have some strong opinions about a number of your colleagues, Agent Vega," said Weir.

"I guess I do. I guess if I'm going to get bounced out behind their bullshit, I might at least say what I think for once." She paused and took a deep breath. "What I'm trying to say is, I don't know how much I can help you. I was 'in,' but I wasn't on the inside with them."

Weir stared at her flatly for a moment. "Talk to me about the missing padlock key," he said to her.

Amanda Vega's head dropped. Her voice was strained as she said: "Monroe and Fitzwater were part of the evidence collection team. They failed to log the key properly while they searched for a lock it might fit." She swallowed hard. "And I failed to supervise them properly."

"You see how this looks," said Weir.

"I do," said Vega.

Back in room three, Jimmy May was thinking about how it would look when he was released. "I mean I guess I ain't that worried," he allowed. "Damn-near everybody's gonna know it was FBI anyway."

"How?" said Imogen.

There was a knock at the door. The guard opened it, and an agent stepped in. He held out May's confiscated phone to her.

"This thing's blowing up," he said to her. "Ten or more texts in the last five minutes."

"I thought you said no one texted you," said Imogen.

"Not about a job. No one wants a trail. But now I ain't been on my spot, they're thinking the worst."

Imogen started scrolling though the texts.

"Now that's some bullshit right there," he said to her. "Those are private communications. Isn't there some Freedom of Expression shit or Interstate Commerce clause makes it so you can't be readin' my phone?"

Imogen didn't look up. The texts—12 of them, all from different numbers—took on a frantic tone when looked it in sequence:

"where u at?"
"J text me"
"DRo lkg for u."
"wtf! where you at?
"J you at the 7th?"
"you get scooped by fbi?"
"B says fbi got you—hmb"

"What about Serve and Protect?" May pleaded.

"That's the cops," said Imogen, still not looking up. "We're Fidelity, Bravery, Integrity—F B I."

"*Integrity?*" he yelled. "You're investigating yourselves right now! You're asking me if the boss is in on whatever shit you got goin' on. You're arresting other agents!"

89

Imogen showed May the last two texts. "How do they know this?"

"When do I get outta here?" he asked. He folded his arms and looked at the far wall.

"Answer the question."

"I want a lawyer."

"This is national security. We are way past that now." She paused. "You may go when I say so."

She cringed inwardly at her own words. What was she turning into? she wondered. She and Trey had played fast and loose with the Fourth Amendment stipulations about right to privacy and freedom from unreasonable search and seizure; she and Vega had denied May due process (Fifth Amendment) and now she had just denied him the right to counsel (Sixth). It was only Tuesday. What corners wouldn't she cut?

"It's pretty clear you're not involved," she said reassuringly. "We're working on getting you out of here," she said with practiced calm, though she wondered if they could actually let him go any time soon. Not only did they need to check his story, they needed to watch him for his own safety. She had seen what the conspirators could do. "But we need to be sure," she continued, "and we need to understand what's going on. Now: how do they know?"

"Look, you don't have to be a genius. When I didn't show up this morning, they figured I got rolled. So a couple people who I ain't gonna tell y'all about, probably got worried about where I was—why—and what I might say. But no one could find me at the Seventh District station, so they probably checked the Sixth. By that point, somebody they know saw y'all roust me or heard from someone who had."

"How far can information like that get?"

"As far as it needs to."

Imogen heard a phone ping. She looked at May's phone for a moment before realizing the sound had come from beside her chair. She reached into her bag. It was from Trey Kelly:

"Benny just got a call." She stood up, told the guard to stay with May and went out. She dialed Trey's number.

"He's on the move," said Kelly by way of greeting.

"Where did he start?" she asked.

Trey gave her an address in Bethesda matching Colls' home. "Where've you been?" Trey demanded. "I texted you like 15 minutes ago."

"I just got it. There must be a weak signal in the interrogation rooms. Where is he now?"

"Shit. Well, he's on the move now. He left Bethesda and he's on the road. Right now he's between Cabin John and Tysons Corner."

"Stay on the phone," she said to him, and as she turned to pound on the door to interrogation four, Weir was already opening it.

"Colls is on the move," he said to her, taking his phone away from his ear to speak.

"Benny made a call from Colls' address about fifteen minutes ago," said Imogen. "He's on the road, heading west, near Tysons."

"Well, that's our confirmation," said Weir. "Shit! Tysons Corner is on the way to Dulles Airport. If he's still heading west, he's running!"

"Where is he now?" Imogen asked Kelly.

There was a pause.

"Trey?" she said again.

"The signal's gone dark," said Kelly. "He must have turned it off."

Imogen shook her head at Weir. "We lost the signal."

"Damn!"

"Does your guy have eyes on him?" asked Imogen.

"No. He's not pursuing. I told him to focus on watching the house because we were going to be there soon enough anyway," said Weir. "Stay there," he said into the phone. "Secure the area. No one in or out. We're still going to tear that place apart. I'll call you back." He hung up.

Weir took the phone from Imogen. "Do we have audio?" he asked Kelly.

"No, I was in the process of setting it up. I got the authorization about two hours ago, but it's just me down here at the mo—" said Kelly.

"Shit!" Weir hissed.

"Colls made his call, and then he hung up," Kelly continued. "The new contact called someone else. I didn't have time to establish audio for them. I'll have it in soon if either one calls back or calls someone else."

"Very good," said Weir. He handed the phone back to Imogen, who hung up.

"Colls initiated the call," she said to Weir. "That was the first time he turned on the phone since we've been on him. Until now, he's always been on the move when he calls. The signal came on right at or near his house in Bethesda. He knew we're getting close," she added.

Weir stared down the hallway at the agents gathered there. "How the fuck did he know?"

6

"You said you were being watched," said Agent Brody, sitting across a table from Calder, in his hospital room.

As he looked at Brody, Calder had the impression of looking at an adult sitting in a child's chair. He could not be sure if Brody was just massively tall, or if the painkillers were warping his perceptions. Whatever the reason, the room felt cramped, the ceiling somehow lower. Calder felt tired. His thoughts flowed slowly. It was difficult to focus. And discomfiting to be sitting in a hospital robe opposite someone dressed for work.

"Are you with me, professor?" asked Brody, his voice edged with annoyance.

"Yes," said Calder and stared off at the blinds covering a window on the far wall. What was going on out there? he wondered. Was Imogen OK? Distantly, like a half-formed thought that needed attention, the distant throbbing in his shoulder and torso tugged at his mind. It was as if the pain was all on one side of a heavy door, clamoring to get in. At the thought of a door, his mind turned back to the steel door in the parking garage, the bullets ricocheting off it. He felt again the bullets tear into him as Kurtz had burst through that door. His hand moved involuntarily to his ribs. He saw again the thick blood spreading. It had been a strange sensation, shivering even as warm blood pumped across him.

"And?" said Brody

Calder looked blankly at Brody. He yawned.

Brody took a deep breath. "How did you know you were being watched?"

"Someone broke into my office and went through my files, trying to see what I knew. At the time, I didn't know anything about the plot, which is probably why I'm still alive."

"If it's as you say, surely they'd have wanted to sew everything up. Maybe it was just a break-in. Happens all the time on campuses."

"I doubt it," said Calder, and stared at the contours of the false wood grain on the tabletop. He twisted his head side to side as he gazed at the whorls.

Brody stood up, impressing Calder again with how tall he was, how out of proportion to the room. "Let's try again tomorrow," he said tightly.

Calder stared at him intently, wondering just how far Brody was going to have to stoop to make it through the door.

"Until then," said Brody.

Calder nodded, watching, waiting to see him go out the door, and when Brody dipped his head only slightly, Calder felt obscurely cheated.

He forgot Brody a moment later. It suddenly seemed like a very good idea to crawl back into the bed.

Outside the room, Brody stalked to the nurse's station. The attending physician was there, reviewing Pollack's charts with one of the nurses.

"My God!" said Brody, gesturing back toward Calder's room. "What have you got him on?"

"Agent Brody, I did tell you it was probably too early."

"He's stoned out of his mind!" said Brody.

"He has two broken ribs, a shattered shoulder blade, bone from which tore into his lung; his right arm is broken and his right hand has multiple fractures. We either load him up on painkillers, or he screams day and night and his overall progress is even slower. Either way, he won't focus very well for long. We stepped the dosage down a bit yesterday. Tomorrow we'll do a little less. While he might still tire easily, I think he'll be able to give coherent answers by Friday. Which was my original suggestion."

Brody sighed. He looked at the blank notepad in his hand. "What about Pollack?" he asked.

"He's going to pull through. I want to confer with Doctors Hart and Schwartz, but I think we might try to bring him around on Friday. Still, he's a long way off."

Brody nodded and walked slowly down the corridor.

*   *   *

Hugh Salter sat in his home office, his attention divided between the phone call he was having with Patriot76, a story breaking on a muted television at the far side of the room, and photos on his computer of Imogen and Tom Kurtz.

On the muted television, a rally of Christopher supporters had quickly turned into an ugly skirmish with pro-Redmond counter-demonstrators in front of the Capitol steps. The photos on his computer looked like pictures that must have come from the dead man, Kurtz himself: a selfie on a beach with Imogen, a close shot of the two of them at a café, kissing, his arm draped across the back of her chair; Imogen laughing, clearly trying to avoid being photographed.

From all this, Salter struggled to articulate an emerging pattern, but nothing would come. What, if anything, connected it all? he wondered. On the television screen behavioral norms, trust in the rule of law were disintegrating; on his desktop two FBI operatives were canoodling, flouting the rules of their employment. He looked away from the television and peered at the photographs, trying to divine where they were taken. Did he recognize anything in the café? Who took that picture? Which beach was it?

"Look," he said "I need to know where these photos came from," he said to Patriot76 distractedly. If he kept Patriot76 talking, he might catch a clue or at the very least get some better information.

"We have to protect our source," said Patriot76.

"Uh huh," said Salter, unconvinced. "I mean, where were these taken? By whom? These look like Kurtz's own photos," he said.

"Maybe," said Patriot76. "How to you know I'm not a friend of theirs?"

"Some friend," said Salter. "It still doesn't explain how you got the pictures off his phone. Kurtz is dead. Killed by the Secret Service on December nineteen. This is the twenty-seventh. How do you have access to his phone?"

Patriot76 did not respond. Salter tried another tack. "Look. For one, usually, if the photo is from an iPhone, when I open up the information tab on the picture, it gives me a location, along with the date and time and all that. Here, I've got time and date, but no location."

"These were cagey people, breaking the law."

"Taking a photo that can be hacked isn't very cagey," Salter rejoined.

"I didn't say they were smart."

Salter sighed. "These are from over two years ago. That much we know. How do we know any of the other stuff? Why—if you've got access to this—isn't there something a little more current?"

Salter felt himself on uncertain ground. This was good information, possibly a scoop. And there might be more to come. He didn't want to antagonize Patriot76. For all his clandestine, Deep Throat bravado, he seemed as unsophisticated and thin-skinned as a good many other conspiracy peddlers Salter had dealt with over the years. They were so certain of their information and motives that they became impatient and peevish regarding basic questions or anything they perceived of as a delay.

Salter's intuitive sense was that Patriot76 was just a delivery boy, a zealot that they—whoever they might be—could count on. Salter had to tread carefully. He peered toward the muted television again: the report had shifted locations and a scuffle had broken out among a group of state legislators on the floor of a state house.

"Maybe," he said to Patriot76, "if you could look at the source phone again there would be just a little more detail?"

If he pushed too hard, Patriot76 would find another reporter, someone less principled or guarded, who would break the stories with fewer questions. The information was newsworthy in an atmosphere like this, so it would get out easily enough. The choice he had to make was whether to be the one breaking it or be the one left on the outside, where he and his principles might soon be working freelance, trying to grow a Twitter following. And yet—the earlier story from Patriot76 had hardly advanced his career when the FBI promptly ridiculed it.

"Let's talk in a couple hours. See what you can do about a location tag," he said, "and something about how the photos came to you. Meanwhile, I'll talk to my news director," he said.

"I'll call you tomorrow," said Patriot76, and he hung up.
Salter put down the phone. He pounded his fist on the desk. He still didn't have Partiot76's phone number.

The alert that Weir initiated when Colls bolted, presumably for Dulles Airport, entailed doing everything Weir and Dyer had hoped to avoid about broadcasting their suspicions. Although Weir was in daily contact with twelve Special Agents-in-Charge at various field offices across the country, and received a daily summary digest through Vega from another group of agents detailed specifically to the Faithless Elector Task Group, the information flowed only one way—to him. In a climate where he could not trust everyone he commanded, it was prudent that only he and Dyer have the big picture, however murky that image was.

Weir had been hoping to take down Colls with a limited-scope, low-profile operation involving just a small number of agents and minimal transmission of the FBI's knowledge and intent. The Faithless Elector Task Group was a large, sprawling one, with almost sixty agents, but fortunately the key aspects about the phone tracking—his best line of inquiry—were still largely secret.

Only he, Dyer, Trager, Vega and Kelly knew the extent to which the FBI was moving forward. But now he had been forced to issue an arrest warrant, alerting agents and officers at Dulles to be on the lookout; he had had to issue hold orders for Colls' passport, to flag his credit cards, to place him on a no-fly list; and for the warrant he had had to divulge some information about the "network."

While agents were not talkative by nature or training, the marshaling of forces to arrest a retired FBI agent was going to be impossible to keep quiet. The storm of questions was coming, he knew, from Dyer, from colleagues, from the press. Worst of all, he had signaled that the Bureau knew more than it was letting on—and he had still failed to bring his suspect to ground.

Agent Bishop, who had been scrutinizing Vega's effects, had reported nothing incriminating or even indiscrete, though he had asked for a little more time. Agents were currently turning over Colls' home. Weir sat down to debrief Guthrie, the agent he had sent to observe Colls at his house. The video surveillance was cued up and ready to play on a split screen.

"Before we start it," said Weir, "walk me through. You got there at 2:17 p.m."

"Yes, sir. A moment before the time-stamp on the video."

"Your cover was cable repair. You set up down the block, out of direct sight of Colls' residence."

"Yes," said Guthrie. "At the corner, I started the dash cam—screen one, here," he said, indicating the left half of the screen. "I then deployed the cherry picker, and I had a good view of the house and the street, but the truck and I were mostly screened from the subject's view by a group of trees along the road. I set the pole cam in place and turned it on. The aerial cellular intercept antenna was already on, and I fine-tuned its reception."

"So what happened?"

"I came back down from the cherry picker, confirmed that the video camera was feeding the data backup, and began pretending to work on the box. I had barely begun surveillance when one of the residents, one Byron Wade, came out to ask what I was doing. I showed him my dummy work order, said it was a problem at the other end of the street and that he wouldn't notice any interruption in service. I got an earful about how bad the cable company's service was. He was about to launch into a speech about corporate monopolism when I told him I had a schedule to keep and had to get back to work. Five minutes later, the subject's car drove out of the driveway and headed east, as you'll see."

"And there was no call in to him in the time you were there?"

"Nothing. Only the call the subject made."

"Could the neighbor have alerted him?"

"No, sir. Phone monitoring was in place immediately, and there was no call sent or received at the subject's location before his one outgoing call. I'd approached from the west, so he would not have seen me drive by. I have no explanation."

"No one spoke to him?"

"No one, sir."

"You saw no one else?"

"There was a guy delivering those sales circulars everyone throws away, but he never went near the house. Just threw the bag onto the subject's porch, like he did for every house on both sides of the block."

"Where did he go after he went by you?"

"I can't say, sir. I'm sorry. He didn't seem important. I watched him, his actions appeared legitimate, and he made no connection with the subject. My objective was the subject and his house, and I didn't want to give away what I was doing by questioning the delivery guy."

"Yes, of course."

"He'll be on the tape," Guthrie offered.

Half an hour later, when Imogen popped her head in, Weir and Guthrie's scan of the surveillance tape had offered nothing new. Weir pointed at the man delivering the circulars. "This guy could mean something, or he could be nothing."

Imogen looked at the delivery man, young, black, beefy. "What if we showed this tape to our suspect, Jimmy May?" she said after a moment.

"Why?" asked Weir.

"From the start, he seems to have been hooked in without knowing it."

Weir considered a moment. "It can't hurt. Both couriers, I guess."

"Before we talk to him again," she began, "what can we tell him about his release? His story checks out. He did cooperate. He's worried about his safety, but he feels he can deflect his bosses' concern by letting them know he was picked up by the FBI rather than local cops. Based on the texts I saw, they've already got wind that it was us, so we're not divulging anything new. But I'm worried about his safety."

Weir thought a moment. "What did you say about your concerns?" he asked.

"Only that there were still things going on, and that he might not be safe. He wants out. I'm pretty new at this. Is there any way to keep him?"

Weir sighed. "There's always a way, but he gave us good intel. He cooperated." Weir rested his chin on his hands. "Tell him we're letting him go, but that we have one last thing before we send him on his way."

Imogen brought May to the meeting room with Weir and Guthrie.

"Mr. May," Weir began, "I thank you for your cooperation and per our agreement, you will be released. Before you go, I'd like you to look at this video from earlier today and tell me if you can identify either of the men on the tape."

May shrugged. "Sure."

The first person on the tape was Colls' neighbor. Weir paused the tape and pointed at the neighbor.

"Nah," said May. "Never seen him."

Weir restarted the tape. A moment later, the delivery man came into view, throwing his rolled circulars.

May watched for a few moments. "This is from today?" he asked.

"Yeah," said Weir. "A couple hours ago."

May chuckled.

"You know the man in the tape?" said Weir.

"Nah. Never seen him," said May. "Shit, you got played."

"Wait. So you do know him?"

"I don't know him, but you still got played. I thought FBI was supposed to be these great detectives!" He chortled again.

Weir peered at the screen again.

"Two things," said May. "What day is it?"

"December twenty-seventh," said Guthrie, whose tone made it clear he didn't much care for May's glibness.

"Tuesday," said May. "It's Tuesday." He pointed at the young man on the screen. "He's delivering the Thursday circular on a Tuesday."

"Come on," said Guthrie, "they—"

"—if you don't deliver on the right day, you don't get paid. And if there's a make-up to do, you do it on Friday. That's it. No other day. I've done it. I know."

"You said two things," Imogen interjected. "What's the second?"

"He's throwin' 'em on people's lawns, or just below the steps to their porch. Only one of 'em hits a front door. Your man's—the old white guy's, I'd guess."

"Shit," Weir hissed.

"I've done this, too," he went on, indicating the courier on the screen. "Get a message to someone who needs to know something. When the cops are all over you, they're everywhere. And they think of everything: tap your phone, stakeout your girlfriend, put a tag-trace on your car. If you even try to deliver a message inside a fortune cookie, they know it. But you have some broke down old man or a kid delivering yellow pages or Thursday circulars, no one looks twice. Damn, you're all so smart, but you don't see the obvious. Why's a man delivering Thursday circulars on Tuesday?"

Guthrie was anxious not to make eye contact with anyone in the room.

"Any idea who would take a job like this?" asked Weir.

"Nah. Could be anybody."

"This could be an insurance policy," Imogen offered. "It's known in the neighborhood that the FBI's got Jimmy. Maybe Co—" she stopped herself saying her former colleague's name. "It's possible the subject had it set up: like, 'if the FBI comes snooping around, get a message to me'."

Guthrie scowled.

"It was obviously something that'd been worked out well in advance," said Imogen.

"Can I go now?" asked Jimmy. Weir directed Guthrie to take May to be processed and released.

"This just gets worse and worse," began Weir, leaning heavily on the meeting table. "Colls probably knew we were onto him, if not the whole group. His running forced our hand—and he didn't go to Dulles or any other airport. By putting so many agents on alert we showed way too many of our cards. I have now confirmed to him and his pals that we know way more than we're letting on. The operatives are going to roll up fast now. I need you and what's-his-name at IT—"

"Trey Kelly," Imogen supplied.

"—You and Kelly to get on it. I'm sending Davies, too, to get you both up to speed. Find out how large it is . . . how far it goes. And I'm bringing Vega back in as soon as I get final word from Bishop."

* * *

Senator Eliot's Chief of Staff, Casey Hague, stepped out of the briefing room to answer his phone.

"You're going to be hearing some things over the next few days," said the voice at the other end. "Things about the investigation. Things that might worry you. Don't be worried. Keep everyone else calm. Stay on task. It may seem like a big deal because it's local, but I assure you it's incidental to our purpose. No information has leaked, nothing links back to anyone of consequence. They don't have a clue what's going on. Nothing changes."

"I don't even know what you're talking about," said Hague.

"By design. Only a very few people do." And the line went dead.

* * *

102

In Newton, New Jersey, Patriot76's phone rang. He pulled two phones out of his pockets. He looked at one, realized it was the other the one ringing. "Yes?" he said, putting the other away again.

"Okay," said the voice at the other end. "It's in hand. We should have confirmation shortly."

"Okay," said Patriot76. He walked over to a bench set back from the High Street facing the Sussex County Courthouse and sat down. "How did it happen? How'd they get close?"

"I don't think they did get close. In a way, it was probably only a matter of time, what with three known associates."

"But they seem to have picked up on the cell phones," said Patriot76.

"Doubtful. It's true they picked up the courier."

"Do you think he talked?" asked Patriot76.

"What could he say? He doesn't know anything damaging," the man on the phone pointed out. "He probably didn't even know what was in the package. At any rate, we're in the process of settling it. But trust me: the investigation is going nowhere. They're chasing their tails."

"Listen," said Patriot76, "there's someone new in the picture. I want to send you some photos I took outside Trager's building to see if you know who the new guy is."

"Okay."

Patriot76 fumbled with the phone. "I hope this comes through. These flip phones aren't very good." He pressed 'send.' As he waited for confirmation at the other end, he said, "I had a pal run the plate on the car. His name is David Douglas Kelly. Heard of him?"

"Yeah, I know who he is. Jesus! They've brought in a computer guy!" he scoffed. "Like they can find a god dammed algorithm for what's happening." He laughed.

"Yeah," said Patriot76, laughing as well, though his eyes suggested he wasn't quite sure of the joke. "Of course, you know, what if . . . I'm just saying: what if he's some kind of hacker?"

"There's nothing to hack. We followed your design. We were very careful. There's no trail anywhere to follow."

"I've used a computer," said Patriot76.

"To communicate with the press. Not the same thing," said the man on the phone. "How's that going?"

"I had some nosey questions from that reporter, trying to get more than he's given, but he's poking around in the dark. It'll work out. I'm going to call him tomorrow."

* * *

Hugh Salter stood with his news director in the newsroom, watching a report from another channel: "Beginning yesterday," it began, "and continuing through today, the FBI has descended on this quiet Bethesda neighborhood, apparently investigating one of their own. FBI sources aren't saying much of anything, but there is strong speculation that retired Agent Andrew Colls is a suspect in the Faithless Elector plot."

"Shit," said the news director. "How do they know that?" He stared pointedly at Salter. "How come *we* don't know that?"

"The silence here," continued the reporter on screen, "says more than the little official word we are getting from the FBI, who will confirm only that an investigation is underway. Neighbors tell us they think the house has been under surveillance for at least twenty-four hours, and that former agent Colls left quickly late this morning. You can see, just behind me that federal agents are removing boxes and what look like computers."

The news director muted the television and turned to Salter. "We didn't get any of that today," he said. "What can you give me that they won't have?"

"How about: 'Continued Missteps at the FBI'? Even though it's an open secret within the FBI that their agents Tom Kurtz and Imogen Trager were an item—and I have pictures— they not only continued to work without reprimand, but were allowed to work together on the Illinois vote fraud investigation."

The news director picked up his phone. "Jeanne," he said, "come in here, please. I'm putting you on something with Hugh Salter." Jeanne Hammond walked in a moment later.

"And," continued Salter as the producer sat down, "it was Agent Trager's analysis that, first, served as the basis of the Justice Department's finding that the Illinois vote results should stand; and second, she was the one who broke the story that the Faithless Electors were anything but conscientious stewards of the public trust—but were actually bribed or coerced into switching their votes.

"We can say," Salter continued, "that today's screw-up is just the latest in a ham-handed investigation. Once again, the FBI is one step behind. They've failed to clean up their own house. They've clearly missed Colls, as they missed out on Kurtz—"

"Okay, good," said the news director. "Get to work."

"What quotes do you have?" Hammond asked Salter as they left the room.

* * *

At the Bus Rental building near the Stadium-Armory Metro stop, Imogen and Trey Kelly were at work tracking the number Colls had called when he ran the previous day. "It's Wicked," Trey confirmed. "And Wicked immediately called someone new, in Frederick, Maryland . . . and then Figgy."

Imogen filed another backdated wire tap approval to get tracking on both numbers, though the data was already coming through. For good measure, Trey requested any other available data from Mike at NSC. Even though they were still tracking past movements, Imogen felt a thrill because they'd caught up a lot and this was so recent. They were getting closer.

Imogen's phone rang. It was Vega, back on the job. "Colls' phone was on until he reached somewhere around Cabin John, is that correct?" she asked in lieu of greeting.

105

"Yes," said Imogen. She wondered if it made sense to say something like "good to have you back," but decided against it.

"I'm in the traffic situation room," said Vega. "I have access to all the traffic cameras in that area. Where was the last time you had contact and what was the time?" In the background, Imogen could hear agents talking heatedly.

Imogen peered at her screen. "He was heading west on 495. He had just crossed the bridge at mile-marker 41 at 2:41 p.m. He's driving—"

"—I've got all that," said Vega, and hung up. "You're welcome," thought Imogen.

"Okay," said Kelly, "Wicked and Figgy go dark immediately after their phone calls, but I've got our guy from Frederick heading down US-15. At Leesburg, he turns onto Route 7, heading southeast. And then we lose him."

Imogen's phone rang. "Here's what we have so far on Colls," said Vega: "we see his car passing the camera at mile-marker 43.01 at 2:46 p.m., but he doesn't pass the camera at marker 46.69. He doesn't turn up anywhere after that—north or south—and he didn't take a winding route to Dulles, because we would be able to see him entering the airport. We don't have cameras on the other roads. He could have turned off—going north or south—at Georgetown Pike or at Old Dominion. Either way, he's in the wind. What else have we got?"

Imogen looked at the data for the other subject, driving from Frederick. "Amanda," she asked, "are there any cameras on US-15 or Route 7, coming from Frederick down past Leesburg? We're trying to track someone who may have been going that way to meet Colls." Imogen gave her two mile-markers and their times.

Vega covered the phone, but Imogen could still hear her barking muffled orders. "Nothing on Route 15," she said when she came back on. "I've got four cameras in that target area along Route 7. But I need intersections, junctions; not mile-markers. I've got cameras at the junctions for Routes 659, 28, 286 and 606."

"I'll get you junctions and times. Hang on," said Imogen. Kelly looked up from his readouts. "What are you going to tell her to look for?" he whispered, urgently. "We don't even know what the car looks like." He stood up and walked over to her screen. "And he turned off his phone just there," he said, pointing at the screen, "between Routes 286 and 606."

"I know. And he only turned it back on for a minute, forty-eight seconds, traveling in the opposite direction about half an hour later."

Trey shook his head, his face grim. "Twenty minutes before we established audio."

Imogen thought for a moment before picking up the phone again.

"Okay," she said to Vega, "this will be difficult. We need to flag the cars heading south-east along Route 7 beginning at junction 689 at 2:55 p.m. He turned off his phone somewhere between Routes 286 and 606, so we can't be sure if he made it as far south as 606."

"Wait," said Vega, "it's not crazy traffic, but it's pretty heavily traveled. It could easily be eight or ten cars we have to flag. How do we know which one?"

"He turned his phone back on at 3:37, heading the opposite direction for just under two minutes while he called his Boston connection. He was between Routes 28 and 659 on his way toward Leesburg. If any of the cars you flagged going south are returning at exactly the same time—"

"—Got it," said Vega. More muffled orders to her staff. "Give us a few minutes," she said. "I'll call you back."

Vega did not call back right away. When she did, more than an hour later, she was already in her car, en route to Frederick. "We're on him," she told Imogen. "We flagged the only one of twelve cars heading back along the same route, a Ford Bronco with Maryland plates that led us to an Aaron Deptford. He works security for the Army at Fort Detrick. We know where his car is. We're pretty sure he's at home."

"Excellent," said Imogen, a bit dismayed to find herself annoyed not to be included in the man-hunt. "Do you have agents in place yet?"

"Negative," said Vega. "We don't have any agents closer than us. Given all the shit that's gone down, we're playing it close to the vest. I don't want anyone else slipping through our hands or more people alerted than necessary. I was about to call the MPs, ask them to look around, but if our target works with them . . . ."

"Yeah, I get it," said Imogen.

"So, I'm taking a bit of a chance. But I asked the Maryland Staties to drive by. They confirm that his car is in the drive, and now they're staked out at either end of his block. I'm still about twenty minutes out. If he runs before we get there, one of the Staties will pursue and the other will secure his home. I need you to keep an eye on any phone activity."

"Got it. Trey and I will get to work on his personal phone, too. See if that can give us anything."

Vega gave Deptford's home and work address to Imogen. "Listen," she said, "be careful: he works security for Battlecreek Logistics, which is a subsidiary of Sloane Street Defense Corp. They're a big outfit, with ties all over. So maybe tiptoe a bit. There's no telling what the Sloane Street spooks are paying attention to—or why. If it somehow pops up that FBI or NSA—or whoever else you have up your sleeve—is scrutinizing a Sloane Street employee, things might get weird."

"Good points. Thanks." She paused. "Listen, Amanda . . . about—"

"—Look: we both had jobs to do. And we still have jobs to do, thank God. I can see how this looking-over-your-shoulder can get to you. It's messing with me right now. I have to double-check everything I'm thinking about doing, everything I say . . . everyone I talk to. On top of that, shit-stains like Deptford and Colls and fucking Kurtz are making us look like idiots. I will get Deptford, and I will wring him dry. And he'll lead us to Colls. I think for the good of the Bureau I'll let Weir interrogate Colls when we find him, 'cause I'd probably kill the fucker." And she hung up. Imogen stared at her phone for a moment.

"All good?" asked Trey.

"I think so."

7

Trey and Imogen had been able to lock on to Deptford's personal phone, and had tracked him to a secluded area outside River Bend Park on the Virginia side of the Potomac, where he stayed about twenty minutes. Weir had dispatched a team there to follow up for clues.

Vega took Deptford quietly and without incident. Deptford was thick set and fit. His thick bushy hair was dark for a man in his mid-forties, and made him appear younger. He sat in silence on the trip back to Washington, his face slowly draining of color. As they were arriving and transferring him to the interrogation room, Vega's phone pinged. Weir's team had found Colls' body, dead, next to his car, an apparent suicide. Vega paused. "Take Deptford in," she said to the agents with her, "I'll be there in a minute."

She dialed Weir. "A suicide?" she asked when he picked up.

"Apparently. I've got crime scene looking it over right now. I don't believe it for a second, but from the photos my team sent, whoever killed him did a good job making it look that way. Point blank to the head. Brains skull fragments all over his car. Gun still in his hand. How are you doing with Deptford?"

"Nothing yet, sir. Just got to interrogation. I'll let you know the second I have anything."

Imogen arrived some moments later, meeting Vega outside the interrogation room they had used for Jimmy May.

"Has he said anything?" asked Imogen.

"No," said Vega, "but they found Colls' body. Apparent suicide." She let that sink in. "No one believes that," she added. "Let's get to work." Vega opened the door to the interrogation room.

"Do I get a phone call?" asked Deptford as Vega and Imogen walked into the room. "You have to let me contact my lawyer."

Imogen and Vega seated themselves. "That is indeed the law, Mr. Deptford," said Vega, "and we will give you that opportunity. Only . . . you know, suddenly I'm thinking that might not be in your best interest under the circumstances."

Imogen stared at the table top, wondering which Constitutional right she would be complicit in violating today. But just as quickly came a flash of anger. Deptford was engaged in a dark, murderous network conspiring to subvert the electoral process, and corrupt the Constitution. Now he wanted it to protect him?

Deptford looked straight ahead.

"You do not have to answer questions without an attorney present. That is correct. But you can listen to me for a moment or two before deciding further how you would like to proceed—in your best interest."

Another agent arrived, handing papers to Vega and to Imogen. Vega looked at Imogen.

"We have tracked your personal phone to exactly the spot where you met FBI agent Andrew Colls, just outside Riverbend Park. We have recovered his body there."

Vega leaned in toward Deptford. "See, we've been monitoring Colls. He called someone. That someone called you. You drove to meet Colls, and now he's dead."

"I want my phone call," said Deptford.

Vega nodded. "Colls called someone—looking for help, I suppose. Instead, he got you, and a bullet to the head. You go ahead and call someone." She sat back. "I wonder if you'll even make it home alive." Vega twisted a bit in her chair to look at Imogen. "You know, Gen . . ."

"Yes, Amanda?" said Imogen.

"The interesting part is not that Deptford here will be killed by whoever he's really working for."

"No, I agree, Amanda. That's really just a fact."

"What will be interesting—more to us than you," she allowed jocularly to Deptford, "—is how they'll do it."

"They've been really creative so far," Imogen assented.

"There was the Elector with the wine bottle just after the election?"

"Yes, that was good," said Imogen. "In Oregon. He had these champagne bottles, and they made it look like one of them exploded."

"That thick bottom with that dimple thing—"

"—the 'punt,' it's called," said Imogen.

"Yes. The punt. They took a large, thick triangle shard of glass from the bottom of the bottle and drove it straight into his neck. It hit the carotid, so he probably bled out quickly. I doubt he actually drowned in his own blood. He certainly didn't get to share the champagne."

Imogen flipped through her papers as though looking for some detail that might confirm which had killed the man first. "There was that woman in Iowa," she offered. "Supposedly slipped on the ice while taking out her garbage. I expect they crushed her skull pretty well, but she froze to death, slowly. One guy drowned."

"Yeah, he used to be in the Navy. They sure have a sense of irony." Vega chuckled.

"Another was burned to death in his farmhouse . . ."

Vega turned back to Deptford. "How do you think they'll get you?"

Deptford stared straight ahead.

"Any hobbies?" Imogen asked brightly.

"Fuck you," he said. "You ought to be worrying about yourself, Agent Trager."

Vega and Imogen stared at him.

"What the hell does that mean?" Vega demanded.

Imogen felt the blood rushing to her head, heard it pounding in her ears.

"Just that," said Deptford matter-of-factly. "They don't leave loose ends. You fucked them. They don't forget."

Imogen felt sick. She had been exhilarated by the work she was doing. Taking the initiative in the investigation and uncovering leads had pushed aside her lingering feelings of helplessness and fear, and now they were rushing back at her with astonishing force. It was like falling and seeing the rope that will save you but not catching it.

"Do you know something specific?" Vega asked. "How do you know her name? I didn't introduce her."

Deptford looked away.

Vega turned to Imogen, seeming to gauge her state of mind. After a moment, she turned back to Deptford. "Then you know how right we are," she said. "But the difference between Agent Trager and you is that she has the FBI on her side, and just at the moment, you don't. She has several thousand people to look after her, but if you ever leave here, you're on your own unless you enlist some help by doing us some favors."

Deptford shifted in his chair.

"It's possible your lawyer," Vega continued, ". . . who is their lawyer . . . would get you out on bail. Maybe even somehow see you cleared of all charges. But you know these people even better than we do. As you say—you wouldn't want to be a loose end—or suspended from one."

Deptford looked at the table.

"Now talk to us," said Vega.

"You don't have the authority. I don't think either of you can protect me or guarantee me immunity from prosecution if I do help you."

The door opened. Weir and Deputy Director Bill Dyer stepped into the room. "I can," said Dyer.

* * *

The next two days were full of purpose and excitement for Kelly and Imogen. For his safety, and to maintain a low profile, Deptford had been removed to the secure detention

113

where Imogen had been held. Vega took to escorting Imogen from headquarters to the Bus Rentals building each morning. Kelly was officially seconded to the task group.

As they worked to untangle the new cell back at Bus Rentals, Imogen and Kelly began by feeding numbers and locations to Weir and Brody as they interrogated Deptford. With a little more thought, he'd decided that he'd very much like to help, after all, and as he remembered more and more, the network sprawled.

Before the end of the first day they had identified two numbers likely to be other low-level conspirators, probably on a par with Trebor and Covington, taking orders from Deptford. The tracking that Imogen and Kelly provided checked out against Deptford's testimony and demonstrated that he was giving good information.

They sent the information to Brody, Weir and Vega, who had Adam Kimball and Noah Carpenter brought in. They were truck drivers with military certification and clearance, who did short- and long-haul runs, trusted with certain kinds of sensitive loads. Kimball lived in Lancaster, Pennsylvania, and Carpenter in Harrisburg, and both often worked at Fort Dietrich. At Vega's direction, they were taken quietly at their respective homes by Pennsylvania State Police detectives.

Looking at the calls, it appeared that though this new cell group covered a broader geographic area, it was structured and functioned much the same as the first one, with Colls at the head, directing Kurtz, who directed Trebor and Covington. In this new cell, though, it was not immediately apparent where Deptford ranked. Was he on a level with Colls or with Kurtz? And who was Wicked, whom Colls had called? Was Wicked at their level, or were they now looking at a more senior controller?

Deptford claimed not to know the identity of Wicked, known to him only as "Mr. Fisher," the man who had given him his instructions to meet and kill Andrew Colls. Without knowing his a name, and since he only seemed to turn on his phone at pre-arranged times, isolating his location and following him was proving difficult.

114

The other number they had been able to isolate belonged to a Frank Reed, a.k.a. "Figgy," a game warden from Newton, New Jersey. In the network, he was known as "Cooper." Surveillance on his house had so far not found him, and if he used a personal phone, he had probably registered it in a different name.

The task group had barely ten days' worth of information on the network at the start, presumably because these SIMs too were regularly changed. Kelly asked for more detailed information on the way the SIM cards were distributed: where and when were the meetings? What were the protocols?

"We would meet—" Deptford began

"—Who is 'we'?" interrupted Brody.

"First, I would meet Mr. Cooper; that is, Reed—we would meet. I would get the new SIMs from him. Then, Kimball, Carpenter and I . . . we would meet so I could distribute them."

"Did Kimball or Carpenter have code names?"

"Yes. Kimball was 'Miller' and Carpenter was 'Tillman'."

Brody scribbled on his notepad. "If you knew their real names, why the code names?"

"In case we were ever overheard. And, if we ever intersected with another cell, they would only know our code names—and we would only know theirs," said Deptford.

"Okay," said Brody. "When did you meet?" he asked.

"The seventeenth of each month just outside Harrisburg. There's a Walmart a little east of there on Route 322. The parking lot at the side of the building toward the back, near the South 63rd Street entrance to the shopping complex. I'd meet Reed there at about two p.m."

"Always there?" asked Brody.

"Yes."

"Any deviation?"

"No."

"Didn't you worry about people noticing a pattern?" asked Brody.

"No," said Deptford.

"Then what would happen?"

"I'd wait in my car. When I saw Kimball's or Carpenter's truck, I'd make sure there was no one else around. Then I'd drive over to this big garbage can and put the package in it as I drove away. They'd drive up moments later and retrieve it."

"Then what?"

"I'd make a call to the lead—Mr. Fisher's new number. He'd pick up, and I would hang up, which let him know I had delivered the SIMs. Carpenter and Kimball would do likewise, indicating they had received and installed the new SIMs. Then we'd destroy the previous SIMs, usually by throwing them away."

"And then what?"

"I'd drive back to Maryland, and we'd all go on about our lives. Wait for contact. Wait for instructions from Mr. Cooper or Mr. Fisher."

"And who is Mr. Fisher?"

"I don't know."

"But you know Reed's real name, as well as Carpenter and Kimball's. How is that?"

"I knew Reed from the military. He recruited me. I recruited Carpenter and Kimball."

Weir texted Imogen and Kelly about where and when the numbers were enabled, and they got to work with NSA trying to identify the numbers from the earlier SIMs. For once, thought Imogen with some satisfaction, they had the warrants and requests in ahead of time.

Unfortunately, the parking lot from which the conspirators called was an area of heavy phone traffic. Filtering was also difficult because the cell towers were farther apart in that part of central Pennsylvania, which diminished the accuracy of the traces. Identifying numbers, testing them and gathering the information—all of which had taken barely a day and a half in the DC area—was much more time-consuming here.

Each of the captured suspects was held as a material witness. So far as the task group could tell, the conspirators higher up the chain were not aware the FBI was holding their operatives. There had been no calls from Kimball or Carpenter or Deptford as they were arrested and nothing had come from Reed's phone. Not one lived with family. So far as neighbors and friends were concerned, there was nothing out of the ordinary about their being gone. They were often gone for weeks at a time on work trips, clandestine or legitimate.

Reed, being further up the hierarchy, didn't leave his phone on much, but seemed to turn it on at agreed times—half-an-hour at 3 p.m. on Monday, Wednesday and Fridays. Though they couldn't track him by his phone, since it was off, that fact meant he hadn't used it to contact anyone else and so was probably not up to date regarding his Dark Network colleagues. His house in Hampton, New Jersey, and office in Newton were staked out.

In his interrogation notes, Brody observed that the upper reaches of the network were very well guarded. Even if captured, no single member knew enough about his bosses to be of any investigatory use. Capturing Reed, or Mr. Cooper as he was known to the network, would be crucial, as would identifying and arresting Wicked/Fisher.

Imogen was enjoying the hunt. And her seclusion and Kelly's kept the political cacophony of the outside world safely at a distance.

Just as well. What was happening was alarming. As the year came to a close, demonstrations took place daily across the nation and violent confrontations were becoming almost as regular. On the street, in the television studios and online, the invective seemed to grow with each passing day: a former political pundit turned candidate darkly exhorted his followers to hold firm, for "the harder the conflict, the more glorious the triumph", while another party leader sounded an ominous, nihilistic tone when he told a crowd, "We have it in our power to begin the world over again."

A sitting governor declared in a speech that "the tree of liberty must be refreshed from time to time with the blood of patriots and tyrants." There was no shortage of self-appointed patriots. Many in the nation clung to a hope for some kind of constitutional resolution—these things always blow over, don't they?—but as time passed a remark made almost casually at a rally by Robert Moore, Christopher's vice presidential candidate, reverberated sympathetically across the nation in these unsettled, disorderly days: "It does not take a majority to prevail," Moore insisted, quoting Samuel Adams from centuries earlier, "but rather an irate, tireless minority, keen on setting brushfires of freedom in the minds of men." The Secret Service had been busy chasing down threats and persons of interest since the Faithless Elector plot was revealed back on December 19.

The election had divided as never before. And the uncertainty of the outcome had hardened those divisions. Almost everyone, if the television was to be believed, was angry, and each side was recklessly accusing the other of whatever it could think of. The killing of the Electors had been blamed on immigrants, the KKK, the Russians, ISIS, Mexicans and, inevitably, the FBI. Bob Moore's profile was rising, too, as he was increasingly deputized to clarify and distance his running mate's and his party's positions.

Online, the echo-chambers were cacophonous. Overall US social media traffic was up by 20 per cent in a month, even after the unprecedented levels of the election itself. The slogan that someone had proposed to discourage sharing of fake news—"Think before you click"—had itself gone viral, though few people seemed to think it applied to them. In this atmosphere, it was growing harder to know what was going on at all, nor what information to trust. The Constitution was straining at the seams.

* * *

Casey Hague, the chief of staff to Senator Drew Eliot kept a weekly appointment with his contact, this time at a coffee shop in Fairfax, Virginia.

"There's a nice table there at the window," said the waitress as he arrived. An unwelcoming winter sun glared across the room. The waitress was in her mid-forties, cheerful, but with what seemed an underlying sadness, a kind of doleful, austere resignation, much like the shop itself. The brightness of the room, the high-gloss cleanliness of the counter, the black-and-white tiled floor, the smart spindle back chairs—all hinted at a robust, meticulous business strategy focused on looking the part of a fashionable, successful coffee spot, yet it left the place seeming tired, arid, soulless. And it was empty.

"Thanks, I think it'll be warmer in the back." He rubbed his hands briskly together. He ordered black coffee and a lemon poppy-seed muffin. When the coffee arrived, he pressed the mug in both hands, letting the warmth permeate.

As the door opened, and his contact arrived, Hague rose to shake his hand. "What a difference a week makes," he said.

"Oh?"

"I don't mind telling you, I was worried when we spoke last time, in Georgetown."

"I could tell," he said as removed his scarf. He paused before taking off his overcoat. "Tea and a banana muffin," he said to the waitress.

"Sweet tea?" she asked.

"Hot tea," he said tartly, sitting down, his overcoat still on. Then, to Hague he asked, "What's changed?"

"Well, this Illinois thing just won't die, thank God. Two weeks ago, there was a lot of dithering, a lot of can-I-get-back-to-you-later? when the senator or I spoke with other members."

"And now?" he asked Hague.

"They're coming around, I'd say."

"What does that mean, exactly? Do you have a list of firm supporters?"

"Yes."

"May I see it?"

Hague was about to hand over the sheet when the waitress brought the tea.

"Here ya go," she said putting the mug and saucer on the table.

Both men stopped talking and smiled at her pleasantly.

She smiled back primly, an automatic, practiced smile. There was no warmth in her eyes, no gracious, small-town "where y'all from?" inquisitiveness, as though like the shop itself, something essential had been painstakingly eradicated from her in favor of a bland imitation.

When she had gone, Hague's contact scrolled quickly through the list. "I only count 34," he said bobbing the wretched teabag up and down in a glass mug with his free hand. He looked up and scowled at the infusion's pallor.

He looked around for the waitress. Not seeing her, he resumed agitating the teabag.

"Those are firm," said Hague, indicating the list. "And we're getting close—probably forty-seven or forty-eight."

"Based on electoral math, forty-eight is the number you should have started with." He folded the paper and put it into the inside pocket of his overcoat.

"I couldn't get commitments. Finally, I'm getting them. I don't see any problem getting to fifty-one now," said Hague.

"There are ten states with split representation."

"Good."

"They like the notion of a split ticket," said Hague, indicating the names on the list. "Given the irregularities in Illinois, it looks like a statesman's compromise, a healing act."

"What if it isn't a split ticket? What if the House votes for Christopher?"

"Then we tell them it's important to show unity at a time like this." Hague grinned.

"Fine. What are you hearing on the other side?"

"It's a shit show," said Hague with a laugh.

The waitress, who had suddenly appeared with a fresh coffee pot, let out a barely audible gasp.

"Forgive my language," said Hague quickly.

The waitress smiled tightly and poured him more coffee before quickly returning to the kitchen, leaving them alone again.

"Who owes us, in the House? I mean big. There ought to be enough votes there for us."

"It really is a shit storm there. It think it might break our way, but we can't be certain."

"I'm going to need you to do something. As you know, we lost our man with contact on the inside."

"Lost him?" said Hague archly.

"Yes. And he had a man on the inside."

"Can't one of your operatives just take him over?" asked Hague.

"It's not that simple. He's not an operative. He doesn't work for us. As far as he knows, up until now he was just keeping his old boss and former mentor in the loop, swapping gossip. If this guy had even a whiff of what's really going on, he'd sink us."

"Why the hell would we risk making contact?" asked Hague.

"Because without him, we're blind at a critical stage. And I think I see a way to make it work that's safe, and it certainly gives you plausible deniability."

"I'm listening," said Hague.

"Your senator is the Judicial Oversight Committee chair."

"You can't be serious. The senator cannot be seen to—"

"—The senator will not be seen to do anything. Hear me out. First, put pressure on the Director to bring in some more manpower, fresh blood, that kind of thing. Tell them that the Public Integrity Division needs a bigger role."

"That's it?"

"It should do the trick to get our man better placed. Frankly, that was the course we were going to follow even before we lost our man. If your pressure works, he's an obvious choice."

"So how do we get him to keep feeding us?"

"I think a quick private conversation. Appeal to his sense of patriotic duty. Let him know that his mentor was helping the committee in its oversight capacity before his untimely demise. Here's the name." He slid a small, folded piece of paper toward Hague.

Hague put it in his pocket. "I'm glad you're bringing up this sudden . . . blindness, as you call it. Your call the other day telling me not to worry about what I was hearing in the news," said Hague, grabbing a sugar packet, "had the opposite effect. I'm assuming it was about that retired agent's suicide. What would that have had to do with our efforts?"

"Nothing. I just wanted to reassure you. None of it—nothing—connects back to you. There are separate spheres of activity, and none of them overlap."

"Yes, but frankly that call feels careless on your part," said Hague, stirring his coffee.

Hague's associate was quiet for a moment, eyeing him carefully. "I don't see how," he said finally.

"The person in question—" Hague looked around the empty shop for the waitress or anyone else—"had not yet committed suicide when you called. If this ever came back on us, it could be asked why you were calling to reassure me about something that hadn't yet happened. Someone might be led to believe you had prior knowledge of the unfortunate man's actions—actions which would seem on the face of it to be of a deeply personal, private nature."

"Given your frame of mind at our last meeting, it made sense."

"I need you to be more careful in future," replied Hague.

The man stared straight ahead, his jaw clenched. "You're right, of course," he said finally. "And in future, can we see about finding a place that knows how to make tea?" He stood up and began winding his scarf.

Vega and her team had been quietly looking into the backgrounds of the various cell members, to find what they had in common. For Colls, Kurtz, Trebor and Covington, it had been their university, Princeton, and their club, Jefferson's Tigers. Colls, a Virginian, came from a venerable line of West Pointers, politicians and State Department officials. Vega couldn't help but speculate there might also be a plantation owner or two.

First, Colls had joined the military out of college, leaving it at age 26 for the Bureau, after serving with distinction in the first Gulf War. His FBI intake interviews stated he seemed disillusioned, possibly even a little bitter about his service, but there was nothing specific. The interview notes also remarked that he was intelligent, adept and seemed like a natural leader. Kurtz, some fifteen years younger than Colls, came to Quantico after getting his law degree. He was mentored by Andrew Colls, though he never served directly in any of Colls' groups. Right up to the moment they were exposed as traitors, there was nothing but success, promotion and praise for either man.

Trebor and Covington, by contrast, had tried and failed to make careers in the Army and Navy respectively. Their service records showed poor performance ratings, poor leadership skills, though short of grossly incompetent. Turning their hands to the FBI, they had both kept up with the fitness requirements during the training period, but their test scores were poor and they did not finish the training. The only definable link for all four until the Faithless Elector plot was revealed was the Jefferson's Tigers club. The Tigers was an enthusiastically reactionary club at Princeton, known for stunts, pranks and sneering letters to the editor about the corrosive effects of "political correctness" on free speech, but little else. Annoying, Vega allowed, but harmless.

For Reed, Deptford, Kimball and Carpenter, the link was the military. Based on their files, Kimball and Carpenter could have looked forward to being career non-coms, which had been their trajectory before leaving the service and joining Sloane Street Defense Corporation. Again, like Trebor and Covington, there was nothing good or bad, or otherwise distinguishing: they weren't loners or malcontents, hadn't been dishonorably discharged, hadn't been in trouble with the law; like Trebor and Covington, they were just work-a-day guys, busy under-achieving. All four had Facebook pages, and they weren't shy about shouting down perceived "snowflakes," "whiners" and other assorted "losers." But, Vega allowed, so did tens of thousands of other people who never bothered to pick up a gun or join a conspiracy.

In contrast, Reed and Deptford's careers, like Kurtz's seemed to destine them for substantial, prestigious positions. Deptford had distinguished himself in the Army as a marksman. Kurtz had distinguished himself at every level.

Reed was something of an outlier, difficult to pin down. Though he continued to be promoted, the vagueness of his military record and his movement in and out of active service suggested there might be something more than what she was seeing. Outwardly, all six of them were just the kind people not to recruit for such an enterprise.

Over the next few days, Vega's team looked deeper into associations, connections, and other groups they might have joined—anything that might have put them on the recruitment radar for whoever was masterminding the plot. She asked Weir to direct Brody to dig deeper in his interrogations to get at how the broader network had formed. Meanwhile, she was following up the leads Imogen and Trey were providing. With so much data, though, the Bureau was wasting thousands of hours driving down dead-end streets.

During the first week after their capture, Brody's interrogation revelations had provided or confirmed solid, much-needed detail about the conspiracy. But since that initial flood of usable testimony, Vega noted, Agent Brody's scoops had slowed to a trickle. He continued methodically probing and cross examining the connections of his charges, but seemed to be coming to the end of their usable data as he worked farther backward in time.

Reed, a.k.a Mr. Cooper, had known Deptford while both served in Afghanistan. Kimball and Carpenter had served there, too, and while their deployments overlapped in time, Brody couldn't find any event or mission or group that would have thrown them all together. Brody's notes to Vega confessed that he wasn't sure whether he sensed there was something they weren't telling him, or whether he hoped that was the case. He refused to believe it was just random, he stated in his summary notes, but so far, that's what their testimony suggested. The three confirmed that while Kimball and Carpenter had known one another in the military, it was not until they were all working at Fort Detrick that Deptford had recruited them.

While Vega saw that each network cell appeared to be a closed system, closer scrutiny showed occasional overlaps:

Covington and Carpenter, for example, weren't from the same cell, but they appeared together in Park Terrace, New York, just outside Binghamton on November 15 to kill the Elector there. She flipped through the file of Brody's interrogation notes. She read:

> Brody: "how did that happen?"
> Carpenter: "I got a call. It said meet this guy and 'service the target'."
> Brody: "you mean 'kill'?"
> Carpenter: "Yeah."
> Brody: "And you'd never met him before? Was that normal?"
> Carpenter: "There was no normal, no routines. You get an order from a verified source, you execute the order."
> Brody: "You weren't still in the army, you know."
> Carpenter: [scoffs] "Tell me about it."

There were, as yet, still no leads regarding the widow in Iowa City, the boat owner in Seattle or the winemaker in Yamhill, Oregon.

The Treasury Department investigators were faring no better, Vega thought as she turned to their report. The investigators had quickly been able to establish the outlines of the "gift card" payment-withdrawal structure as funneling through various Swiss private banks. Those leads, unfortunately, traced back to a network of Special Purpose Entities: orphan and limited liability companies, whose owners were further shielded by another layer of SPE's.

They had peeled back enough to secure a lifting order for a set of accounts linked with the payments through one of the private banks, but rather than revealing who was behind the curtain, this only showed more drapery. Vega closed the file, shaking her head.

What did they know for sure? Vega wondered as she looked at what specific crimes they could charge. It was clear from the cellphone trails that Carpenter and Deptford had been present at the death of the Elector in the burning farmhouse in

Maine on November 12. And it was pretty certain that Trebor and Covington had caused the motorcycle death of the Elector in Bedford, Mass, on the same day. On November 13, Carpenter and Kimball had been in Bellefonte, Pennsylvania, the day the Elector there died in a freak car accident. He owned a car dealership just off I-80, and had been crushed savagely between two cars when the parking break failed on a used car.

* * *

Early next morning, New Year's Day, Agent Vega appeared at Bus Rentals. Trey let her in, and conducted her to the pit, where they'd been working. Imogen brushed aside some takeout beside her to make room for Vega at a terminal. The "pit" was so-called because the offices elevated all round gave it the appearance of being below ground; but the name had new resonance after a week when agents and computer geeks had been at work and cleaners had not.

Vega perched primly on her chair, surveying the scene, uncomfortable about putting her hands down anywhere. "Can you run the last few weeks of the networks?" she asked. "I'd like to look at December seventeen through our latest data."

Trey sat down, brushing a box from Chicken Palace further along the desk. He picked up his keyboard, turned it upside down and shook it, letting crumbs and dust fall on the table. He swept the detritus delicately into his hand, as a waiter might the crumbs from a meal, then brushed his hands together and let the crumbs fall to the floor. He wiped his hands on his trousers and began.

"Okay," he said. "December seventeen through today, January one."

As each line coursed across the map a little phone icon would pop up next to it whenever a call was made or received.

"Is there another explanation for what they're doing?" asked Vega.

"What do you mean?" asked Imogen.

"Restart it, please," she said to Trey, who returned the playback to the 17th. "I mean, there's a good bit of chatter and activity leading up to the nineteenth, when they got their three Electors to overturn the result. That makes sense. Then, Gen, you and Pollack blew it wide open. But while there's still communication going on, it's drastically curtailed."

"Three of the four cell members were dead, which doesn't leave a lot of scope for chatter; and now the fourth is dead, killed by his superiors," said Imogen. "And the two out there that we know about are still talking."

Vega paused the playback. "Maybe they were talking about closing shop," she said. "Here's Deptford on the nineteenth, in New Hampshire, presumably out to kill Henry Porter, one of the Faithless Elector there," she said and pointed at a call signal from Wicked. "The other two Faithless Electors were in Colorado and Minnesota, probably not part of this cell." She resumed play. "Everything up to and including the nineteenth makes sense." She pointed at the screen. "This is probably the order to watch you, Gen, since right after it, all three go to your building. This here is probably the order to kill Novaczeck, the campaign manager.

"But what's the new activity?" Vega continued. "Are we getting it wrong? What if their chatter is just about winding everything down? What if the three we have on ice right now were next in line to be killed? It could be that this was always the plan, and we should be looking at how to flush out Wicked and Reed rather than focusing on their new strategy to influence the election. I mean, how do you keep something this big quiet? And: if we investigate them trying to turn the election, how do we differentiate between legitimate politicking and a conspiracy?" she asked. "How would we prove it?" Her gaze wandered toward Trey, clicking away at something.

"You need it to be a small, tight group," said Imogen. "I think that's how you keep it quiet, below the radar. The more people, the greater the chance that one of them gets careless. The smallest number possible is best."

"I guess that makes us a bit like them," said Vega, not liking the idea. "Weir's deliberately keeping it small. Discrete units work on pieces of the puzzle, not the whole—"

"—Shit!" said Trey, pointing at the screen. "I haven't been focusing on texts because they never use them, but look there," he said pointing to what looked like a call. "This is from just before we got audio capability on them. But that's not a phone call. That's a text." He peered at it more closely. "Actually, it's a phone call and a text. I didn't notice it because Wicked calls Reed and then Reed sends him a text." He pulled the keyboard closer to him. "We've never been live with them so we can't record what they're saying. But a text stays in the system. Hang on," he said.

Wicked had deleted the text almost immediately, so it took Trey a couple minutes to fashion a workaround to retrieve it, but he got it. "Here we go!" he said and hit "enter" with a flourish. All three stared in silence at a grainy picture of Imogen standing outside Trey's car in front of her building.

"When was this taken?" asked Vega.

"That's gotta be from Christmas night," said Trey, unable to take his eyes off the photo. "That's the only day Gen didn't have a car," he added distantly. "I dropped her off."

Vega was already on her phone. "Davies?" she said, "I need you to take a drive."

Davies sped toward Imogen's apartment in the fading light under flat, grey skies. Wind whipped at the Potomac, tiny whitecaps showing against the dull gunmetal water. As he turned the corner onto Imogen's street, Davies slowed to a deliberate pace and began scanning the rank of parked cars on the opposite side of the street, where it was permitted.

The eighth car in the row was a grey Buick Lacrosse. Davies was almost past it when he noticed someone in the passenger seat. Their eyes met, he and the man in the car. Involuntarily, Davies touched the brake. A car honked behind. He stared a moment longer, fixing the man's features in his mind, then accelerated toward the end of the street to turn around. As he stamped on the accelerator, he cursed himself for not getting a license number.

Quickly, he reached a cross street where there was room to turn around. The car that had honked was still behind him and honked again as he doubled back. He was still at a distance when he saw the Buick pull out of the parking spot and speed away. Davies pushed harder on the accelerator as the Buick turned a corner at the top of the street.

"Call Vega," he enunciated carefully into his phone, taking the corner at speed.

Amanda Vega's phone rang deafeningly through the car's speakers, then: "This is Agent Vega. Davies?"

"I'm in pursuit of a grey Buick Lacrosse. Couldn't get a license number. He was parked across from Agent Trager's apartment building. Now heading southeast on Virginia 27."

Both cars weaved death-defying curves in and out of traffic, the Buick far ahead. As they approached the Columbia Pike interchange, Davies thought he saw an advantage as the traffic slowed through a construction area. The Buick continued to veer from side to side. At one moment, as they headed up an onramp, Davies reckoned he might be able to make a move to overtake. The Buick broke left as Davies broke right around a slow-moving Prius. In what seemed the same moment, the Buick driver slammed on his brakes and dived through a break in the concrete barrier dividing the opposing lanes. The traffic that side was lighter, and he was lucky there was a break that allowed him to turn and race back the other way.

"Fuck!" Davies yelled. He scanned ahead but saw no other break in the barrier. Already he couldn't see the Buick. "Vega," he said, "I've lost him. He turned back toward the pike: heading south. I didn't get close enough to get a plate number."

"Our closest trail is six or seven minutes out. He's lost. Dammit."

"I did get a pretty good look at him."

"That's something," said Vega. "I'm on my way back to headquarters. Meet me there." She turned to Imogen and Kelly. "You two may not leave this building."

8

Don Weir's phone pinged with a text from Dyer: *"youre gonna need to see the news. AG says mess of shit coming down."* Weir put aside the reports from his team, including the photo Reed had taken of Trager and Kelly, and turned on the office TV.

". . . old business still very much unresolved at the FBI," the anchor was noting. "Senator Drew Eliot of South Carolina, the ranking member of the Senate Judiciary Committee, is calling for hearings . . ." Vega, just back at headquarters, knocked at the door, and Weir waved her in. "Hugh Salter has more."

"When the so-called Faithless Elector plot was revealed two weeks ago to the day in a hastily called White House press conference," said Salter, standing in front of the Capitol, "the President entreated the nation to trust the process and let the Justice Department do their job. But many here in Washington are now saying the Justice Department can't be trusted."

The report cut away to Senator Eliot in his office. He was grave, judicious: "No, there are good men and women doing important work at the FBI. But I'm not at all satisfied with the findings of the Public Integrity Office regarding the voting mess in Illinois, and I'm calling for hearings to determine whether these missteps by a few are the product of incompetence, gross negligence, dereliction of duty—or worse. We have left them to do their jobs, but there seems to be a lack of progress and a systemic lack of accountability, possible undue political interference . . . and I want to know why. The American people want to know why."

Back to Salter. "At the heart of these concerns is Agent Imogen Trager. It was her analysis that served as the basis for Public Integrity's finding in Illinois, which has become so controversial." An inset video graphic showed Imogen standing next to the Attorney General at the press conference, then braving the gauntlet of reporters outside her apartment building on her first day back at work. "CNN has since uncovered evidence not only that Agent Trager was romantically involved with another agent, against FBI rules, but that her lover was Agent Thomas Kurtz, the man gunned down in the Old Executive Building parking garage on December nineteenth."

As he spoke, the inset video turned to the still pictures sent by Patriot76 of their beach selfie, kissing at a café, Imogen laughing, trying not be photographed. Weir, sitting at his desk, put his face in his hands. Vega stared blankly at the screen.

The report cut again to Senator Eliot in his office: "I'm shocked," he said, "utterly shocked. How was she able to keep her job? Was there a reprimand in her file? Who thought it was okay that she be put back to work, and on the Faithless Elector Task Group, no less? And with questions still unanswered about her conduct and findings on the Illinois election results?

"Did her liaison with Agent Kurtz cloud her judgment in any way? I'm hearing from you that he was the lead agent on the Illinois investigation. Was there collusion? Did she deliberately mislead her superiors? These are all questions we need to get to the bottom of."

Salter once more, on the Capitol steps. "Further questions remain. What were the circumstances of the shooting in the Executive Building garage? What has happened since to FBI Executive Assistant Director Pollack? Where is Professor Duncan Calder, who was shot and wounded? What light can their testimony shed?"

Weir's phone rang. He paused before picking up, muted the television, relaxed his breathing. It was Dyer.

"Yes, sir," he said into the phone. "Yes, I'm watching it. No, sir. As we discussed, I felt Trager would be an asset . . . and she has been . . . Yes, sir. Yes, I did know. Well, nonetheless . . . yes, sir. Thank you, sir. Right away." He put down the phone and turned to Vega. "I need you to go get Imogen," he said to her.

"Are we detaining her?"

"No," he said, glancing again at the surveillance photo.

"We're getting her out of harm's way—harm to her and us."

Sharon Voth knocked on the door frame as she entered. "I'm sorry. I happened to overhear some of that. Can I help?"

Sharon and Agent Vega arrived together at the Bus Rental building driving separate cars. Trey Kelly met them at the door and the guard buzzed them in.

"Has there been anyone hanging around here?" Vega asked the security guard when they were inside. "Anyone trying to get in?"

"Nope," he said. "No one."

"We need to keep a sharp eye," she said. "Are there cameras for the perimeter?"

"Yes, right here." The guard pointed under a desk on his right where four small screens were mounted.

"Do you know how they're backed up?" Vega asked.

"There's a server here inside," said Kelly. "Has something else happened?"

"We need to talk with Gen," said Vega. "And we need to go over the perimeter tapes here beginning on Christmas Eve. I'll put someone on it."

Vega introduced Sharon and Trey as they walked quickly along to the pit.

"Hi, Amanda . . . Sharon?" said Imogen.

"Have you seen the news today?"

"No. We've been working all day," Imogen answered. "Did you catch him?"

"No, I was about to debrief Davies, when . . . It's not good. Somehow it's got out in the press that you and Kurtz were an item," said Vega.

"Ugh," Imogen groaned, rolling her eyes.

"It's being taken seriously, and that's not the worst. They've got pictures of you two together. Senator Eliot, the ranking member of the Senate Judiciary Committee, is calling for hearings; wants to re-open the whole Illinois investigation, wants to review where we are on the Faithless Elector plot."

"Fuck." Imogen's mind was racing.

"None of that's happened yet," Vega reassured her. "Dyer will do his job, but we've got to get you out of harm's way."

"What?" said Imogen. "So I get shuttled off like some wayward woman . . . like I'm fucking Mata Hari?"

"Yes," said Sharon. "You do. It's ugly and it's wrong, but these are tiny, small-minded people—"

"—Powerful," Vega interjected.

"They will eat you up and spit you out," Sharon continued. "And honey, while they're chewing on you, you'll be vulnerable to whoever is still out there looking to finish what they started."

Imogen slammed her fist on the table. Trey stepped out and walked up the stairs into his office.

"So, I just sit at home?" Imogen asked.

"I can't imagine that would be helpful . . . or safe," said Vega. "If there was anything normal about this case we'd get you to one of our safe houses, like we do for witnesses, but they're all known or pretty easily discovered by anyone inside the FBI. We still can't figure out how that reporter got hold of photos from Kurtz's phone, and it's pretty clear someone's after you."

Imogen stared blankly at a dark computer screen.

"We could put you back at the detention center," Vega said.

"No!" said Imogen. Her thoughts were scrambled. She felt sick at the thought of her life and reputation being dragged out in the open and scrutinized, furious that her character would be questioned without being able to answer. Wouldn't it be better to stay and fight? she thought. "Couldn't I just stay here?" she asked. "Trey and I have practically been living here for the past few days. There's a cot . . . "

"What about Philadelphia?" Sharon offered. "You hid out there before. No one official knows the address. It's not your family's is it?"

Imogen shook her head.

"Does anything connect you to it?"

"No," said Imogen. "It's a friend's house and they're away."

"Can you go back?" asked Sharon.

Imogen thought. Her friends were still away on sabbatical. The renters wouldn't take over until the end of February. It was a possibility. "Yes," she said. Then, petulantly, she hissed: "This is bullshit!"

"Okay . . ." said Vega, clearly not liking the idea.

"So, that's the plan then?" said Imogen.

"No. No, it is not," said Amanda glaring at Sharon. "I don't know anyone in the Philadelphia office well enough to trust them to watch you. Not under the circumstances."

"If I may," Sharon began, "Dyer wants Weir to remove Imogen from the Task Group, effective immediately. I'll process the orders when I get back. But she is not being put on administrative leave; she is not being subpoenaed—yet. To be out of the official loop when we don't know what's coming next or whom to trust probably makes her safer."

Vega was nodding. "It's not a good option," she sighed. "I thought the detention center made sense, but Philadelphia sounds like the best of the bad options. It gets you out of the loop, dark to anyone but us, and it keeps you safe. You have your laptop with you?"

Imogen nodded.

"Then you can still keep your hand in, keep helping . . . at least until they suspend your account, if that's one of the things that ends up happening. We should see if Trey can help with keeping your account from getting hacked." She looked around, but Trey was in his office. "Give Sharon your apartment keys. She's going to get your things—changes of clothes, whatever else you need. Do you have a sidearm at your place?"

Imogen nodded. "In the dresser, second drawer down."

"Ammo?"

"Same drawer, in a box next to the gun."

"Okay. When she gets back, if the coast is clear, you'll leave directly from here for Philly."

"Is that safe for Sharon?" asked Imogen.

"Nobody knows me, hun. Hell, if anyone's still watching your building or looks twice at me they'll figure I'm the cleaning lady."

"And I'm sending Ron Guthrie back with her to keep an eye out," said Vega. "I'm confident she'll be safe with Guthrie along. While she's away doing that, I want you and Kelly to go over everything you've been doing, get me up to speed on where you are so we don't lose any ground."

Calder wished the morphine drip were a little stronger. The narcotic meant the pain from his shoulder was still subdued, but the dosage had been decreased significantly, and inklings of the pain he was really in, of what was really going on in his body, broke through. He wasn't sure if he was imagining, or whether he could feel exactly where the bullets had torn through his insides.

As annoying and impatient as Agent Brody had been, Calder wished he would come back. He looked forward to anything that might interrupt the tedium or take his mind off the damage in his body. There was nothing to do but pace around his room, or pad softly down the hall in his non-skid socks past the off-limits television room.

His request for books or a newspaper was met by a "we'll see" from the nurse. He had wanted to call the Political Science Department office at the university, but had been told he was not yet cleared to make phone calls.

"Could someone at least call the university on my behalf and let them know I'm okay?"

"We'll see, professor."

His strength was returning slowly, and the twenty or so yards down and back along the hallway no longer left him exhausted and panting for breath. It felt like progress, for which he was grateful. Still, every now and again the trauma of what had happened to him would burst in on him seemingly out of nowhere, and for no discernible reason, sapping his strength, blurring his focus.

One moment, he would be lamenting being stuck, a prisoner in all but name, feeling the annoyance at his situation growing into outright anger, then suddenly he would be shuddering, weak, sick to his stomach, his breath coming short. At such moments, he would find the nearest chair and sit down, or if there was no chair, steady himself against a wall until the wave passed.

Brody did not come back. Although Calder could not know it, he was busy interrogating the network cell members Vega had captured. Finally, Don Weir showed up to check on Pollack and to finish Calder's debriefing.

It was a hasty, perfunctory session, with Weir merely double-checking Brody's questions and Calder's answers to them. And it was short, leaving Calder with the realization that the long days of tedium were far from over.

"For the time being," Weir said at the conclusion of their interview, "we will continue to hold you in protective custody, officially as a material witness."

"So I'm not going anywhere."

"I'm sorry, but it's mostly for your safety." Weir closed up the file and placed it in the satchel next to him. "I can let you get newspapers in, and have access to the television, but you still won't be able to make outside contact."

"What about the university?" said Calder. "Classes begin soon. I'm supposed to be teaching a class. Could someone at least call the Dean?"

"We'll see."

Calder sighed deeply. "How is the investigation coming?"

"It's going," he said.

"It's not like I could tell anyone," Calder offered.

"No, that's true."

"Or is there a conspiracy of homicidal nurses?"

Weir smiled, but still said nothing.

"And Imogen? Is she all right?"

"She's fine," said Weir. "Safe . . . for now." He reached into his bag and pulled out yesterday morning's Washington Post. "Illinois Questions Unanswered," blared the headline.

Calder's heart sank as he scanned the article, thinking about how Imogen must feel to see her work maligned—wrongly—in the press. He wanted to reach out to her, to help her. "When can I get out of here?" he asked Weir.

"It's as much up to the doctors now as it is to me," he said. "We'll see." Weir left Calder reading his newspaper and went to look in on Pollack, who, though awake, was still groggy and drugged. Weir hoped he could focus for a few minutes at least.

* * *

Amanda Vega sat down with Gus Davies in her office to debrief him about what had happened when he first made the reconnaissance pass outside Imogen's apartment building. He sat silently and stiff in a chair in front of her desk as she reviewed his report, looking straight ahead, his gaze fixed a little above and to the right of her head. His thick black hair, though cropped short, grew thick and bushy, making him look like a seated Royal Foot Guard still wearing his busby.

"Grey Buick Lacrosse," said Vega finally. "Current model?"

"Not new," he said meeting her eyes, "but certainly not old—two, maybe three years old."

"No license plate." She turned over a page.

Davies returned to looking above and past Vega. "No," he said. "The car was parked between two others. He rabbited before I could turn around, and while in pursuit, I never got close enough."

"But you did get a look at the driver?"

"Yes. He was seated on the passenger side, blocked from my vision as I was scanning the row of cars. I didn't see him sitting there until I was right next to the car."

"The Buick?"

"Yes. Our eyes locked."

"And you think you can identify him?"

"I believe so."

Vega opened the middle drawer of her desk and pulled out a file. "Describe him?"

"White, late forties, early fifties. Grey hair, medium length, receding hairline. No distinguishing marks I could see."

Vega looked at the description he had submitted on his report and nodded. "I have six photos in here," she said, her hand on top of the file. "I'm going to lay them out, and I want you to take your time looking at them. They're not mug shots, so it may be difficult."

Inside the file, Vega had five suspect photos from various past surveillance details, but she had also included the government-issued photo for Frank Reed, a game warden, or "conservation officer" as they were called in New Jersey, which she had reprinted as black-and-white to match the others.

She laid them out one-by-one, a series of middle-aged men. She never looked up, never paused; she made sure nothing gave away which photo she hoped he would identify. Reed's was the third photo she put down.

"That's him," said Davies as she reached for the fourth.

"Let me put them all out," said Vega, and she laid them down quickly.

Davies surveyed the group slowly, quietly. "That's still the man," he said finally, tapping the third photo—Reed's.

*   *   *

Imogen took the same route to Philadelphia as she and Calder had taken just over two weeks earlier, along Route 50, past Annapolis, across the Chesapeake Bay Bridge and north through Delaware. It was a cold, clear day, the sun shining flat and stark across a bleak winter landscape. Once-abundant fields now lay quiet under a dusting of snow, cornstalk stubble peeking out in dun-colored rows that seemed to yawn open and snap shut as she raced past.

Running away again, she could not shake the feeling that they were all missing something obvious. Her previous retreat with Duncan had been tactical, undertaken because they were in immediate danger, the conspirators getting close. Was she in danger now? she wondered. How seriously should she take Deptford's threat or the photo?

She had taken the precaution of withdrawing $800 in cash, so she wouldn't have to use either her credit or debit card, just like before. But whereas previously running had seemed the best—the only—option, this trip felt more like an interruption, like an intense conversation that moved off in a different direction before she had a chance to make her point.

The timing of it all seemed odd, too. She had seen the photos the press was using, and they were from over two years earlier. How had they been obtained, and why were they only coming to light now? Why was the Illinois investigation still news? That Senator Eliot might respond to public pressure by holding hearings made sense, but there were ways to go about it that would not have stoked the controversy. He had won re-election. Why keep fanning the flames? The car's engine hummed its tune as the countryside rocketed by.

"Listen," Vega had said back at Bus Rentals, "be careful. I want you to think like you're on the run, because as far as I'm concerned, you are. I don't know why this Illinois investigation is still going. It's clear someone is keeping it alive for some reason. And it all keeps coming back to you. I don't think it's just political. I don't know why they're staking you out, but given the way they operate, it can't be good."

Inside the car, Imogen scratched at her head through the heavy wool cap Vega had given her. "Wear this whenever you're out," Vega had said. "Keep your hair tucked into it. And maybe get a long overcoat. The press and the bad guys are going to be on the lookout for every leggy redhead on the eastern seaboard after today."

"Leggy?" Imogen thought with a smile. She leaned back in the driver's seat and glanced down toward her feet as she drove. The smile faded as she thought again of what she was headed toward—nothing. She glanced toward the dashboard. The car radio beckoned. Her finger hovered over the switch for a moment, but she let it drop. She couldn't face it. The news was a ravening frenzy of speculation and hearsay. It had ceased to give insight or clarification, served only to amplify partisan outrage. She sighed, bitter that her work, her involvement, was now abundant fodder.

* * *

Phil Jezek felt someone rush up behind him as he pulled the door closed against the rush of freezing air. He was at his favorite lunch place, a Japanese restaurant in Penn Quarter, a few blocks from his office. If his mind had not been so focused on a steaming, fragrant bowl of Udon noodles, he might have noticed that Senator Drew Eliot's Chief of Staff, Casey Hague, had been following him on the opposite side of the street for the better part of two blocks.

"Sorry," said Hague, as he bumped into Jezek.

Jezek nodded and smiled, acknowledging there was no harm done and moved to get in line.

"Phil Jezek?" said Hague, touching him on the shoulder.

"Yes?"

"This is perfect. I just stopped by your office, but they said you were out." Hague leaned in confidentially, "I don't usually get to come here. The Hart Senate building's only like a mile away, but it's just too far most days. I come here whenever I can. What's your favorite?"

"Today, I really want a bowl of noodles."

"Oh, that sounds good," said Hague ingratiatingly.

"You wanted to see me?" asked Jezek. "And you are?"

"Sorry. Casey Hague." He extended his hand. "I'm Chief of Staff to Senator Drew Eliot."

"Of course," said Jezek, taking his hand. "We met at that luncheon—"

"—Could you and I have lunch together?"

"Sure, I guess," said Jezek.

Just as they were getting to the front of the line, Hague's phone rang. Jezek turned to look at him. Hague turned the phone so Jezek could see "Senator Eliot" displayed as the caller. Hague sighed, shaking his head. "Yes, sir?" he said brightly, answering the phone. "Just getting a bit of lunch before I headed back. Yes, my favorite place." He smiled at Jezek and gave a wink. "Well, sir, I was able to find Agent Jezek. We were about to . . . yes. I see. I'll call you back in two minutes." Hague disconnected and put the phone back in his pocket.

"How about if you and I got this to-go? Eliot's car can be here in a minute. He'd like to talk with you as well."

"The Senator?" Jezek looked uneasy.

"We'd have you back before anyone misses you."

"What's this about?"

"Half an hour of your lunchtime. A crucial half hour."

*　*　*

It was early afternoon, and the sun was low in the sky, casting bleak shadows across Catherine Street as Imogen arrived in South Philly and pulled the car to the curb half a block up from the house. Though it glinted starkly, bleaching the red-brick row house fronts, the sun did not warm what it touched. She blinked into the light, her green eyes watering in the cold air as she walked from her car to the front door of the row house, dragging her case behind her, the air biting at her fingertips.

She let herself quietly inside, closing the door and leaning back on it. She had hoped the physical act of walking in and shutting the door would bring relief; that she would feel safe, relieved and grateful to be there, freer; but the work that needed doing, the questions, her anger, the puzzle of it all—

141

none of it had stayed on the other side of the door. It followed her inside.

There was a rush of mixed emotions as she realized that the house was exactly as she and Duncan had left it: a mess. They had left in a hurry back on December 20, and there were still dishes on the counter, coffee cups in the sink, garbage from their cheesesteak takeout. She touched the phone in her overcoat pocket, and for the second time in as many minutes she chided herself for doing it. She had switched off the phone as she started the car in the Bus Rental parking lot and had thrown it casually on the passenger seat, a gleaming, mute piece of tech. Still, that hadn't stopped her looking in its direction every few minutes throughout the drive.

Imogen took stock of what was available in the refrigerator, the cupboards. She would need to stay close to home, not draw attention to herself, but she would also need a few things. She put her bag in the second-floor bedroom. She made a list of things she would need and ran to the store for coffee, pasta and other essentials. After days confined in the bunker of Bus Rentals, she was glad of the air and the exercise. Good to be out, she thought, and stretch her legs.

Back at the house, she went to the basement and began on the laundry left over from her last stay. The towels and bedclothes were smeared with bloodstains. She shuddered as she looked at them, thinking of how Duncan had been beaten and almost been killed when he went to see Jim Novaczeck, Diane Redmond's campaign manager. She could see him, the raw skin, multiple cuts; the bleeding nose, the swollen eye; the bruises on his ribs and neck growing, darkening like ominous storm clouds.

She stood over the washing machine in the basement, staring at the bloodstains Duncan had left and wondered if they would ever come out; wondered if this nightmare would ever be over; wondered if she would ever see him again. She sighed deeply and decided she should just pay to replace the towels and sheets. She took off her work clothes and bundled them into the washer with everything else. Then she trudged half-naked up the stairs to put on sweatpants and a sweatshirt.

She sat on the edge of the bed upstairs and despite her better judgment turned on the news: "The FBI can't even keep their own house in order!" thundered some pundit. Imogen changed the channel. "Our process—admittedly imperfect—worked," said a campaign spokesman. "The Electoral College chose James Christopher. We need an investigation of the FBI—" She turned it off and set about tidying up.

She had hoped the process of getting settled would take the better part of a day, but the house was back in order in less than an hour and a half. Whatever psychological distance she had hoped would open up during the drive from DC, whatever fresh perspective might have grown within her during the long wait in the checkout line at the Acme grocery or as she did necessary drudgework, had not been forthcoming. She needed to get to work or she would go mad. Moreover, she disliked leaving so much undone at a crucial point. Amanda was probably right about the need for safety. She'd been vigilant and helpful; but Imogen feeling grateful was different from liking her and wanting her to take too much credit.

From the outside, the house was the familiar "Federal" style, similar in size to every other row house along Catherine Street. Inside, it was quiet, comfortable and nicely designed, an open plan with high ceilings where each room, though distinct, flowed into the next, allowing available light to be drawn through from the front and back. Each piece of furniture was sturdy, well made, and well chosen. Imogen noticed none of this as she set herself up at a teak wood Danish-modern Planters desk in the living room. She pushed some papers onto the floor, opened her laptop, pulled out the hard drive Trey had given her and plugged in.

When Trey had stepped out of the pit while Imogen was talking with Vega and Sharon, it had been to get a new portable hard drive. He had dumped a "light" version of the cellphone matrix data onto the new drive, essentially a copy of the animated portion without the underlying data. She would still be able to follow the cellphone trails, but to drill down any further, she would have to email or call either Trey or Vega.

Imogen pulled out a notebook Trey had also given her. She logged on to the house's wifi connection, and then, following Trey's written instructions, began working through two proxy servers, first, a middle school in Takoma Park, Maryland, and then a bike rental shop in Adams Morgan.

"Why two?" she had asked. "And why these?"

"The middle school is where I went as a boy. Let's just say I know those backwards and forwards," Trey had said.

"And the bike shop?"

"It's an FBI front. We use it for all kinds of things, mostly to lure cyber-thieves and hackers. So, if there's someone hunting you from inside the FBI, they may know enough to search for people using the bike shop IP. But it's a Chinese finger trap. If they start trying to trace you I'll be able to track them. So, first go through the Middle School, then through the bike shop. If the bike shop link gets compromised, we will learn something, but you'll still be safe. And then I'll send instructions to route you through a different, second server. I've done it for Agent Vega's email, and I'll reconfigure Weir's tonight. We can't afford any hacked leaks."

"What if they're as good as you at all this?"

"As good as me?" said Trey, amused. "Please," he scoffed.

She would only be able to use Skype for phone calls, too, routed through the same IP address. The hiding and misdirection felt like before, like she was still running, and once again, she didn't know from whom or what.

Imogen ran the program Trey had given her. After a while, the loops and orbits made by the phone trails took on a hypnotic quality. She realized she wasn't really absorbing information so much as just watching.

Imogen opened her email and typed: "I'm here. All is well so far. Anything new?"

Almost immediately came Vega's response: "Glad you're safe. Confirmed: Figgy = Frank Reed, aka Mr. Cooper. Davies ID-ed him. Wicked still a mystery. Reed/Figgy still in the wind. Watch yourself." Attached was Reed's photo.

*　*　*

Senator Eliot's black limousine pulled up to the curb along D Street NW. It had barely stopped before Hague had the door open and he and Jezek piled in. Hague wedged himself comfortably into a corner next to the senator and Jezek took the seat facing him, behind the driver. Jezek put the plastic carrier bag holding his noodle bowl on the floor between his feet.

"Phil," said the senator, "it's great to meet you. I'm Senator Drew Eliot."

Jezek leaned forward, extending his hand. "Senator Eliot. It's a pleasure . . . an honor."

The senator smiled pleasantly. He, like Colls, had the air of someone accustomed to admiration and deference. "I'm sorry to interrupt your lunch, Phil, but we need your help."

"Mine?" said Jezek.

"Yes. I don't think I'm disclosing anything untoward when I say we're worried—and by 'we' I mean key members of the Judiciary Committee." The senator's easy South Carolina accent was kindly, warm, paternal. "There's a lot that's gone wrong at the FBI lately—"

Jezek looked down at his lunch.

"—don't mistake me Phil. I, like you, have the best interests of the Bureau in my heart . . . as I know you do. This discussion is not about attacking the Bureau. It's about saving it from itself."

"Saving it from itself, Senator?"

Hague sat in the corner stuffing tonkatsu in his mouth. Jezek looked again at the bowl resting between his feet.

"Maybe that's a little melodramatic on my part," allowed the senator genially, "but with this business of the Faithless Elector plot . . . Tom Kurtz . . . the shooting. This tangle with the Illinois elections results that won't go away . . . and then this business of the affair between Kurtz and Trager comes out. The Bureau looks sloppy, inept. Or worse, Phil: corrupt."

Jezek looked between both men. The senator was still smiling pleasantly at him, and Hague was digging with his chopsticks deep into his food container. Jezek smiled back weakly.

"So why am I talking to you about this? you're wondering. I've heard you're honest—true blue. True red-white-and-blue." The senator smiled at his own witticism.

"Well, thank you," said Jezek.

"I don't have to tell you how vital the FBI is to the nation's safety and security, nor how vital it is that it be a transparent, effective, well-run agency. Your mentor, Andy Colls—may he rest in peace—certainly thought so. He mentioned you as an up-and-comer, someone we should keep an eye on."

"I'm flattered, Senator—"

"Someone who would do great things," said the senator. He looked off, his gaze falling just to the right of Jezek, as though he were seeing Colls sitting there. He nodded absently as though hearing Colls' words of praise again. "And," he said finally. "And I say this kindly: maybe you're not living up to your potential?"

Jezek was about to interject when the senator raised his hand.

"I'm not running you down, Phil. It's not a lack of skill, or effort or commitment on your part, but a lack of . . . sharpness, shall we say? Aggressiveness. When opportunities are placed before us, we must first recognize them as opportunities . . . and then we must seize them."

"I think you're probably right," said Jezek staring down at the rapidly cooling food he held between his feet.

"And maybe, Phil. Maybe there haven't been a lot of opportunities to seize. Ambition—the good kind, like you and I have—grows dull the longer it stays in the shed. I sense that you're still keen."

"I am," said Jezek.

"Of that, I am sure." The senator patted Jezek's knee. He looked over at Hague, still eating. "Before he retired," Senator Eliot continued, "Andy would make sure we knew things he felt we needed to know. Since his retirement—and before his untimely death—he continued to help us, mostly by corroborating or refuting things we were hearing from other sources, and occasionally bringing new issues to our attention. He told us that you had been a great help to him in that endeavor."

"Me?" asked Jezek.

"Yes. He said you were unusually perceptive; that you saw through things to what was really happening. Phil, we need that kind of insight right now. And we need someone we can trust. I need someone who's willing to take this on aggressively."

"Take what on, Senator?"

"On the surface of things, we're getting what looks like cooperation from your bosses, but how can we be sure?"

"Agent Colls told you I was supplying information?"

Hague and the senator exchanged a quick glance.

"No one suggested you were spying, Phil," said the senator delicately. "But rather, that in your friendly talks, you were able to help Andy Colls—and by extension, us—to see what was really happening more clearly. And by helping us, you and he were helping the Bureau."

Jezek stared out the window.

"I wanted us to have this talk, Phil, because with Andy gone—"

"—Senator, I don't know how to say this, but I'm hearing that Agent Colls may have been mixed up in something. He committed suicide."

The senator put a comforting hand on Jezek's arm. "Phil, I know this must be hard. You were very close to Andy . . . as we all were. No one saw this coming. But you can be sure in your heart: Andy was not mixed up in anything . . . untoward. I don't want you thinking even for a minute that he was. I can tell you that the current investigation on him is just standard procedure. Given all that's gone on in the Bureau, it's necessary, if distasteful."

Jezek nodded, still looking out the window.

"And, Phil, with all that's going on, it's vital that there be proper oversight. This is your time, Phil. Your time to step up. I think you're sharp enough to see an opportunity to do the right thing when it's right in front of you."

Jezek nodded.

"Without you, we're blind to the missteps or malfeasance in the Bureau. And without you, things can still be covered up. Think about that. People who do not support the mission of the FBI—people who should not have been admitted in the first place, people who may have held you back . . ." The senator smiled. "A shake-up at the Bureau is coming, Phil. You need to ask your ambition—" the senator tapped Jezek's chest—"your ambition for your career, for your country—you need to ask it whether you want to be on the inside"—the senator spread his arms to indicate the cozy limousine—"or out in the cold." He nodded at the icy streets just outside the window.

"I can see you're worried. Your reticence does you credit. You feel there's some possible conflict. I assure you: there is not. There's no skullduggery, Phil. It is perfectly within your remit to report to us in our capacity as the Oversight Committee.

"And there would be nothing formal about it. I'm just hoping that you and Casey here might continue the chats you and Andy were having. Keep us up to date on the what's and why's: has this Trager woman been disciplined, for instance? Or, have they made any headway on the Faithless Elector plot? 'Cause they sure don't seem to be making any. Are there any more gaffes or scandals we should know about before they hit the news? I think you'll agree there's been more than enough of that."

Jezek was nodding. "Yes," he said. "Yes, I could do that. Unofficially?"

"Exactly," said the senator. "Officially unofficial." He smiled again as he reached out to shake Jezek's hand. "Andy Colls trusted you, Phil. I'm glad I can trust you. This is important in many ways."

"Thank you, Senator. I'm honored to help."

"Don't mention it, Phil." The senator sat back, contemplating Jezek. "I think you'll find that I can be helpful, too. Right now, for instance, you're in—?" he looked searchingly toward Hague.

"—He's been detailed to Public Integrity," said Hague.

The senator pursed his lips as though mulling something over. "I'm sure they do great and important work, but I think we can all agree your talents are probably languishing there." He looked out the window. "Oh, this is your stop, Phil."

The car pulled to the curb and Jezek opened the door. He stepped out of the car and shook the senator's reassuring hand one more time.

"And Phil, when you get transferred to the Faithless Elector Task Group, try to act surprised." He smiled and winked, then motioned for Jezek to close the door.

* * *

Imogen closed her email and went back to tracking the loops and orbits, staring through, rather than at, her screen. Something about Boston tugged at her, seemed to hover indistinct in her mind, like something glimpsed in the depths of a pond. Its form and shape were trying to resolve, trying to swim up into her consciousness.

Amanda thought the conspirators' talk was only about final cover for themselves as they wound down, but Imogen was convinced there was something more. As horrible as the conspirators were, they were efficient, no wasted movement, no unnecessary risks. If they were winding down and had wanted the people in Deptford's cell dead, it would have already happened.

Her focus had just come back to the screen wanderings of the known conspirators when she saw Kurtz's timeline jump rapidly to somewhere just outside Chicago, Illinois, in mid-November, barely a week after the general election. He had been in Illinois for three days. This detail had been noticed before, of course, but it had also been put down as essential Bureau business. So far as Imogen knew, it had not been followed up. Who had sent him, and what, specifically, had he done? If he had gone at the behest of Colls, they could be onto something.

Just as she was getting ready to close the screen and open Skype to contact Vega and Kelly, she saw Kurtz's timeline jump again. To Boston.

Back at headquarters, Weir asked Sharon Voth to come into his office. "And close the door, please," he added.

Sharon did so and sat down in front of his desk, some files, a notepad and pen at the ready.

"First," he said, "I've been to the hospital, and I wanted to let you know that Doug Pollack is definitely out of the woods. He's nowhere near a hundred percent, but he's out of the coma, he can sort of answer questions, and the doctors say he will keep the arm. They've done an amazing job, the doctors. He's going to be okay."

Sharon's eyes welled up.

"He specially wanted me to let you know he's okay, and he hopes you're doing well. I told him you'd been a great help."

"Thank you," said Sharon quietly, her voice overcome with a storm of relief.

Weir stared at the top of his desk for a moment, as though unsure how to proceed. After a moment, he began: "Pollack also said he used to bounce things off you . . . department things . . . things he wasn't sure about."

Sharon nodded.

"I wondered if . . . I wondered if I could count on you that way."

"Of course," she said. "I'll help every way I can."

"Thank you. For instance, what do you know so far about this investigation, about the Faithless Elector Task Group?"

"I know that Andy Colls was the leader of a network cell that involved Tom Kurtz and the two other assassins; that you appear to have found another cell . . . one outside the FBI, thank the Lord; that Trey and Imogen's work helped get us all rolling again. I know you were worried about Agent Vega, but now seem satisfied. And I expect you're pretty worried about Jezek being assigned to the task group, since he's pretty closely linked with Colls."

"How do you know about Jezek being reassigned? It's only just happened."

"I got the same email order you did this morning. I'm cc'ed on everything like that. I printed out the order for you to counter-sign so I can file it. It's right there on your desk." She pointed.

"Right," he said. "Right. Of course."

"I know that Colls is dead. It's officially a suicide, but no one who knows about it believes it. By the way could you sign that order transferring Jezek? I'd hate for it to get lost."

Weir signed the papers.

"Since you're asking," Sharon ventured, "it is definitely a worry that Jezek has been assigned here. I don't know to whom he's answering ultimately, but you'll have to be careful."

"Yes. That's what I wanted to talk to you about. The order came from Dyer. Should I be worried about Dyer now, too? I don't think so, but . . ."

"I see that," said Sharon.

"There's nothing I've kept from Dyer. Everything I know, he knows. He doesn't need to watch me."

"I think Dyer's probably on the level. That is to say, as much as anyone in his position can be," she added with a wry smile. "Though I don't know it for a fact, I'll bet this comes from Senator Eliot and the Judiciary Committee. They're clamoring for arrests, results. The Task Group has been pretty quiet."

"I know. But I can't let on what we do know . . . certainly not yet."

"Which is probably why they want someone on the inside. Someone like Phil Jezek. He's true-blue, follows orders like a dog; and he can sniff out the alpha dog in any group faster than anyone. The key will be to freeze out Jezek somehow without him knowing he's being isolated."

"Agreed," said Weir. "My thoughts exactly. I've just never had to do that to an agent before."

Sharon nodded her head sadly. "But you do now, Don. And: I'd take this as an opportunity to maybe play some offense; make this forced inclusion work for you."

"What do you mean?"

"I'd suggest you feed Jezek some kind of false information. Then, if that false intel starts coming back at you from higher up or in the press, or in hearings, you'll know it came through him. Which will expose a bit more of who is connected to whom. And if it doesn't come back on you, you can be a little surer of him. Because we don't know for a fact that he's in league with Colls and them. Vega wasn't."

"Yes, I see," said Weir.

"Also, I think you should sign the documents approving Imogen's vacation request. I have them here."

"Trager wants vacation time?" he asked, bewildered. "Now?"

"Well, officially your only directive was that she be removed from the Task Group. It's possible—in fact, probable—that the next directive will be for you put her on administrative leave," Sharon began patiently. "And if she's on admin leave, she will need to be available in the case of a subpoena. The language on the form states: 'Because the employee remains in paid status during an administrative leave/investigatory suspension, Bureau work rules and policies continue to apply. For example, the employee must remain available.' So, I suggest you approve her vacation request. If the higher-ups tell you to put her on administrative leave—which they seem likely to do—you can state absolutely that you will do so just as soon as you can; that she will be informed of it, and the admin leave will go into effect as soon as she makes contact."

Weir stared at her.

"You've got some wiggle room with Imogen. She's an analyst, not a field agent. This wouldn't work for Vega."

"Is this the kind of thing you learned from Pollack?" asked Weir.

"Oh, no." Sharon chuckled. "Doug's a straight-shooter . . . like you. There's not a devious bone in that man's body. He's got a law degree, but he's mostly a cop. I'm mostly an administrator—I wouldn't know the first thing about organizing and conducting a full-field investigation, for instance—but I understand the politics of organizations . . . at least of this one."

"Do I need to watch you a little more closely?" Weir asked, playfully.

"No, Don. Only if you want to learn a little cunning. Besides, I only use my powers for good," Sharon affirmed with a grin.

* * *

Hugh Salter's reports had led the evening news two days in a row, and his reporting had made the break before the first commercial on another occasion. The other news organizations were now playing catch-up, and Salter's news director was happy, which was dreadful to behold. News directors were naturally perverse, misanthropic, high-functioning paranoids. This abrupt bonhomie came across as awkward and out of character. Salter wished he could share the feeling of contentment.

As he sat looking out at the newsroom through a glass wall, the reservations about how and why Patriot76 was feeding him would not go away. Disclosures that uncovered official secrecy, or that unmasked the workings of government decision-making, or that exposed venality at the top levels government were one thing, but the information he was getting felt like something a political hatchet-man would invent to destroy a rival or punish an enemy. Agent Trager wasn't powerful. She was an FBI analyst.

Her work, now that he'd had time to fully digest it, looked sound. He worried that something different was wrong with the Illinois vote count, something no one was seeing. The more he thought about it, the more probable it seemed that someone was trying very hard to discredit Trager. Why else would they go after a relative non-entity like her, a wonky, if photogenic analyst?

If anything, the success Patriot76's scoops had brought were making Salter more concerned. As part of the mainstream "legacy" media he had felt largely exempt from the existential crisis in journalism brought on by revelations of the outsized role "fake news" had played—and continued to play—in the election. The memes, half-truths and outright lies given a Frankenstein-life as they were indiscriminately shared on Twitter and Facebook had so far had little effect on him or his colleagues. But now that one aspect of the news environment had been colonized by this stuff, what if his reporting had become the leading edge of some darker manipulation? When he interviewed Senator Eliot, the senator had said he was "shocked" at what was allowed to happen in the Bureau. But in Salter's estimation the senator hadn't seemed shocked or even surprised by the revelations.

Everything kept coming back to Trager. It could be that everything Patriot76 was feeding to Salter he was also feeding to Senator Eliot and his aide, Casey Hague. It made a kind of sense that they would be in the same loop. But presumably Eliot had analyses as reliable or better than those he and his press colleagues had seen on the vote results. Why bang on about it? What was to be gained?

When this had all started, Hague had more or less admitted he knew Partiot76's identity. Was this a wedge into the FBI? he wondered. Was Patriot76 an FBI agent? Because the main question that had been bothering Salter for days remained unanswered: who would have access to a dead agent's phone in the midst of one of the most intensive investigations in the nation's history, when that agent was the central figure in it? Who would have access to inter-Bureau emails like the one he exposed between Trager and Pollack?

Salter picked up the phone and dialed the FBI public information officer, David Lewisham. "Yes," he said, when the receptionist picked up, "it's Hugh Salter from CNN for David Lewisham."

"That's it! Feet to the fire," said his news director, who had just popped his head into Salter's tiny fishbowl office. He grinned at Salter and rapped his knuckles good-naturedly on the doorframe before continuing down the hall. Salter smiled pleasantly and gave the news director a thumbs-up. A happy news director was definitely harder to stomach than an unhappy one.

* * *

"Phil, come in!" said Weir jocularly to Agent Philip Jezek. Weir walked around his desk to shake hands. "Glad you're on board. We're swamped. Is there anything you're still working on back in Public Integrity?" He steered Jezek toward a chair.

"No, sir," said Jezek.

"Excellent. All in for us, then!" he rubbed his hands together. Weir pointed at the files in Jezek's hand. "Good. You got those. Have you had time to review them?"

"I've made a start. This was all so surprising."

"Yes. But we need all the good help we can get." Weir moved to close the door. At the door, he and Sharon exchanged a meaningful glance. "No interruptions, please," he said and closed the door.

Weir sat down in the other chair in front of the desk and leaned toward Jezek. Quietly, he said, "I think you can see, we're not making much headway."

"I didn't want to say that right off the bat, sir, but there isn't a lot here."

"No. When we stumbled onto Colls, we thought that was our big break."

"Is there something to the rumors, sir?"

"What rumors?"

"That he was involved in the Faithless Elector plot."

"It sure looks that way. With Agent Colls, we caught a break. One of our informants was talking about someone making drops that didn't sound drug-related, and Agent Vega followed it up. We pulled the courier in for questioning, but unfortunately, we didn't learn much of anything from him. Then—we think—someone who was part of that group who

155

led us to the courier somehow alerted Colls that we were on to him . . . even though, frankly, we weren't."

"I don't understand."

"Poor bastard. It's not widely known . . . well, you've seen it in the files . . . he killed himself."

"Yes," said Jezek.

"Probably, he thought we were closer than we really were. Couldn't stand the thought of the scandal."

"How do you know he was involved at all, then?"

"I barely believed it myself," said Weir, shaking his head sadly. "He was a good agent. But we found an old SIM card in his car under a floor mat when we found the body . . . and, by way of confirmation, his car matched the description the courier gave us. It probably went to a burner phone he ditched somewhere."

"That's all you have on Colls?"

Weir nodded sadly. "It's enough." He looked at Jezek a moment. "You worked closely with him on a number of things. How are you holding up?"

"It's difficult, I admit. This job, you have to be ready for shocks, for the untimely death of colleagues. But this. It doesn't make sense."

"I know," sighed Weir.

"What's a SIM card got to do with it?" Jezek asked casually.

"We were able to match it to a number that Kurtz had called from his own burner. The one he had on him when he was killed."

"I see."

"But that's all we got . . . And that's another tragedy: Kurtz."

"Are the events in the parking garage accurate?" asked Jezek.

"It was Pollack who shot him. Pollack's still in a medically-induced coma, by the way," Weir lied. "I'd like to get more of the specifics, but for now, we're looking at two rogue agents. I know that's distasteful, and hard to believe, but that seems to be the full extent of the Bureau's exposure, which is of course my first priority."

"Of course."

"But we're sure they weren't acting entirely alone. This is big . . . you know that. You've looked at the files." Weir paused, stared at Jezek for a moment. "I tell you, I've got a feeling Illinois is the key."

"That may be," said Jezek. "I was detailed there, you know, just after the election."

"I didn't know that. So you know the players, the ground . . . this is good."

"I do. But isn't this Agent Trager working on something there?" Jezek asked.

"Not anymore. She's on administrative leave. There's just way too much going on for her to be effective, or helpful. You've seen the newspapers. And frankly, between us, she wasn't all that effective even before this crap about dating Kurtz broke in the news. She's a stats person, a wonk. And she's good at it. But she's not an agent." He sighed heavily. "I tell you, if he knew about those two, Pollack's gonna have some explaining to do if he ever recovers, that's for sure. But let's be honest, we brought her in mostly for show. She'd been on the news—in a good way, originally."

"So where is she now?"

"You know, I said we'd put her on leave. Actually, I think she saw the writing on the wall. She claimed—maybe rightly—exhaustion . . . "

Jezek scoffed.

Weir nodded, indicating that he and Jezek were on the same page when it came to her lack of stamina. "At any rate, she took vacation time. She said she was headed for Myrtle Beach or something."

"Maybe she's a flight risk?"

He nodded approvingly at Jezek. "Good. But I'm ahead of you. Her passport is flagged, so she can't leave the country. Right now, I don't need the distraction of trying to find her on some sunny beach. But if we do need to, we'll flag her credit cards and trace her down pretty quick."

"Yeah. A woman wouldn't be too far from her credit cards," said Jezek.

They both had a good chuckle.

The smile on Weir's face dwindled. He looked hard at Jezek for moment. "I need you to go Illinois," he said finally. Weir stood up and walked to his desk, where he picked up a thick file. As he handed the file over, he said: "We've checked Trager's work, but I need someone who can do some real detective work—not some analysis. I need it to be someone from my task group who I can trust. I need it to be someone who will get in amongst the election officials and get me some intel, a lead. Something we can sink our teeth in."

Weir walked quickly to the door. "Sharon?" he said as he opened it. "Slight change in plan: I'm not sending Vega to Illinois. She stays here. Phil here's going instead."

"Very good," said Sharon, "I'll make the changes. Is Davies still going?"

"Yes. No change there." He turned to Jezek. "You and Davies will work together. You're the lead. Work out your travel arrangements with Sharon here. I'll let Vega know what's happening, and get any work you'll need." He headed off down the hallway.

"Very good, sir," Jezek said after him.

Sharon smiled at Jezek. "Nothing like hitting the ground running, eh?"

Next day, Agent Vega sat at her desk, the door to her office closed against the tumult. The 115th Congress would convene in 24 hours, and every federal department, the FBI included, was gearing up for the day and taking extra precautions.

As she worked, tracing information from her computer screen to the files on her desk, she cursed under her breath. In the first days after December 19, she had exhaustively checked Kurtz's movements, but she had found no non-official movement and so had moved on to other potential leads, focusing on unofficial movements. What she had failed to do was pay attention to who had sent Kurtz on specific details. Now she was going back over it all again.

As she sifted through case files, reports, requisitions, and personnel requests, it became clear that while Kurtz was rarely part of Colls' direct task force, Colls had requested and detailed Kurtz numerous times over the past two years to various locations. He had done so most recently, and pertinently, to Illinois just after the election, and he had sent him to Boston in July and again on November 6, two days before the general election.

9

At Fort Belvoir Hospital, Duncan Calder knocked on the door to Doug Pollack's room. "May I come in?" Pollack peered at him a moment. "Imogen's professor . . ." he said distantly.

Calder shuffled into the room. "Yes," he said, smiling, "Duncan Calder." He held out his hand automatically and then stopped. He stared awkwardly at the bandaged, splinted right hand and withdrew it. "I wanted to see how you were doing," he said.

Pollack cleared his throat. "Still here," he said, his tone implying that it was a status about which he still had some doubt. His eyes were alert, but they were the only things about him that appeared to have revived. He was haggard and colorless.

"I'm glad. I wanted to say, thank you," Calder began. "It's strange to owe so much to someone I barely know."

Pollack smiled weakly. They stared at one another silently.

"I wonder if they'd let me get up for a while," said Pollack. "I'm sick of this bed."

"I'll go ask," said Calder. He turned and padded over to the nurse's station, expecting a non-commital "We'll see."

To his surprise, the doctor and nurse seemed warm toward the idea.

"It's doubtful he can walk very far at all," said Dr. Hart. "But it might be good for both of you to get out and about, at least here on the floor."

It took some time but the nurses rigged up a wheelchair to carry Pollack's various IV solutions. Calder was glad of any novel activity and watched their work with interest. Pollack could walk, they instructed, and push the wheelchair, which would lend him some stability—and then when he was tired, he could sit, and Calder could push the chair. Pollack made it about ten paces out of his room walking behind the wheelchair before it was clear he was overwhelmed and had to sit. Calder took over and wheeled him down toward the elevators and then back along the hall. Not quite the blind leading the blind, but the halt and the lame making the best of it.

"I'm afraid this is the extent of our world at the moment," said Calder as they doubled back to head toward the elevators again, rolling silently across the bright oak floors.

Back at the familiar end, next to the elevators, there was a view out over the hospital grounds and beyond to the Potomac. Calder pushed the chair to the windows. The sun, pale and low in the sky behind a shield of unbroken clouds, swathed the countryside in cold light.

"It all looks so peaceful, doesn't it?" said Pollack, his eyes fixed on the river.

"Lovely," Calder agreed.

"But it isn't real. There's shit going on out there." He indicated the broader world with a tilt of his head, the silent, dormant trees, the icy waters moving unalterably past them. "Imogen's on the run again," he said. "Alone, this time."

Calder said nothing. Whereas Pollack looked out and found a deceitful serenity in the landscape, Calder's aspect was inward, silent.

"My replacement, Don Weir, thinks there might still be a mole in the Bureau."

"Is there anything we can do?" Calder asked.

"Not from here."

*　*　*

On Catherine Street in South Philadelphia, Imogen was looking inward too, but with no grand vista. The windows at the front of the house looked straight out at the houses facing, and the windows at the back looked out at a deck barely twenty feet deep. Her thoughts felt crowded too.

161

She closed her laptop and stalked to the front hall. She had been inside for two days, and her Pilates-at-home workout routine was no substitute for fresh air. She stuffed her feet into a pair of fur-lined winter boots, pulled on an overcoat and knotted a scarf. By the front door she stopped at a mirror and tucked her hair into the heavy wool cap Amanda had given her, pulling it down tightly across her ears. She reached into her purse and donned a pair of Ray-Ban aviator sunglasses with green lenses. Surveying herself in the mirror, she felt she looked anonymous if a bit dowdy. She turned the collar of her coat up as she went out the door, locking it behind her.

She found a pair of gloves in her pocket. Even with them on, she found herself walking with her hands deep in the pockets to keep them warm. She set off east toward the Delaware River, head down. A raw wind grew stronger as she neared the water, stinging her cheeks and nose. Despite the biting cold, it was good to be out. Fortunately, since she was trying to avoid being seen, the weather seemed to keep most everyone else off the streets. Or would that make her more visible? she wondered as she plowed on, chin tight to her chest.

At Front Street she decided she would make a broad circuit, first heading north along Front to the South Street bridge; across to the water, then along the river, south toward Christian, where she could turn back toward Second Street and Catherine. The wind blew bits of garbage, sand and leaves into strange eddies. One block would be clear and clean, free of debris, the next would have piles deposited by the wind in specific locations, in the lee of a lamppost or filling a depression in the pavement. Again, she seemed to be trailing in T. S. Eliot's wake: "The grimy scraps Of withered leaves about your feet", she thought, "And newspapers from vacant lots."

She marched across the South Street bridge over I-95, and felt it was mistake. On a warm day, she could see, it would have been lovely, but the bridge was totally exposed. The wind whipped, hard and biting. She licked her lips and wished she had brought her Chapstick. She pulled her cap a little snugger across her ears as she paused mid-span and considered turning back.

Imogen looked back toward the city, then out, toward the riverfront. It was as bad as it was going to get, she thought . . . she hoped. Cars rocketed along I-95 below her. A lone jet, angling toward the airport, settled into its approach pattern above her. Rooted momentarily to the spot, she looked out at the Delaware River. George Washington had famously crossed it up by Trenton on Christmas night, 1776, a desperate gambit at a crucial time.

Her thoughts returned to the dark network. Could the threat—to herself, to the nation—be any worse than it already was? She thought of Macbeth, contemplating his doom or his fortune: "I am in blood Stepped in so far that should I wade no more, Returning were as tedious as go o'er." Hardly a model for an analyst-investigator. Yet the combined impulse toward acceptance or defiance, making sure all the bloodshed had not been in vain, was a strong one. Even if that meant more blood would be shed? she wondered.

Still musing, she found herself across the bridge and at the riverbank. She walked up to a railing and leaned on it, taking in the river, finally at a spot where her thoughts too could flow downstream, less constrained.

The Illinois result, she now saw, had been central to everything from the very beginning. First, it got the FBI and Kurtz involved. Then the disputed result became the sham reason given by each of the Faithless Electors for switching their votes. And the result was still being disputed. She wondered if it had been an invention from the very beginning.

As a wedge issue, Imogen thought, it should have been a non-starter. Redmond, the Democratic candidate, had won a close but legitimate plurality of votes. Imogen had demonstrated that herself. The manufactured votes had padded the win, but there wasn't even a hint that the engineering had altered the outcome. The whole mess should have withered, become a historical footnote, an anecdote tucked away among many others in the already bloated file labeled "Bungling Corruption: Illinois."

Tom Kurtz, she remembered, had seemed angry when she had found ballot stuffing from both major parties, not just the Democrats. As she turned the results of her analysis over in her mind, the tampering had seemed small and not well coordinated on either side. She would need to confirm the timing of the late returns when she got back to her laptop.

She began walking again, chin still to her chest against the wind as she moved south along the river, turning the late returns over in her mind like the leaves in the wind. It struck her now that she had been quick to dispense with her findings in order to move on to Duncan's Elector data—so quick that she had missed the central question in the whole Illinois fiasco: why would anyone add votes when they were already winning? Why would the Democrats have risked it?

She quickened her pace, eager to get back to her laptop and notes. Her eagerness was shaded with concern because it now seemed probable that she had been set up, steered toward those precincts, as a magician forces a purportedly random card on an unsuspecting audience member.

* * *

The 115th Congress convened on January 6. News coverage began on every channel, every cable news outlet and online early in the day, teasing out and examining each detail of law, procedure, history and lore. For the second time in less than a month, Imogen was a spectator, hiding out, watching on the same television in the very bedroom where she and Duncan had watched the Faithless Elector plot play itself out on December 19.

Her mouth twisted bitterly as she watched the pages bring in the wooden boxes containing the Electoral votes. In years past, the pages had often been photographed walking in a line bearing their boxes, smiling their awkward, self-conscious young-person smiles, looking generally pleased with the attention. In contrast, many now bore a look of apprehension. Rather than making a grand, ceremonial entrance to solemnize a foregone conclusion, many of the young pages looked troubled, pensive as they picked their way along the no-man's-land aisle between two warring camps.

The unofficial count, after the three Faithless Electors had switched their votes, was 270 for the Republican James Christopher, and 268 for the Democrat Diane Redmond, who had a modest half-million-vote lead in the popular vote. The outgoing vice president, acting in his final capacity as Senate president, read the votes aloud. When Colorado's votes were read, one Senator and one Representative each objected, and provided their objection in writing, as was required by statute.

Since 1873 there had been a statute requiring that "no votes or papers from any other state shall be acted upon until the objections previously made to the votes or papers from any state shall have been finally disposed of." As it was well known that Minnesota's and New Hampshire's votes would also be contested, the joint session agreed, without objection, to consider all of the Faithless Elector votes presented. Each House then went into separate session to consider the three votes.

Less than an hour later the two Houses reconvened, each having unanimously agreed not to accept the three tainted Faithless Elector votes. The secretary of the Senate reported and recorded the action.

The President of the Senate announced "no candidate having the necessary clear majority of Electoral votes, the House will use the constitutional procedure whereby each state has one vote, as provided for in Article Two." Additionally, the Senate would vote separately for vice-president, each senator having a vote. In the House, a majority of 26 votes for president would carry the day for one candidate or the other. In the Senate, the vice-president would need a majority of 51 votes. As this procedure would require state caucuses, the Speaker called for a motion to adjourn until the next day.

* * *

At Fort Belvoir Hospital, the television coverage was like wallpaper to everyone except Duncan Calder and Doug Pollack.

"So, what do you think, professor?" asked Pollack.

"Tomorrow they come back and all the states vote for the actual Electoral College vote-winner—fifty to zero?"

Calder stared at the screen, wondering how many ballots there would be over the coming days before there was a winner. "Heart-warming," he said. "But improbable."

He pulled out a sheet of paper and began writing down which states had voted for which party in the election. He turned the paper to show Pollack: "If they go strictly by the popular vote in each state, the Democrats might have just enough votes for their candidate to win. The vote was very close, though, in Florida, Ohio, Virginia, North Carolina and a few others, which in a caucus could conceivably go to the Republicans.

"A lot of the states that went for Redmond, nevertheless returned Republican majorities to the House, and it's those House members, voting in caucus, who will determine the vote for their state—the one vote for each state. It's sort of ironic that the Senate gets two votes when the House only gets one: I spend multiple lectures on American government talking about how anti-democratic and disproportionate the Senate is." He smiled. "But—again—they're pretty much evenly divided Republican versus Democrat, so that vote could go either way, too."

"It's two weeks from today to the Inauguration deadline. I don't even know what happens if we don't have a president by then," said Pollack.

"The President of the Senate will serve as acting president," Calder replied. "Unless the Senate has been able to make a choice for vice-president, at which point the VP choice becomes acting president until the House can wrestle something across the line."

"This is nuts!" said Pollack.

Imogen, watching the proceedings and doing the same vote calculations as Calder, also felt the insanity of it all. If the goal of the conspiracy had been to undermine Americans' faith in their electoral system, everything was going to plan. She looked down at her laptop. That destabilization had started with Illinois.

She switched off the television and called up her work on the vote-tampering report where she began looking again at the timing of the release of results. Two late-reporting precincts, one in Chicago's 16th Ward and the other in the 49th, looked suspect. They were late returns, but if those precincts were adding bogus votes, they were adding them to what was already a comfortable win for the Democrats in the state, and in the Electoral College.

* * *

Amanda Vega switched off the high politics on her phone— not her concern, she thought, but what a way to run a railroad—and went back to combing through Kurtz's assignments. Kurtz had been seconded to Colls' operations numerous times before he retired. The two obviously worked very closely together. But that closeness continued after Colls' retirement in September. She could see from the phone trace data Trey and Imogen had provided that twice in the time since he had retired Kurtz had been in touch with Colls before leaving on what was ostensibly FBI business before going to Illinois.

No wonder the FBI was chasing its tail, thought Vega. On both trips to Illinois Kurtz noted a lack of evidence on the fd-302 interview forms he filed after talking with a number of local officials. His summary covering the file referred back directly to the non-finding detailed in the 302's. At the bottom of the summary was a note to "HQ" stating Kurtz was "placing the matter in RUC," meaning "referred under completion," FBI-speak for "we're done with this unless you tell us differently." For a moment, she was shocked to see Pollack's initials at the bottom. But why wouldn't he have signed off? One of his best, most trusted agents had filed a thorough report saying there was nothing to investigate.

It was clear now that Colls had talked with Kurtz, and Kurtz had gone to Illinois with the intention of not gathering evidence and then written his report not finding anything, on Colls' order. And they had sewed it up tight. Any agent picking up the investigation and searching the relevant files would have concluded Illinois was a dead end. His trip to Boston in July had been before Colls retired, and it had not been on a case, but to give a counter-terrorism briefing to the field office there. Vega recognized a number of the names of those who attended, but one jumped out at her: a friend from academy days, Tracy Wilder.

Following up on Boston, even though Kurtz had been to Illinois twice, seemed like the better bet, and she could stay under the radar with Tracy. With Jezek and Davies in Chicago, it might seem strange to have her following leads there. Vega paused for a moment before calling her friend, deciding to call Wilder's personal phone rather than her Bureau office phone.

Wilder picked up on the second ring. "Amanda?" she said.

"Yes, how are you, Trace?" Vega asked warmly.

"Better than you, I expect," she said playfully. "I used to think of being here in Boston as kind of a backwater, that I really wanted to be in Washington. Now, though . . . not so much. Everything okay?"

"No, frankly. Every time we get a lead that looks good, it turns into a dead-end." Vega paused. "Where are you right now?"

"About to leave the building. I'm guessing that with all the shit going on down there that you calling my personal line means you want to speak without prying ears, so I'm heading over to the Common Grounds cafe."

"Thank you," said Amanda.

"Pretty rough?"

"Yeah," said Amanda. "The worst of it is that we can't know who to trust even within the Bureau. It's not normal

168

bullshit like someone taking credit for work they didn't do. I mean, I think we have fucking spies."

"Jesus. So it's true."

"What is?" asked Amanda

"About Kurtz, about Colls?"

"What have you heard about Colls?"

"That he was mixed up in the Faithless Elector plot and killed himself rather than be taken," said Tracy. "Is it true?"

Amanda paused before answering. It wasn't necessary, even to a friend, to divulge everything she knew. "Yes," she said.

"Unofficially, yes."

"My God," said Tracy. "It must be awful."

"It is, but we will clean this shit up, and in the end the Bureau will be the better for it. I firmly believe that."

"Excellent," said Tracy. "How can I help?"

"Well, it's about Kurtz, actually. He was up there back in July, right?"

"Yeah, Kurtz was here delivering one of his anti-immigration, er, I mean, counter-terrorism briefings." Tracy giggled.

Vega smiled. "You attended the briefing, didn't you?"

"Yeah. I remember it. It sticks out in my mind as one of the most pointless briefings I've ever had. And that's saying a lot."

"Pointless how?" asked Vega.

"There was nothing new, nothing we hadn't already heard from our own specialists. It just seemed perfunctory, pointless."

"Was there anything out of the ordinary? And I mean anything. I'm grasping at straws. Colls detailed Kurtz to give the briefing, and I need to follow up everything those two did together."

"I'm thinking," said Wilder. "There was nothing that stands out from the presentation. "

"Was there anyone attending that seemed odd? I'm looking at the list of everyone who was there, but I don't know all the names."

"No," said Wilder. "It was everyone you'd expect. I remember we were all grateful it was short—"

There was silence at the other end.

Amanda waited. "Tracy?" she said finally.

"Kurtz had a meeting right after ours," she said. "As we were leaving, I was trying to get by the knot of brown-nosers at the front of the room trying to get some face time with Kurtz. I overheard him say he had to rush off: he had another meeting before heading back to DC. With Alec Nash of all people."

"Who's Alec Nash?" Amanda asked.

"Well, that's why it's kind of weird. Now, he's nobody. He's back working at some PR firm here in town. But he used to be former governor Moore's press secretary. Or should I say our maybe-vice-president-elect Bob Moore?" She paused. "Is that at all helpful? I'm sorry, I can't think of anything else."

Vega was looking through the files on her desk. There was nothing about a second meeting. No Alec Nash. "Thanks, Trace," she said. "That might be something. I really appreciate it."

"Glad to help. Do you want me to make any inquiries?"

"No, Trace. Thanks. If you hear something that seems relevant, please let me know. But we need to keep this as quiet as possible."

"Got it," she said. "Be safe. Let's talk soon."

"I'd really like that," said Amanda. "Bye for now."

She hung up and immediately began an email to Weir, Kelly and Imogen: "Just found a possible connection in the Boston area. Boston field office confirms that Kurtz met with an Alec Nash on July 7. He's not listed on Kurtz's itinerary, so it wasn't official business. It could be nothing, but we should follow up. Alec Nash is the former press secretary for VP candidate Bob Moore, back when Moore was Gov of Massachusetts. Don—please authorize phone track data on Nash to see if there is any overlap with 'Wicked'."

Imogen, from Philadelphia, wrote back immediately, hitting "reply-all": "Fantastic, Amanda! Sounds like it could be a break. Is there anyone you trust in Chicago? I need someone to scrutinize the 16th and 49th ward districts there. Maybe even rattle their cages a bit."

Don Weir sat at his desk, staring at the emails. He replied immediately to Vega and Kelly: "approved," he wrote. "I'll get Sharon going on the warrants" and clicked "send."

He clicked "reply" to Imogen's email. Then paused. "Sharon?" he called.

She came to the door.

"I just sent you an email requesting warrants on the new targets."

"Yes, I saw," she said. "I'm right on it."

"First, though: what am I going to tell Imogen?" He gestured at his computer screen. Sharon walked to his desk and stood behind his chair, reading the email.

"Did this come through on Trey's shielded server?"

"I think so."

Sharon leaned past him and checked. "Yeah," she said. "It did. Ask Gen what she wants and we'll figure out how to get it to Davies and Jezek without giving too much away to Jezek. I'm not sure there's a need to put in an email that you're worried about one of you agents."

"Isn't it encrypted?"

"Yes, but later, if it's subpoenaed . . ."

Weir nodded.

Trey Kelly had not waited for Weir to respond, but had begun hunting for Alec Nash's phone number the moment he saw the email. He found the number quickly, and within an hour of Vega's message began the process of downloading the call and processing location data for the past 18 months.

Nash seemed to travel a lot, much of it on airplanes, so his phone was switched off more than the others he had tracked before. The sudden jumps across the virtual landscape, made it slow going.

When the official approval came in, more than four hours later, Kelly was sorting through the data dump and getting ready to run a bullshit test on it before synchronizing Nash's personal phone data trail to compare it with the one he had already from "Wicked."

Weir sat down again to respond to Imogen's request, cc'ing Vega (and Sharon): "Let me know what you want exactly, Imogen," he wrote. "I will get Jezek and Davies on it. They are landing in Chicago now. Ideally, figure out a way to detail them so they have to split up. I'll put Davies on the more sensitive info you need."

Imogen responded immediately: "OK. We really need to understand better what happened in the precincts around the 16th and 49th wards of Chicago. I'd like to get a picture of what went on in McHenry and Kendall Counties a bit to the west of the city, too. Those are the Republican districts and might also tell us something, since they're two of the districts that were padding results.

"The key question that Davies has to get an answer for is: why did those two Democratic districts manufacture results when they were already winning statewide? These districts reported late, so by the time they were adding bogus votes they must have known where their party stood. And the Republican side reported late, too: why did they risk being caught chasing a lost cause?

"To cut short the denials our agents are likely to get, I've attached the data specific to all four regions. It's circumstantial but compelling. It shows them we know they did it. You can distribute it to Jezek and Davies. They need to get with whoever is the ranking election official and hold their feet to the fire. Tell them: we know you did it; here's proof; now tell us why."

Back at Bus Rentals, Kelly leapt up from his seat. He pointed accusingly at the computer monitor. "Got you!" he shouted. He grabbed his phone and texted Weir, Vega and Imogen. "Nash=Wicked!" he typed.

Amanda Vega had pulled an old bulletin board out of storage. She needed clarity, and in the hope of gaining some had begun

172

a conspiracy board in her office, showing the name and where possible the pictures of the actors in the known cells. Just as she was beginning to stick each one up, she saw Kelly's text confirming Nash as Wicked. She smiled, then printed out a picture of Alec Nash from his PR firm's website and wrote "Nash/Fisher" on an index card. She had two discreet known spheres:

> Alec Nash/Fisher at the top, directing
> Frank Reed/Cooper, who directed
> Deptford/Plumber, who was responsible for
> Kimball/Miller and Carpenter/Tillman

To the right of that she put up the other cell:

> Andrew Colls, directing
> Tom Kurtz, who oversaw
> Trebor and Covington

She pinned four conspirator codenames for others named by Deptford, but as yet unknown, in the top left corner:

> "Postman," "Pilot," "Baker" and "Weaver."

She then printed out the timescale she had been working from, detailing where each had gone, dates and which crimes they had committed.

Vega stood back from the chart and stared, her arms crossed. Deptford and Colls were in similar positions within the hierarchy, though they weren't known to each other until the day Deptford showed up and killed Colls. Both took their orders from Nash.

She stared closely at Nash's photo: he was handsome, with dark blue eyes and thick lashes; late forties, short salt-and-pepper hair styled to appear sporty and spontaneous; his stubble beard, darker than his hair, was well sculpted and flecked with grey. Reed, roughly the same age, looked scruffy and unkempt in comparison, though it was an honest, outdoorsy look; and Deptford looked like who he was: ex-military, precise, well-tended, steely-eyed. "You look like a PR guy," Vega said to Nash's picture. "Where are you getting your orders?

Just then, Weir stopped into her office. "Who are you talking to?" he asked.

She turned around, embarrassed. "I was looking at the board here. I was telling Nash we're going to bring him down."

Weir nodded. "Good," he said. "I hope he believes you and he's shitting himself."

"What's bugging me now," she said "is that he looks like a PR guy; he is a PR guy. How is this man-scaped fashion plate the one giving orders for all these murders? And if he is, why's he doing it?"

"Yeah, what's the plan?" said Weir. "We're pretty sure they're still trying to get Christopher elected, but we don't know who's really calling the shots."

Vega nodded. "And how do we prove collusion?" She sighed. "It's clear we're not seeing everything. But now that Trey's proved that Wicked is Nash, I'm going to do some more digging. First, I'm going study his timeline and match up his movements, see what we can glean there: find out who he's been meeting with. Maybe something'll come of that. Shit, I sound like Imogen," Vega added, shaking her head.

Weir smiled. "There are worse wonks to emulate, I suppose."

*　*　*

FBI Agent Phil Jezek pulled into the McHenry County Administration building parking lot and found a spot as near to the door as he could. It was an enormous lot, and parking close still meant walking 50 or more yards to the front door. He sat with the car running and the heater blasting, zipping up his coat and pulling on his gloves. The gauge on the dashboard indicated the outside temperature was 5 degrees Fahrenheit.

Jezek turned off the car, flung the door open and began walking purposefully toward the front entrance. He could feel the material in his trouser legs growing stiff, the cold biting at his ears and nose. He wished he had boots on.

Inside, in the brightly lit, overheated modern atrium lobby the young woman who met him at the front desk acknowledged his FBI identification and conducted him back past the front desk to the office of Meghan Percy, the County Clerk.

"Yes?" she said, looking up from her work.

"I'm Special Agent Jezek from the FBI, Office of Voter Integrity," he said. Jezek presented his ID again.

Percy glanced at it, and then fixed a flat gaze on him.

"Yes?" she said.

"I have some questions," said Jezek sitting down.

"Don't you guys talk to each other?" asked Percy her tone angry, but edged with weariness.

"I'm not sure what you mean," said Jezek.

"No. I guess you wouldn't, probably because you don't talk to each other." She shook her head in disbelief.

"Someone else from the FBI has been here?" asked Jezek.

"Well, that prick Kurtz, for one," the County Clerk began.

"Why don't you talk to him? He's taken care of it I guess."

"I'm afraid Agent Kurtz is dead. Taken care of what?"

"Well, I didn't do it," she said, "not that I'm sorry to hear that little prick's gone."

"Agent Kurtz was a friend of mine—" Jezek began.

"—Well, I'm sorry you had to hear it from me. But it's true."

"Ms. Percy," Jezek began. "I have strong evidence that you engaged in—or at least abetted—voter fraud. If I don't start getting some cooperation, I will throw a cordon around this whole fucking building, bring in a swarm of agents, arrest you and begin investigating everything you've ever done. I will—"

"—Yeah, yeah, Kurtz said all that, too. But here I am."

Jezek studied Meghan Percy, perplexed. He had been an agent for 17 years, and this was new. People had one of two reactions to finding out they were being questioned by the FBI: solid citizens, and even some criminals, tended to fall apart quickly, whereas career criminals tended to remain calm, self-possessed. For this latter group being investigated or even arrested was just a part of doing business, and they treated interrogations as regrettably unavoidable annoyances. Percy, though she was clearly rattled, as a "citizen" would be, acted with a bravado that seemed out of place, more like someone at the end of her rope, like the resignation of someone backed into a corner.

"I get it," she blurted out. "We fucked up. Okay? I know!"

Jezek, still perplexed, looked down at the printout of the evidence he was going to present to demonstrate that the FBI knew what had happened.

"You've got a printout there," she said, pointing at the papers he was holding. "You're going to tell me you know which precincts fudged the numbers, which election judges will be on the chopping block with me."

"Okay. And?"

"And then . . . and then"—she was crying now—"then you're going to threaten my kids, my husband—"

"—Ma'am, I'm with the FBI," said Jezek incredulously.

"If I don't tell you who was behind it all, who gave the order," she gasped between sobs.

"Who did give the order?" Jezek asked quietly.

"I did!"

"Okay . . . "

"So I fucked up, okay? I'm not from Chicago," she spat.

"Ms. Percy, I am unaware of any exchange or agreement you had with Tom Kurtz—"

"—Yeah. We've established that," she said regaining her composure.

"The only threat currently hanging over you is that of legal reprisal for having broken the laws of your state, misuse of office and violating the public trust. You may indeed go to jail, as may others; but I am a sworn officer of the United

States Justice Department, and the United States government does not threaten its citizens!"

Percy eyed him carefully. She was older than he, tall and thin, with short, auburn hair. Her mouth and eyes were stern. She was hard—not a stout, robust resilience but a strained brittleness.

"Ms. Percy, I need to understand fully what's going on. Start with election night and work up to Kurtz. Before I leave, I will need the original vote records, results of your audits. I will need to see affidavits, certificates and a lot more. It's all listed here." He held up a single sheet of paper. "And I have the authorization here." He raised a separate sheet.

"Okay," she began, making no move to comply or get her staff moving. "This is a Republican-majority county. But you have to understand, Illinois hasn't returned a Republican majority statewide since 1988. We do our bit here in McHenry county . . . Kendall County, too, but most years, the Democrats run 54% or better statewide. In 2008 they won 62% of the vote. This year we all thought it might be close. You know?"

Jezek nodded.

"But as the results started coming in, as we started looking at it and making projections, it looked like it was going to be a loss again, with the Democrats taking their usual 53 to 54% of the vote. Then, while we were still compiling late returns and a few Republican districts were lagging, the Democrats showed a big push."

"In Chicago."

"Right. A big push. All of us here looking at those returns knew they were padding. And we thought—why do that now? We looked at what was counted, at what was projected. It didn't make any sense . . . " She let that sink in. "Unless—we thought—unless the Democrats had intel on some late-reporting Republican leaning districts performing better than we ourselves had anticipated. Which would mean that if we added some here, we might just tip the balance." She paused. "But, as we now know, there were no phantom fucking districts that performed better than expected. Everything

177

performed exactly as expected . . . so I have no idea what the Democrats were doing," she sighed.

Jezek was squinting in the snow dazzled light glaring through the windows. "You told Kurtz all this?" he asked.

"He *knew* it all," she rejoined flatly, staring straight ahead. "What he wanted to know was who told us to do it . . . who we'd told."

"He didn't arrest you? Detain you?"

"No."

"You weren't a material witness?"

"No."

"What files did he want?"

"None."

"And you say he threatened you? Your family?" asked Jezek, the incredulity creeping back into his voice.

"Not him," she said, "but the message was obviously from him."

"What message?"

"Two men met me in the parking lot by my car one night after work. They handed me pictures of my house, my husband, my little granddaughter getting dropped off at school. They told me to keep quiet about what had happened here."

"Why are you talking to me now? Aren't you afraid?"

"I'm sick of living in fear," she said. "I need help. Have you ever had your whole family threatened? The ones you love the most in the world? Have you ever had to turn off the news because the investigations all around are too close to home? But if—as you say—Kurtz is dead, maybe if I come clean . . . " She paused, looked down at her desk for a moment. When she raised her head, she fixed her eyes on Jezek: "So, if you're for real, I can help, but you have to help me too; if you're going to want me to testify to any of this, I'm going to need some immunity, some guarantees . . . some protection."

Sixty miles to the southeast, in Chicago, Gus Davies had arrived at the Ward 16 storefront office. One of the few occupied commercial spaces on that block, it was itself empty, but for a receptionist, sitting alone. "Yes?" said the young woman at the reception desk. Her hair was twisted intricately into braids that wrapped stylishly around her head. She stared intently at her computer screen.

"Good morning, I'm hoping to talk with George Johnson." He pulled out his FBI identity card. "He was—"

"—He's dead," she said matter-of-factly, not looking up.

"Dead?"

"Murdered back in November," she said to the screen. "Looks like it might have been a robbery. They jacked his car somewhere and left him to die in the weeds in some vacant lot. Sickening."

"Do the police have any leads?"

She shook her head. "Not that we've heard," she said, finally seeming to realize he wasn't going away and giving him her attention. "The car turned up a few days later, chopped and stripped." She twisted the end one of her braids between two fingers.

"Is there someone else I could talk with? Maybe one of the other election judges?"

"The alderman's assistant will be back this afternoon," she said. "You could make an appointment." Her suggestion sounded less like an offer, and more like a challenge.

Davies drew her attention again to his FBI identification. He placed his business card on the desk. "Miss, I'll be back around two. Make sure he makes time for me."

She shrugged. "I'll see if he's available," she said, her tone implying that she might or might not relay the message.

Davies leaned in close. "He'll be available," he said in a low, menacing voice. "I've offered to do this pleasantly, more or less informally, at two. But if you can't make that happen, I can come back here at three with twenty agents, search warrants—arrest warrants—and turn your shitty little world inside out."

She stared at him blankly.

He straightened up and smiled. "Your choice." He tapped his business card. "See you at two!" he added cheerily and walked out into the frigid Chicago wind.

At the northern border of the city, Davies stopped in at the 49th Ward headquarters in a strip mall storefront. The alderman's aide, a heavyset man with an improbably boyish face, came out to greet him. "How can we help the FBI?" he asked jovially, shaking Davies' hand. He conducted Davies to his office. "Please tell me you're not here about the election again," he said as they sat down.

"I have some questions," said Davies, almost regretting the pall he was about to put over the interview, ". . . about the election."

The aide's pleasant expression faded to resignation.

"I wonder," Davies began, "if I could speak with Paul Porter, and I'd like to get the ball rolling reviewing the returns. We should have the proper paperwork and the subpoena by tomorrow morning, but I'd like to speak with him first. He was the election judge . . ."

The aide leaned heavily on his desk, his head in his hands. "I think we'd all like to talk with Paul," he began. "But he died in a car accident last month."

"He's dead?"

"He drove off the Skokie Valley highway a bit north of here in a blizzard, poor bastard. A little too much Christmas cheer, or something." He shook his head sadly. "Great guy. He was a bow hunter, you know."

"Straight as an arrow, was he?" asked Davies.

* * *

Dyer, Weir and Vega stood around the desk in Weir's office, poring over the evidence and clues. On Weir's monitor, turned to the front of the desk, Imogen's face, Skyped in, floated above the papers.

"Walk me through what you know," Dyer said to Weir, "including what you think you know."

180

"Okay," said Weir, "this conspiracy has been operating for at least eighteen months. We have identified two distinct cells operating within the network. At the top is Alec Nash, a PR executive, who used to be Bob Moore's press officer when Moore was Governor of Massachusetts. Nash is the highest person we've found, but we don't think he's at the top. We have three unidentified code names in addition to the names we do know. Nash is directing Frank Reed, who we're still having difficulty locating. He's on leave from his job, and we can't locate his personal phone.

"Below Reed is Deptford, a retired Army marksman. We have him in custody. We also have the foot soldiers he directs in custody, Adam Kimball and Noah Carpenter. Deptford has been very cooperative, and his information has allowed us to unravel his cell. Kimball and Carpenter have been essentially useless—they don't know anything—but we have been able to use them to confirm Deptford's information. As far as we can tell, neither of the higher-ups—Reed or Nash—knows we're holding their people. You already know all about Colls, Kurtz, Trebor and Covington."

"Right. So these are the players we know," said Dyer.

"And," Weir continued, "with the phone tracking, we have been able to place specific individuals at locations where murders of Electors have occurred, including the surveillance on Agent Trager and the murder of Redmond's campaign manager, Jim Novaczeck."

"Don, how reliable are the warrants? What's the likelihood that any of this evidence gets thrown out when we go to court?"

"Practically zero. At each step, we've obtained proper warrants."

"What about these co-conspirators you have on ice?"

"They're being held as material witnesses, and none has asked for counsel. They know that having been apprehended, their bosses will kill them if they get the chance."

Dyer nodded. "Good. Good," he said. "What else?"

"We recently learned that Kurtz met with Nash in Boston in June," said Weir, "probably on Colls' orders. We can see

181

pretty well what these two networks were up to based on their movements and connections, and we're confident that our reading of their command and control is accurate.

"But it's also clear that we don't have the whole picture. And the fact that Nash's trace has no connection or apparent involvement in the killing of Electors in Iowa, Colorado or Oregon leads us to believe there are more—or at least one other—network cell out there we haven't found. Worse, it was still operating as of late December. It's pretty clear the Faithless Elector conspirators had two election judges in Chicago murdered, too."

"Yes, talk to me about that. I don't fully understand," said Dyer.

"Imogen?" Weir said to the screen.

"It's conjecture," Imogen began, "but it fits what we know. For the moment, our operating assumption is that this conspiracy exists to put James Christopher in the White House."

"That much seems clear," agreed Dyer.

"But for all its effective ruthlessness, I'd argue that this is really just an intelligent, calculated gamble on their part—"

"A gamble?" asked Dyer.

"Yes, with contingencies built into each step, imposed on a dark network, terrorist cell architecture," she said. "I don't think we could even call what they're doing a 'plan' in the strictest sense. They have a goal—Christopher in the White House—and they seem to be proceeding along an informal decision tree model. The other thing is that even though they ultimately want Christopher in the White House, I don't think this is operating from the Republican party. I'll get to that part in a minute.

"We figure their Option 1 was to win the election by tipping the scales with some fake news and conspiracy theories put out just before the vote; and as we know, they came damn close to swinging it, apparently with help from social media abroad—but all that's now under media and political scrutiny, of course.

"Option 2, having failed to win that way, they went to work undermining faith in the election process, and getting three electors to switch their votes—enough to win in the Electoral College, even though they lost the popular vote by half a million votes or so. That almost worked, too, if it hadn't been for Matthew Yamashita, the grad student killed in Seattle."

"So . . ."

"And that's where Illinois comes in. Going back to election night, when it became clear Christopher wouldn't win, which was Option 1—and remember, Illinois' final count came in later even than California's—the conspirators got two Democratic election judges in Chicago to pad the Democrats' win in the state; and they did it in a way that would be easy to spot, so potentially bringing the whole election into dispute.

"So now, having lost, the conspirators could gin up a public outcry about a rigged election and point to malfeasance in the Illinois result. And the Illinois result could serve as sham cover for the three Faithless Electors' supposed vote of conscience—as their reason for switching their votes to Christopher. You'll recall that each one made a fuss about Illinois as their reason for switching their vote. Which, again, almost worked."

"Right, right," said Dyer.

"But we don't think it was the Republican party behind all this because there was no coordination. The ballot-stuffing I uncovered during my analysis in Kendall and McHenry Counties was done by precinct-level Republicans. If they had known about the plot—if it had been a party led effort—they wouldn't have done what they did. In fact, according to Jezek's report, Kurtz and his goons interrogated and threatened these county people to find out who had given them the order to falsify the results."

"They'll need protection," Weir said to Dyer, "and some kind of deal in exchange for testimony."

"What have they been promised?" Dyer asked.

"Nothing firm," said Weir.

"Fine," said Dyer. "I'll take those files with me and make a determination." He paused, then looked toward Imogen on the screen. "Agent Trager, if, as you say, it's not the Republicans, who's doing this?"

"I don't know, sir," she admitted.

Dyer sighed. "But you don't believe they're through yet—whoever they are—do you?" he said.

"No, sir" said Imogen. "They're not done yet. We just don't know what Option 3 is."

10

Next day, Thursday, January 12, with the House still deadlocked on the vote for the president, the Senate held a vote for the vice-president. With the President pro tempore presiding, the Senate voted 51-49 in favor of Bob Moore, the Republican vice-presidential candidate.

Imogen, still in Philadelphia, watched on television as Hugh Salter gave his report, her mouth twisting into an unbecoming sneer as he came on the screen.

"Today, the Senate voted 51 to 49, approving Bob Moore as the next Vice-president of the United States. If the House remains deadlocked past January twentieth, a little over a week from now, then Moore will become the acting president until such time as the House votes for either Diane Redmond or James Christopher.

"Why is the process taking so long? And how can the Senate reach an agreement when the House seems perilously close to not awarding the presidency in time for the Inauguration on January twentieth? What's proving difficult is the coalition-building. Earlier, I spoke with Professor Walter Bellamy, Professor of Political Science at Rutgers University to understand why."

The news report cut to a taped segment, with Professor Bellamy in the studio. "Like a great many things," he began, "what looks simple on the outside is actually rather complex. If you go through the representatives of each major party in each state—and it is they who will be voting—and sort them into Democratic or Republican columns, it turns out that twenty-nine states have Republican majorities.

"So, since the vote state-by-state in the House needs only twenty-six such states to award the presidency, it would seem obvious that the Republican candidate would prevail. And indeed the Republican candidate, James Christopher, may prevail, just as his running-mate did earlier today in the Senate.

"But the House is different: if you look at the electoral map, seven of the states with Republican majorities in Congress were won by Redmond in the Electoral College, which means that a great many of the Republican representatives in those states were elected in districts that voted for Redmond. And in other cases it may be that their win in the election was very narrow . . . or both.

"Party matters," Bellamy continued, "but so does re-election. Which means Republican representatives in those seven states are having a long, hard think about what to do, and how they will justify their decisions to their constituents and to their party. At the moment, there are twenty-one states firmly voting for Redmond and twenty-two states solidly for Christopher, with seven up for grabs."

"What do you think is happening on the hill?" Salter asked.

"I wish I could tell you definitively. As someone who studies elections and American government, I would love to be in on some of the discussions taking place right now; what kind of pressure is being applied, what favors called in, what incentives dangled?"

Imogen turned off the television.

* * *

Phil Jezek, back from Chicago, was running late to his meeting with Casey Hague at the Bethesda bar he had frequented with Colls. As he hurried around the corner, he saw what he took to be Senator Eliot's limousine standing at the curb. It was growing dark, but the car was shining and glinting directly under a streetlamp. Jezek slowed his pace, grateful he wasn't late.

186

The limousine door opened on the street side. Jezek raised his hand to wave, but quickly dropped it to his side, as he didn't recognize the man getting out into traffic, a man in his late forties or early fifties wearing a dark green, well-used military style jacket. It didn't bear any insignia, Jezek noticed, but it looked official. The man's grey hair was medium length, and scruffy in a way that suggested his usual style favored a crisper, tighter cut, but he had not attended to it in some time. The man looked at and through Jezek, his gaze like that of a man accustomed to long distances. He pulled on a camouflage baseball hat, tucked what looked like a file under his arm and darted between the cars to the other side of the street.

Jezek lost track of him as Casey Hague stood out of the car on the curb side. He waved at Jezek, smiling brightly.

"And I thought I was going to be late!" Hague called jovially, walking briskly toward Jezek, his hand outstretched. "When did you get back from Chicago?" he asked as they drew together and shook hands.

"Late last night," said Jezek. "Did I tell you I was going there?"

A puzzled look passed across Hague's face. "You must have," he said, flashing a smile again. "Let's get a drink!"

When they were seated together at a table at the back of the bar, Jezek leaned in toward Hague. "I think the senator will be pleased," he said. "The Faithless Elector Task Group is definitely making headway."

"Excellent," said Hague sipping at his drink.

"But, unfortunately, it looks like Kurtz was somehow in on the whole Illinois thing."

"Illinois thing?"

"The election results that have been called into question."

"Right."

"Davies was interviewing two Democratic precinct judges in Chicago, and I spoke with two Republican officials in McHenry and Kendall County, just outside the city. The ones I spoke with were scared. Kurtz had been in to see them and apparently threatened them to keep quiet, gave them tactics to delay and obscure what they had done."

"And what did they do?"

"They added bogus votes to inflate the result in their counties."

"And what did the Democratic ones say?" Hague asked casually. "He spoke with the election judges . . . this Agent Davies?"

"He spoke with aldermen for those precincts. I'm not sure where it all stands. I'll know after tomorrow, when I meet with Weir. It may be that Davies and I go back, or we detail someone from the Chicago field office to follow up."

"So this is good," Hague ruminated. "Maybe we can put this Illinois thing to bed soon."

"And," said Jezek, "we may also be able to find out how deep this conspiracy goes in the Bureau. I know that's something Senator Eliot really wants to know. I'm going to find out who detailed Kurtz to Illinois back in November. Vega has those files. I'll see her tomorrow morning, first thing."

"You're doing great work," said Hague. "You've really taken the bull by the horns."

"Thank you. I will say I'm worried about what I might find."

"How?"

Jezek looked around him, but there was no one else at the tables to either side of them. "Well, obviously, we'll follow the truth wherever it leads, but . . . what if I find that Colls sent Kurtz? It could mean he was in deeper than any of us knew. And it could mean that you'll need to double-check the intel he passed along. It might also go a long way toward explaining why the Bureau seems so opaque to the Oversight Committee. You've been getting mixed and/or incomplete messages."

"I see what you mean," said Hague. "Have you talked with anyone else about this?"

"No, of course not."

"Excellent. Please don't say anything yet. Let's take this one step at a time. Confirm what you need to, and report back to me. And only me. Can you do that?"

"Yes," said Jezek.

"Thank you, Phil. Listen, I'm sorry to cut this short, but I have to get back."

"Yes!" said Jezek. "Of course. I guess congratulations are in order. Please give the senator my regards: I hear he was key in pushing the vote through in the Senate."

"I will. Thank you."

"This has been a terrible, messy business," said Jezek, "but things are getting sorted out. The system is working. Step one is now in place."

"Yes," said Hague, buttoning his jacket. 'Yes, it is."

Don Weir and Deputy Director Bill Dyer sat grouped at one end of a long meeting table in the Attorney General's office, the Attorney General at the head of the table.

"I understand your reluctance to go forward with arrests and go public about the conspiracy," she said, "until you're sure you have all the players in your sights. Under normal circumstances I would follow your recommendation, but these are not normal times."

"Agreed—" Dyer began.

The Attorney General held up her hand. "It's seven days until the Inauguration," she began. "You have presented me with clear evidence of a plot to steal the presidency on behalf of one of the candidates. My time is up in seven days. Who is to say that whomever Christopher appoints as the new Attorney General will make this a priority? The clues point to him. Even if we don't have a president by January twentieth, Bob Moore, his running mate, has already been made VP, and he would become the acting president. There's no telling what mischief he could cause, or what priorities he would seek to pursue, what lines of inquiry he might allow to atrophy.

"I'm not saying either one is in on the conspiracy, but they certainly have no tactical reason to advance an investigation that would likely lead to arrests of some of their supporters or their own possible impeachment."

"Yes, Madam Attorney General," said Dyer. "But this suspect Reed is still at large. You see that we don't have a complete view of the conspiracy. They seem to be geographically organized, and we only have the two East Coast cells in the network. If we show our hand too early, he's likely to disappear or be killed to keep him quiet. None of which helps us."

"And the three you're currently holding?"

"They've told us everything they know, which frankly isn't much. It's a well-planned, highly disciplined group. They can't tell us anything because they don't know anything. By design. This Reed is the key. We need time."

"We don't have time, Bill."

"How about this," said Dyer, "we bring in the county clerks from Kendall and McHenry counties, offering them reduced sentences in exchange for testimony; depose them, gather evidence. We have sufficient evidence on Colls, Kurtz, Deptford and his flunkies. We're watching Alec Nash.

"The moment we have Reed, we arrest Nash. We confront them with everything we know, the murders, the outlines of the conspiracy. We see which one wants a deal first. Give us three more days, ma'am. Please."

The Attorney General stared past them toward the windows looking out on the city. After a moment, she pulled her gaze back and looked down at the papers in front of her. "Let's not be coy," she said. "Because Nash is involved, it's likely the Vice-president will shut down this investigation once he's sworn in." She took a deep breath. "Two days," she said finally. "Go forward as you have just outlined to me, and be ready to charge and make arrests in two days with whatever you have—first thing Monday morning."

* * *

Amanda Vega was in her office, the door closed speaking to Imogen on Skype. "I'll say something to Weir, Gen, but I think it's best you stay there."

"Maybe he could send me to Chicago," said Imogen, "I could work directly on deposing the election officials there."

"Not likely, they—" there was a knock at the door. "Gotta go. Stay safe," she said, and closed Skype.

"Yes?" she said as the door opened and Agent Jezek walked through.

"Hey, Phil, welcome back. What can I do for you?"

"I'm looking for a file. The catalogue says you have it. I need to follow up on some things about Kurtz and the Illinois investigation."

"Yeah, sure," said Vega. She started hunting through the stacks of files. "Which time?" she asked, still not finding the file she wanted.

"Either . . . both, I guess, but I really want to see the notes for his November visit."

As Vega turned from her desk to a stack of files on the floor, Jezek's eye was drawn to the conspiracy board on the wall. Amanda found the files she was looking for, and glanced up just in time to see the color drain from Jezek's face.

"What's this?" he asked.

Vega noticed him looking at the conspiracy board. "Oh," she said. "Yes. That." She eyed him warily. "What do you see?" she asked.

" . . . nothing."

"You recognize someone, don't you?" she demanded.

"What does this represent?"

"Fuck, Jezek! Tell me who you know? Where did you see him?"

"What is this?" he asked again.

Vega shook her head slowly as she stood up, her dark eyes burning at him. "You first."

"I saw this man," he said, tapping Reed's photo.

"Where? When?"

Jezek drew a deep breath. "I can't," he said.

"Phil, you need to talk to me." Her voice became gentler, but any warmth she hoped to project was belied by her fierce demeanor. Jezek looked away.

"Phil, we are farther along in unraveling the Faithless Elector conspiracy than perhaps you know. Everyone you see on that board is up to his eyes in conspiracy and murder."

Jezek visibly winced. Vega picked up her office phone and dialed Weir. "Don," she said, "it's Amanda, can you come over to my office right way? It's urgent. Thank you." Jezek sat down in a chair next to Vega's desk and put his head into his hands. As she was carefully replacing the receiver in its cradle, she could hear Weir's footsteps in the hallway. He knocked as he entered. Just inside the threshold, he stopped, taking in the scene. He looked back and forth for a moment between Vega and Jezek.

"Jezek just ID-ed Reed," Vega said.

"Where?" he asked. "When?"

"Phil's having a little difficulty coming clean."

Weir's expression hardened. He reached behind him and closed the door. "The men you see there," he said indicating the conspiracy board, "have each committed murder, or ordered the murder of more than a dozen people in order to carry out and cover up a plot to steal the presidency. Whatever they're trying to do, they haven't finished yet. Unless you come absolutely clean, I will add your name as co-conspirator to the arrest warrants we are preparing."

"Who sent Kurtz to Illinois back in November?" Jezek asked, his forehead resting in his hands.

"Pollack," said Vega. "Colls was retired by then. But we know from our wiretaps that Kurtz went on Colls' orders."

"And," said Weir, "Colls sent Kurtz to Boston in June to meet with that man." He tapped Alec Nash's photo.

Jezek sat up a bit in his chair, though he still looked at the ground rather than meet the eye of Vega or Weir. "I'm sorry," he said.

Something about the way he said he was sorry bothered Vega, and she unsnapped the safety clip on her gun holster, preparing for the worst.

"I thought I was helping," Jezek continued.

"I need to hear everything, Phil," said Weir. "What's going on?"

"Since the end of last month, I'd been meeting Agent Colls for drinks after work. It was just informal shop talk, a little gossip. I hoped he might still be able to help me . . . give advice, put things in perspective . . . you know."

"Okay," said Weir.

"Then, a week or so after he killed himself—"

"—He was murdered, Phil, by this man." Weir pointed at Deptford's picture. "Made to look like a suicide. On this man's order." He tapped Nash's photo again.

Jezek shook his head in disgust. "So maybe a week after his death, I ran into Senator Drew Eliot's aide, Casey Hague, in that Japanese noodle place a few blocks from here, and we ended up getting into a car with the Senator."

"The Senator was present?" Vega asked.

"Yes. They told me that Agent Colls had been helping them with their inquiries. They told me that they were worried about the lack of progress in the Faithless Elector Task Group, in the opacity of the Bureau in general. They told me that Colls had been passing on information from our discussions. They asked,"—he took a deep breath—"they asked if I would continue those conversations with his aide, Casey Hague. Informally. Officially unofficial."

"Christ!" Vega hissed.

"And you agreed," said Weir evenly. He flashed an intimidating look towards Vega, telling her to keep her emotions in check. She looked away, her thumb and forefinger absently pulling at the free holster safety clip.

"Yes," said Jezek quietly.

"Is Senator Eliot how you got transferred into the Task Group?"

Jezek nodded. "I think so."

"How many times did you meet?"

"Just twice. The second time was last night."

"What did you talk about?" Weir asked.

"I told him about what we'd found in Illinois; that Kurtz had been there and had threatened the election officials."

Weir's eyes widened. "Amanda, get on the phone to the Chicago field office, tell them to double the guard on the election officials. Then phone Dyer, tell him we need to serve the subpoenas for records today. And we need everything by the book. No one cuts corners just because we're under pressure. I don't want anything getting kicked out because we didn't follow procedure. Tell them, dual control on everything; that we might have a rat and the officials' lives are in danger."

Vega walked quickly out the door to call from Weir's office.

"I'm not a rat," said Jezek quietly. "I never . . ."

"How does Reed figure in all this?" Weir asked impatiently.

"I saw him with Hague, the senator's aide. The car was parked outside the bar."

"What car?"

"Senator Eliot's limousine," said Jezek. "I saw Reed get out, and then I saw Hague get out."

"Had you ever seen them together before?"

"No," said Jezek.

"I'm so sorry," Jezek began, "I thought I was doing the right thing."

"You thought you were doing the right thing for yourself. You didn't look at the broader picture. You didn't think about your fellow officers."

"I won't see them again, I swear!"

"Phil," said Weir. "Phil, look at me. Yes, you will."

* * *

Casey Hague kept his other weekly appointment, this time with Alec Nash, meeting at a West End tearoom. Nash walked in to find Hague seated at a table behind a broad, square column in the center of the room.

"They'll know how to make a proper cuppa here, I should think," said Hague with a grin.

"Yes," said Nash dubiously. "Awfully public." He eyed the Saturday crowd warily as he pulled off his scarf and began unbuttoning his coat. In contrast with the barren, chilly cleanliness of the coffee shop in Fairfax, Virginia, the previous week, this tearoom was warm, crowded and colorful, with eclectic art covering the walls.

"Well, yes," Hague admitted. "But it's young people and hipsters, hardly a demographic that's likely to give us a second look, except maybe to wonder how the hell we wandered into their space. Most won't even look up from their laptops."

Nash looked around. He nodded. The customers were indeed engrossed in their work, headphones in, eyes, ears and minds plugged in. Those who did look up, did so only to stare distantly out a window at the glaring January sunlight.

"Excellent work on the Senate vote," said Nash when he returned from the counter some minutes later with a pot of Assam tea and a cup. "What's happening in the House?" he asked as he lifted the top off the teapot. He bent his head toward the pot and waved some of the steam toward his face. He lifted his nose and smelled deeply. He smiled and closed his eyes.

"We've got a bunch of nervous ninnies," Hague reported. "Pennsylvania will turn our way, I hear, though it hasn't happened yet. Which gets us to 23 states. Virginia and Ohio might come around, but they're still an open question. Michigan could go either way, as could Wisconsin. Colorado we can forget about, and I think Florida is hopeless."

"And what have you done so far?" he asked, taking a long sip of his tea. "Which of our people have you targeted?"

"That's part of the problem," Hague admitted. "We've twisted all the arms we can. The problem children are the ones who never took money from our friends, or who barely won their seats in districts that voted heavily for Redmond."

"I see," said Nash.

"I'm at my wit's end."

"I'm not," said Nash. "Maybe it's time for new measures. Can you get me a list of the members who are holding this whole thing up?"

Hague looked quickly over his shoulder. "I have a list here," he said. He withdrew a piece of paper from his inside jacket pocket. "Hang on," he said, uncapping a pen. "I'll cross off the Pennsylvania members, since—"

"—No, leave them. We're not counting them until they've hatched." He took the paper from Hague, folded it and placed it in his jacket pocket. He sat back and poured some more tea into his cup to warm it up. "I'll have to remember this place," he said looking around approvingly, "when we're all here permanently."

"There's one other thing," said Hague. "We've been meeting with the agent you pointed us toward in order to keep abreast of the investigation. They know all about what happened in Chicago and the suburban counties. They've taken the officials into protective custody and impounded all election materials. They know about the two dead officials. They're also about to find out that Kurtz was detailed to look into it and hush it up."

"Well, that's sub-optimal," Nash said blandly.

"What are we going to do?" Hague asked in a harsh whisper.

"There really isn't anything to do," Nash replied.

"This could really fuck us, couldn't it?"

Nash stroked his chin, scratched at his ear. "No," he said at length. "It was always going to be a potential problem once those idiots in McHenry and wherever county took matters into their own hands. But it's isolated. Kurtz can't testify, Colls can't testify. The narrative will be that they were dirty cops, tangled up in something crooked in a crooked town like Chicago. The officials in Chicago can't testify, and the county clerks don't know anything, can't implicate anyone but themselves and Kurtz . . . and Kurtz is beyond caring; certainly not a danger to us."

"Okay," said Hague.

"Will you be meeting with Jezek again?"

"Tonight."

"Good. Find out if they've somehow put together more than Chicago because then we would have to worry. Okay? That's your job. I'll work on our friends." Nash patted his

196

jacket, indicating where he had put the list of wavering congressmen.

"What will you do?" asked Hague.

"I'll do what needs doing to get the result we need—whatever that is. There are other ways to twist arms. Other ways—and places—to apply pressure. People have wives, and some of them are painfully possessive. People wouldn't want them to know things that people get up to from time to time with other people. But you just find out if the Feds know anything more," said Nash. "That's your part. I'll take care of my part. We don't want to be the ones on the outside looking in because we didn't have what it takes."

He leaned forward and put a hand on Hague's shoulder, his dark blue eyes burning. "Now's not the time to be squeamish," he said in a low tone. "We're in the home stretch, and we need to get to the finish line first. If we do, our people'll be in charge and it won't matter what anyone else knows or thinks they can prove. We'll be in the clear. And we've done some shit, haven't we?" He patted Hague's shoulder. "If we finish second though . . ." he let that thought trail off. "Stay focused," he concluded, sitting back in his chair. "This has been in the works for a long time. And there's always a contingency."

* * *

On the other side of town, at Bus Rentals by the Stadium Armory Metro stop, Trey Kelly was pounding his fists on the desk. "Goddammit!" he roared from his office.

The lone staffer there on a Saturday glanced up from her work. Hearing nothing more, she went back to work shaking her head. The boss had been far less gregarious since the New Year, keeping to himself more and more. He was not a micromanager, but he did check in regularly with each employee, sitting affably with one or another throughout the day, giving advice, testing something the employee was working on. During such exchanges he was generally warm, helpful. But lately, he merely reviewed their work, leaving them detailed notes. Sometimes a whole day would pass with no interaction from him. It was rumored that his girlfriend had left him, while others noticed that he seemed involved in something classified.

Trey stalked to the office door. He looked out at the pit. "Sorry," he said, smiling sheepishly. He turned around and closed the door. He flung himself into his chair and dialed Vega's number.

"It's Trey," he said when she picked up. "I got the note about making sure not to proceed with the tracking and tapping on Casey Hague until we had the warrant in hand. Unfortunately, I only got the okay about an hour ago, and we missed out on catching Hague together with Nash. They just had a meeting at a tea and coffee shop in the West End about half an hour ago."

"Jesus, this goes deep," said Vega.

"I'll follow up with you in a couple hours. I'm compiling the full eighteen-month tracking. I'll get it to you as soon as I can."

* * *

Dyer and Weir were back in the Attorney General's office. "Please, Madam Attorney General, we need one extra day," Dyer pleaded. "We've discovered that Senator Drew Eliot's aide, Casey Hague, has been in on the whole thing from the beginning. Our phone traces show that he has been having weekly face-to-face meetings with Alec Nash for the better part of a year. It is also clear that Hague knows Reed. I share your concerns about a new administration following through on all this, but the tighter the case, the less chance there is that it'll be dropped. And if it really comes to that, we should maybe think about mobilizing the press."

The Attorney General nodded, looking past them. She looked at the boxes piled to one side of her office, books on the floor; surveyed the blank walls. "One more day," she agreed. "Even if we were charging now, the press would say this case is politically motivated, a parting shot from a spiteful administration. I can't change that framing, but the stronger the case, the more it can withstand those attacks, which is why I'm giving you the extra time.

"But make no mistake," she continued, "every day we delay only makes it look worse, more like there's a grain of truth in that narrative. And with Senator Eliot involved—and he is involved, even if we don't have the evidence to charge him yet—it will be a political fight; and it will be ugly. I want nothing in the press yet—though God knows they're digging."

"Yes, ma'am," Dyer and Weir said in unison.

"And keep me completely in the loop. I need to know and understand everything. I don't want to be caught by surprise."

Weir and Dyer exchanged a look. Dyer nodded.

"There's something else you should know," Weir began. "Prior to Colls' death, he was meeting with Agent Philip Jezek, a series of 'friendly' talks. So-called. Colls was a mentor to Jezek, and he was eager to impress Colls. The information Colls gleaned from these friendly talks was passed to Hague and Eliot."

"What kinds of things did he pass on?" she asked.

"It was mostly who was working on what," said Dyer. "Leads we were following up. Fortunately, Don kept things pretty close, so the damage is limited. They do know, however, that we know about the election judges."

"And Hague's the only person he passed information to?" the Attorney General asked.

"Well, after Colls was killed, Jezek was approached by Hague and Eliot," said Weir.

The Attorney General's eyes widened.

"They picked Phil up in the Senator's limo at lunch time, drove him around, told him that Colls had been supplying them with information for the Senator's Oversight Committee. They told him that the information Colls had passed along was what he had learned from Jezek in their friendly chats and asked Jezek if he would continue to be their eyes and ears in the Bureau . . . on behalf of the Oversight Committee."

"And Jezek agreed?"

"Yes," said Weir.

The Attorney General's hands were clasped together tightly in front of her. "Is there any proof?" she asked.

"Jezek will testify."

The Attorney General looked disappointed. "No photos? Tape?"

"No, ma'am, I'm sorry. Interestingly, though, they needed Jezek on the Faithless Elector Task Group, so Eliot put pressure on Dyer here to hire more men."

Dyer picked up the story: "Eliot's aide suggested to me that someone working in the Public Corruption Unit would be ideal. Jezek was second most senior in that department. They must have known he would be the obvious choice. And I picked him." His mouth twisted bitterly. "To get Eliot off my back I picked Jezek."

The Attorney General nodded gravely, but there was no mistaking that she looked happy again. "By Tuesday," she said quietly. "Get them. Get them all."

* * *

It was getting close to lunchtime and Hugh Salter was making calls around the Hill, trying for updates or inside information, any sense about which way the vote was tending. He was getting little more than the usual stonewalling, even from sources with whom he had a good relationship.

At the fifth call he got through to a congressional aide. As he asked whether there were any new developments, or new strategy for coalition building, the aide cut him off: "I've never seen anything like this," she said. "There's real coercion going on suddenly."

"So, Jill, someone's playing hardball?" Salter had said, his voice betraying a note of cynicism.

"No," she said. "Hardball, we can play. Dirty tricks we can counter. This is intimidation. I'm talking threats," she said in a harsh whisper.

Her tone made Salter who had been doodling on his pad sit up straight in his chair: "Like what?" he asked.

"Nice try, Hugh."

"So they're threatening to leak info. How else have they threatened the congressman?"

"I've said too much already," she said and rang off.

Salter made a note to circle back to Jill before the end of the day and continued working through his list of calls.

"Hi Dan, it's Hugh Salter," he said to the next staffer who took his call. "I'm looking for updates, wondering if there are any new strategies, how close to a final vote you are."

"It's still deadlocked, Hugh."

"Yes, that's what I'm hearing officially. I'm hearing unofficially that a number of congressmen are being subjected to tactics that seem to go beyond hardball. Like intimidation. Threats. Do you have any comment?"

"I won't speak on the record."

"So there is something going on? Where's it coming from? My source isn't sure," said Salter.

"Not for the record, Hugh."

"Fine," said Salter, "not for the record. What can you give me in terms of background, context?"

"Listen to me, Hugh. Lives are at stake." Dan hung up.

Salter stared blankly at his page of notes. The staffers he had just spoken with sounded genuinely frightened. Threats. What kind of threats would shake a veteran political staffer?

He went back to his call list, and began trying again those who had not picked up his first time through. As he was dialing the second number, his phone pinged, alerting him to a new email.

He opened the window onscreen. There was a message from Patriot76: "Someone is passing around salacious material," it began, "trying to influence the election. Florida Congressman Somerset has been linked with a male prostitute and Congresswoman Percy's husband has been paying kickbacks from his construction business." There were attachments.

Hugh Salter sat at the desk in his fishbowl office. He stared blankly out toward the newsroom, not seeing it, his thoughts turned inward, alarm growing within him that he had been played for a sucker. A bitter, impotent rage filled him. His chest felt tight, his hands cold.

"Yeah," Salter said under his breath as he looked again at Patriot76's email, "and you're probably the one doing it."

His concerns about the role he was playing in Patriot76's machinations had faded into the background over the past week as he had filed his reports about the chaos on Capitol Hill. He had even lent his experience and expertise to help other reporters with context and background on the difficult choices facing a number of the representatives. He had felt he was doing good work, cutting through the noise. Now, once again, he felt like a sordid accomplice.

It was infuriatingly Orwellian: leak damaging information, attack a culture of leaks—and the press—but nevertheless benefit from the chaos caused by the leak you have so carefully planted. And as before, it was an ethical quandary. Whoever was supplying the information knew what would sell: it was a scoop, to be sure, so some news agency would pick it up, even if he didn't. If he didn't run with the story, he might have to defend his choice not to have pursued the tip-off, which could make him look partisan. But if he did go with the leaked stories and they were part of this new, larger context of threats and intimidation, he would be contributing to a process that was undermining and eroding the foundation of the country.

Could the FBI be of any help against whoever was threatening the congressmen? he wondered. It seemed possible the FBI was itself part of the threat. If Patriot76 could get compromising photos from a dead FBI agent's phone, it seemed likely there was at least complicity on behalf of the Bureau, or that someone within it was orchestrating events. Possibly Patriot76 was himself an agent. Salter was stuck for a way forward. He dialed his news director's number and asked if he could come over.

* * *

Inside a van positioned in a downtown Bethesda parking deck behind Barnes & Noble, Weir, Vega and Jezek stood, cramped and hunched over. They were giving Jezek last minute instructions and double-checking his recording device. The "wire" he was wearing was taped to his chest. The transmitter was taped to his side, below his right armpit.

"Taking this off is going to feel like getting a chest wax," said Jezek playfully as he finished tucking in the shirt and began buttoning it over his hairy torso.

Vega and Weir stared at him, his quip falling flat.

"You have an opportunity," said Weir, "to get back some of the credibility you squandered. Stay focused. Don't blow it."

Vega glared at him.

"Yes, sir. Yes, of course. Thank you."

"One more time," said Weir. "Let's hear it."

"I'm to bring Hague the news that Colls did indeed send Kurtz, and that I am worried about what that could mean. Further, I am to say that the Oversight Committee will probably need to look into the intel Colls was feeding them, since he was clearly operating independently."

"Good," said Weir. "Tell them you and Vega are following up on every trip where Colls detailed Kurtz. And?"

"I'm to make sure to state on the tape that when Hague, the Senator and I met, the Senator had been particularly concerned about getting a look-in at what was happening within the Bureau. It's crucial that Hague not be allowed to contradict me and say the Senator was not present at that meeting."

"Crucial. Then what?"

"I need to ask Hague what else I should be on the lookout for? Should I delve into anything else Colls was doing?"

"Good. If you feel it's going well and that he doesn't suspect anything, try getting him to maybe boast a bit—how well they managed the Senate vote for Bob Moore, for example; how it still seems a toss-up in the House . . . see if that leads anywhere."

"Right," said Jezek.

"If we lose the signal somehow—"

"—The number you're calling from will display as 'Mom' on my phone; and I should try to go into the bathroom and fix it," said Jezek.

"Good. When you leave . . . tell him you've got an early day tomorrow; that it's a Sunday and you want to look at files in relative peace. When you exit, start walking east on Elm Street. The van will tail for a block or so, but we'll pick you up before you get to Wisconsin Ave." He paused, looked at each in turn. "Okay," he said. "Let's go."

"Phil!" beckoned Casey Hague from a corner table.

Jezek waved cheerfully across at Hague and indicated he was getting a drink before heading over. He ordered a neat Scotch—a double—for himself, and a bourbon and water for Hague.

"So, how goes it?" asked Hague as Jezek sat down. He laid his phone upside down on the table.

"I'm sorry to say, my worries about Colls have been confirmed."

"No," Hague said.

"When I met with you and the Senator in his car that time, I never thought we'd be talking about how Agent Colls was the problem. Now I'm worried about what you both might think of me. Who knows how deep this all goes, or who else is implicated."

"Phil, you have our complete faith."

"Thank you. But I see how this looks: Colls had your complete faith. And he was running Kurtz as a . . . as a . . . traitor. "

"We don't know that, Phil."

"It's going to come out. The Bureau is moving on the election officials in Illinois—"

"—When?"

"Tomorrow," he said, wishing it were true. "What information did you get from Colls? Maybe if you and I went over it."

"We've been over it," said Hague, "I communicated your concerns immediately after yesterday. We've looked at the inside information Colls gave us against what came to pass, and we feel pretty good that he wasn't lying to us. Could there be another explanation for all this? Could Kurtz have been acting alone?"

"I'll know more tomorrow, but I doubt it," said Jezek sadly. "Vega and I are getting together to go over the files, see where else Colls sent Kurtz, and find out who else he met. In fact, I shouldn't stay long tonight. I've got an early, long day tomorrow."

"You've been an amazing help, Phil. I can't tell you how much we appreciate it. And we won't forget. But listen, if you've got something to do, don't let me keep you."

Inside the van on the first level of the parking garage, Weir pumped his fist in triumph. "We've got him!" he said in a low, harsh whisper. "Okay, we'll wait a minute until Jezek's out of sightline of the bar. Let's hope he calls Eliot."

As Jezek turned to his right and headed along Elm Street, Frank Reed, who had been sitting by the window at a bar across the street nursing his beer, stood up. He saw Jezek fasten the top button on his coat, turn his collar up and stuff his hands into his pockets; saw him start down the street at a deliberate pace. Just as Reed was about to leave the bar to go meet with Hague across the street, he saw a white van with Verizon markings come out of the parking deck and stop, waiting to turn. Amanda Vega was driving.

Reed froze. He quickly regained his composure and took a step back from the window. When the van turned and headed along the road, he left, walking quickly to keep the van in view. After a few yards, he slowed his pace, watching. The van stopped and waited at a traffic light. When the light turned, the van proceeded, creeping along. Half a block ahead of it, starting up the hill toward Wisconsin Ave, he could still make out Jezek.

When the van pulled even with him, the back door swung open and Jezek climbed in. The door slammed shut and the van accelerated. Reed quickly lost sight of it. He stood rooted to the pavement. He looked back toward the bar where Hague waited.

Reed took out his flip phone and turned it on. He dialed Nash.

"This is Mr. Cooper," he said. "We have a problem. They know about Weaver. I just saw an FBI audio van pick Jezek up after his meeting. Please advise what to do?"

"Shit!" said Nash. "Okay. I'm thinking . . . Okay: call Mr. Weaver, tell him your meet is off; say something's come up. Ask if you can meet later tonight. Tell him . . . Tell him Nolte Park in Silver Spring. He knows it. Tell him you'll call as soon as you're sure of the time."

"Where is this place exactly?"

"Don't worry. You won't be going there. Stay focused on our problem children. I'll handle this."

11

Ten miles southeast of downtown Bethesda, at Bus Rentals, Trey Kelly leapt out of his seat. Reed's phone had finally come to life and he had dialed Nash. Kelly logged that they were both target numbers specified in the warrant.

He texted Weir and Vega: "Reed/Figgy just called Nash. They saw your van. Know we're onto Hague. Nash says he'll HANDLE IT. Sending you full audio."

Weir, sitting up front with Vega, texted "Thanks!" He called the agent guarding the three cell members, Deptford, Kimball and Carpenter. "Guthrie," he said , "have the confiscated phones ready. Things are happening, and the handler may try to make contact with one of them. We are en route to you, about ten minutes away. If one of the phones rings, note which one—do not answer!—and we will have Deptford or whoever call Nash back."

Vega stomped on the accelerator.

Weir dialed Gus Davies. "This is Don Weir. I need you to stake out Casey Hague's home in Silver Spring. Will transmit the address within the next five minutes."

Vega was flying through traffic. She had turned on the hazard flashers, and was leaning on the horn as she weaved between cars. Weir and Jezek were thrown side to side. Weir sat in the passenger seat staring at his phone, contemplating his next move. Jezek was in the back, wearing a dazed expression. The van continued its belligerent slalom.

Weir called Kelly back. "Great work, Trey!" he said. "Where is Hague right now? Going home?"

"I'm checking. He's still in Bethesda, at the bar where he met Jezek."

"Text Hague's address to Davies, please."

There was a pause. Then Kelly said, "Okay. Done." There was another pause before he said: "Reed's calling Hague right now." He held his phone up so that Weir could also hear the wire tap audio.

"Yes?" they all heard Hague respond.

"Something's come up," said Reed. "Can we meet later?"

"Sure. Do we need to meet at all?"

"Yes. What about that Nolte Park, near your house?" Reed asked.

"Okay. When?"

"Later. Two, maybe three hours from now. I'll call when I know definitely."

"Okay," said Hague. Inside the van and at Bus Rentals, they heard Reed hang up.

"Jesus!" Kelly said to Weir as the van drew near the detention center. "Reed's just up the street from the bar. He must have been watching you all."

The audio van screeched to a halt in front of a sentry kiosk at the detention center facility. The guard came out shining his flashlight, one hand poised at his gun. He shone the light into the van. Vega, Weir and Jezek showed their identification.

Weir, still connected to Kelly, heard Reed disconnect and immediately call Nash.

"Yes?" Weir heard Nash say.

"It's set," Reed said. "The park. I've arranged to call back with a definite time."

The guard waved the van through, and it lurched into the parking garage.

Weir heard Reed disconnect. "We're at the holding facility," he advised Kelly and hung up.

Vega aimed the van at a heavy metal door leading to an adjacent building and accelerated alarmingly across the empty lot. The van came to a stop directly in front of it. Vega, Weir and Jezek jumped out. Weir keyed in the combination code.

Inside, Guthrie met them outside the cells. He had the three flip phones arrayed on a folding table. Each was labeled: "Deptford", "Kimball", "Carpenter."

"Nothing yet, sir," said Guthrie by way of greeting.

Deptford's phone rang. The four stopped in the hallway, staring at it. Guthrie pointed at a door to Weir's left. "That's Deptford's room," he said.

Guthrie keyed the combination code to open it. Weir stepped in, holding the ringing phone. Deptford was lying on a cot to one side of the small room. "Time to earn your sentence reduction," said Weir.

Deptford sat up and held out his hand. "Tell him you're still in Frederick, Maryland, but you can be here quickly. We're taping this conversation."

Deptford nodded.

"Yes?" he said raising the phone to his ear.

Vega stepped out to call Kelly so she could listen in on the conversation. Standing in the hallway, hearing both sides of the conversation, she heard Nash say to Deptford: "This is Mr. Fisher. Do you recognize my voice?"

"I do, sir."

"Very good. You've been briefed on this possibility, now it's a necessity. I need you to meet with Mr. Weaver."

"I understand," said Deptford.

"He's . . . "—Nash seemed to search for the word—" . . . distraught."

"I understand."

"Nolte Park in Silver Spring. Enter on Denver Road. How quickly can you get there?"

Deptford looked at Weir. "Fifteen or twenty minutes to get things together, forty-five minutes to an hour to drive there. I can be there in an hour and a half. Tell him to meet in me two hours."

"He'll be there. Call me when it's concluded." Nash disconnected.

"Okay," said Weir rubbing his hands together.

"Mr. Weaver?" said Vega as she stepped back into the room from the hallway.

"We're not supposed to know anyone's real name," Deptford responded. "I was shown a series of photos when I was brought on, but I don't know everyone. The guy who just called is 'Mr. Fisher.' I've never seen a picture of him. I know Reed, Kimball and Carpenter, but I was still supposed to use their code names: Reed was Mr. Cooper; Kimball was Miller; Carpenter was Tillman."

"Why those names?" asked Jezek.

"How the hell should I know?" Deptford retorted.

"Do you have a code name?" asked Weir.

"What are you?" asked Vega. "Professor Plum?"

Deptford looked at the agents arrayed in front of him. "Plumber," he said.

Vega pursed her lips tightly. "I'd love to meet Colonel Mustard. Is he the leader of your operation?" she wondered.

"There is no Mustard," said Deptford. "Everyone gets a trade, something that sounds like a last name. Except for the guy at the top. Or the guy I assume's at the top because he's only ever referred to. He's designated The Postman. But I've never seen him or spoken with him."

"Walk us through what just happened," said Vega.

"You're supposed to meet with Mr. Weaver."

"Right, but 'meet' in this context means kill."

"Why did he say Mr. Weaver appeared distraught?"

"He means it should look like a suicide . . . or an accident."

"Why did you want the extra half hour?" Weir asked.

"To give me time to reconnoiter the area. That's generally how I operate. I wanted it to seem real, I guess."

Vega held up her phone and opened up the photo application. "I have some photos of conspirators here," she said handing it to him. "Scroll through them, swiping right to left. Let me know who you recognize and give me names."

Deptford took the phone and begin scrolling through the photos. "Right," he said. "Carpenter . . . Tillman." He turned the phone to show the image. "Kimball: Miller; Reed: Cooper. And that's Mr. Weaver." He turned the phone toward them again, showing Casey Hague's picture.

"And Fisher?" asked Vega. "Have you seen his picture?"

"No," said Deptford.

"Thank you," said Weir, and he stepped out of the room.

In the deserted hallway, Weir telephoned Dyer. "We have Nash on tape ordering the murder of Casey Hague. I want to bring Hague in for questioning, confront him with the evidence, let him know he's been marked down for elimination and see if we can get him to roll over. Then we move on Nash . . . No, sir, we're no nearer to Reed. He knows we're on to Hague, which is why Nash ordered the hit."

Back at Bus Rentals, Trey Kelly was staring at the readout of Reed's trace. For once, Reed had not turned off his phone. He called Vega.

"Amanda?" he said. "Reed's still in Bethesda. And his phone is still on. We might be able to track him."

Amanda stepped out into the hallway with Weir. She was about to relay the information to him and ask about trying to arrest Reed when over the phone Kelly said to her: "Nash is calling Reed."

Amanda switched on her phone's speaker and held it so that both she and Weir could hear what Trey was hearing on the wiretap.

"It's set," said Nash to Reed. "Tell him to be there in two hours."

"Listen," said Reed. "They're on to him. So he's probably being watched."

Weir and Vega exchanged glances.

"I'm outside the bar where he is right now," said Reed.

In the background, at Bus Rentals, Weir and Vega heard Kelly whisper "Oh fuck."

"I don't see any surveillance team," said Reed, "but frankly I can't do a thorough scan of the area without giving myself away. If they're here—and we should expect them to be— they're probably waiting to tail him when he leaves the bar and drives away. And if so, they would definitely follow him to the park, which really fucks us."

"What are you proposing?" asked Nash.

"I know where he parked. We drove in together. I was supposed to meet him after he talked with Jezek."

Weir looked frantically at Vega: "Do we know where Hague parked?"

She shook her head, no.

"If there's no one else around," Reed continued, "I'll take care of it when he goes to leave. Make it look like robbery or something. Shit!" he exclaimed. "I see him. He's at the door," Reed hissed. "Go? No-Go?"

Reed could see Hague standing just inside the front door, buttoning his coat and pulling on his gloves.

Standing in the hallway of the detention center, the silence for Weir and Vega was agonizing.

"Go," said Nash.

"Find out where Davies is!" said Weir.

Vega hung up and called Davies. "He's just arriving at Hague's house, like we told him," she told Weir. "He's twenty minutes away at best."

"Damn!" yelled Weir. "We could alert the Bethesda cops, but what do we say to them? Somewhere in Downtown Bethesda there's about to be a murder? There's no way they could mobilize that quickly."

"Should Davies stay where he is?" asked Vega.

"Yes. For the moment. Let me think." Weir stared for a long moment down the empty hall. "Is his phone still on?"

Vega disconnected with Davies and called Trey. "Is Reed's phone still on?" she asked Trey.

"Yes," he said.

"Where's he going?"

"I'm working on it," said Kelly. "He's standing on Elm Street."

On Elm Street in Bethesda, Frank Reed stood in the dark of a recessed bagel shop doorway, closed now. He watched Casey Hague turn down the lane leading to the parking garage. As soon as Hague turned toward the elevators, Reed darted across the street and along the lane. He was glad it was a cold night. There were very few people around.

At Bus Rentals Trey was peering at his screen. "There's this little alley just off Elm Street," he said to Vega over the phone. "It looks like he's running." Kelly paused his commentary and peered closer at the screen because now it appeared that he was standing still.

In the parking garage, Reed sprinted up the stairs to the fourth parking level, taking the steps two at a time. Hague's car was parked in a corner far from the elevators. Reed knew that even if he missed Hague getting off, he would still be able to catch him before he reached the car.

"Fuck," whispered Vega impotently. "Where are they? What are they doing?"

"They're not moving. Maybe one's in a stairwell and the other in the elevator," said Kelly. "I'm guessing, though."

"Wait!" said Jezek. "Call him!"

Weir and Vega stared at him.

"Call Hague!" said Jezek. "Warn him."

Weir pulled out his own phone. "What's his fucking number?" he yelled into the phone connected to Kelly.

Kelly peered at the display on the screen and called out the number into his phone.

Weir dialed. The phone began ringing.

In the elevator at the parking garage, Casey Hague pulled his phone out of his overcoat pocket and checked the number.

"Come on!" Weir yelled from the hallway of the detention center.

Hague stared at his phone, seemingly undecided as to whether to answer. "Hello?" he said finally.

"Mr. Hague," said Weir, "my name is Don Weir. I'm the FBI Executive Assistant Director. You're in—"

"—Who's this?"

"I'm Don Weir with the FBI. You are in grave, imminent danger."

"What the fuck?"

"Mr. Hague, do not get out of the elevator you are in. Frank Reed has been sent to kill you. We believe he's coming up the stairwell right now." In the background, Weir could hear the feminine-mechanical voice of the elevator announcing, "floor four, doors opening."

"There's a stop button on the panel." Weir said frantically. "Hit the alarm. We'll—"

On the fourth floor of the parking garage, the elevator doors were already opening. Hague, desperately looking for the stop button noticed someone standing in the gap and looked up. Seeing that it was Frank Reed he recoiled, only to stumble into the back wall of the elevator. Reed's three shots killed him instantly.

Reed reached down and dragged Hague's corpse out of the elevator by an arm, shoving it against the wall behind a garbage can. He grabbed Hague's wallet and watch, and threw his phone in the garbage before running to the stairs and heading to ground level. Once there, rather than leave the way he had come in, Reed walked to the back of the parking deck, hopped over a low wall and began walking up the alley.

He dialed Nash's number as he walked along.

"Yes?" said Nash.

"You can cancel your order. Let's check in Monday, normal time." They both hung up. Reed immediately turned off his phone. Nash called Deptford to countermand his earlier kill order. Then he too switched off his phone.

Half a block up the street, Reed saw a cab at the curb near a corner bar. He stepped in and was gone.

At the detention center and at Bus Rentals, there was silence. Trey Kelly stared unseeing at his screen; Weir, Jezek and Vega stood frozen, staring bleakly at nothing.

Weir was shaking his head. "We've got millions of dollars worth of gadgets . . . fucking worthless!" No one contradicted him. He looked at Jezek. "That was good thinking," he said. "We were just too slow." He looked up and down the hallway, glanced into the cell where Deptford was reclining on his cot, staring at the ceiling. "Amanda," said Weir, "get to the crime scene. I'll call Bethesda police. Let's keep a lid on this until we've had a time to think." He sighed deeply. "I'll update Dyer, too."

* * *

Imogen, in Philadelphia, knew nothing about events in Bethesda, but she was no less frustrated and dejected. Feeling at sea without a defined project, she had begun looking into who was behind the Illinois election fraud by searching LexisNexis for common threads. Who were the journalists who were writing about it, she had wondered, but she had come up with nothing. Had there been anyone out of the ordinary that the journalists had sought for insight and quotes? Did any names keep cropping up? Again, nothing useful. Her house was a mess again, Imogen noted gloomily. She was finding it difficult to rally any enthusiasm to tidy up.

Thoughts of Duncan Calder and their time here together piqued the solitude of the past days with an aching loneliness, a yearning to be beyond this disaster and to be together. Because she was living again in the only place they had spent time together as lovers, she found herself confronted at odd moments with visions of them as a couple: talking over coffee, conferring over data, the time she woke up to see him staring at her lovingly.

There was also a tincture of dread in these warm remembered moments. Dread that theirs had been a romance built on the needs of the time. The look in his eyes that morning had been unmistakable, she thought—but perhaps that was to double her mistake. Even if it had been the look of adoration she felt it was, could it have been merely the afterglow of a night of passion? Close though they felt in those moments, their relationship had hardly begun. It had been tested in extraordinary circumstances, for sure, but when that heat was taken away, would there still be a flame?

It wasn't a practical line of thinking, and didn't lead anywhere, so she switched her attention, quite deliberately.

There had to be some clue, she thought, to the conspirators' endgame, some indicator that she and her colleagues were missing. The cell they had cracked—Reed, Deptford, Kimball and Carpenter—it was obvious that they were not ideologues.

215

They were mercenaries. But Colls, Kurtz, Trebor and Covington were different. They all had an ideological, authoritarian streak. They were linked by their association with Jefferson's Tigers at Princeton, but was there something else? Imogen pushed aside a half-eaten ham and cheese sandwich and propped her laptop on her knees, opening LexisNexis again.

Vega arrived in the parking garage with an FBI crime scene team. She stood with a Bethesda police lieutenant outside the main ring of activity where the crime scene technicians were scouring and photographing. Hague's body, swaddled in an overcoat filthy from the garage floor, lay where Reed had shunted it. But for the slick of blood beneath him, he could have been a derelict who had died of exposure.

When their measurements and photographs were finished, one of the crime scene techs rolled Hague onto his back. The blood was viscous, all over his hair and face. The photographer took three more shots before a junior tech dragged the body away from the wall and the garbage can, into better light, for the medical examiner to do his ghoulish work. A gelatinous smear of blood followed the corpse darkly across the cold garage floor.

"That's no robbery," affirmed the lieutenant as he looked at the body. "That's a professional fucking hit." He peered a little closer. "Clinical. One to the chest, one to the neck, one in the head. Who is he?"

"He's—he was—a witness in an ongoing investigation," said Vega. "I can't say more. For now, we need to write it up as a robbery-homicide; say that the investigation is ongoing, and we're not releasing the victim's name until next-of-kin have been notified. Nothing more, including FBI involvement. My boss will call your captain or the chief. Okay?"

"Understood," said the lieutenant.

* * *

As it was Sunday morning, fewer of Hugh Salter's calls were being picked up or returned than usual. Finally, David Carr, a Pennsylvania congressman picked up. "Morning, Dave, it's Hugh Salter," he said brightly. "I'm looking for any updates or insight into how the House vote is going. Where's your delegation in all this?"

Silence.

"I'm hearing that a number of congressmen are being put under pressure," Salter continued. "The game seems to have changed. There's talk of intimidation, threats. Does this have anything to do with the killing of the Faithless Electors?"

"I can't say."

"We're hearing about threats in several states, but I don't know how it's playing in the Pennsylvania delegation."

"So this is national?" asked Carr.

"Yes."

"I have to go," said Carr and hung up.

*   *   *

At Bus Rentals, Trey Kelly awoke from a fitful three hours' sleep looking as haggard and distraught as when he had finally dozed off the previous night. As soon as he was equipped with coffee from the pot, he restarted the playback. It was as incomplete as ever, but this time he had an idea. He dialed Vega.

"G'morning," he said through a swig of scalding, bitter coffee. "Can I get you or Weir to sign a memo request for NSA file-sharing? I think we can get Reed that way."

"How?" she asked.

"Pretty much the same as we did before with the others, by giving NSA specific dates, times and locations—only this time it's the burner phone we've identified. Since Reed's personal phone isn't under his name, we haven't been able to isolate it. But we have his burner phone live at specific places at specific times. So if his regular phone is on, it should be pinging. We get NSA to look for the one number that's pinging from all those locations at those times."

217

"I'll have it to you within the hour," said Vega.

* * *

Weir and Dyer sat in Weir's office, huddled around a conference call with the Attorney General.

"Yes, ma'am, we had what we thought was an excellent inroad," Dyer was saying into the intercom. "Nash called Deptford, not knowing we have him in custody. He ordered the hit on Hague. We have it on tape. It was going to be perfect. Nash would set up the meet between Hague and Deptford, but instead of Hague being killed, we were going to arrest him, show him the evidence we have against him and tell him they were going to kill him. Then we could signal to Nash that the job was done, so he'd still think he was safe while we went to work getting Hague to roll over."

"Why didn't you arrest Hague right after his meet with your agent?" she asked. "I'd have thought that was pretty standard."

"Yes, ma'am," said Weir. "I made the determination that it was better to leave Hague out there, possibly until Monday. During that time, he might call Senator Eliot, or make a report to someone as yet unknown to the investigation. He's hooked in with Eliot, Nash and Reed. I wanted to know if there was anyone else."

"What went wrong?" asked the Attorney General, her voice echoing from her empty office.

"Reed changed the plan, ma'am," said Dyer. "Said he could take care of it himself right away. We weren't near enough to stop him or catch him. And there were no leads at the crime scene."

"So even though Hague's his chief of staff, there's really nothing to link Senator Eliot to any of this, is there?" she asked.

"Nothing we could make stick," said Dyer. "He can say Hague just went rogue and was acting for himself now."

"All right," she said, "Pick up Nash. I've—" Down the line there was a knock at the door to the Attorney General's office. "I asked not be disturbed," Weir and Dyer heard her say sharply, before telling them to wait, and putting them on hold.

At that moment, Amanda Vega strode into Weir's office, knocking cursorily on the door as she did so.

"Amanda," said Weir, "we're in the middle—"

"I'm being told that the Capitol Police just contacted Secret Service," said the Attorney General over the speaker phone.

"About what?" asked Dyer.

"That's what I came in to tell you," said Vega in Weir's ear.

"Unclear," said the Attorney General, "which worries me." She paused, searching for what to say next. "There's something happening on the Hill," she said distantly. She was quiet again, but when she spoke next, there was decisiveness in her voice. "Okay. Arrest Nash now. You'll have the arrest warrant in twenty minutes."

Weir pointed at Vega. "Get your team ready."

"Bill?" said the Attorney General, "Come to my office right away. I want you to brief the prosecutor team."

"I'm on my way," said Dyer. He stood up, gathering some of the papers he would need. "Keep me up to date," he said to Weir and walked out.

Vega, still standing near the doorway, said: "And we think we can get Reed now, too. Trey's working on something like what he did to find the initial traces."

"Excellent. But you heard the boss: pick up Nash now," said Weir. "Their last communication said they'd be in touch again at the regular time. That means 3:30 tomorrow. If you can arrest Nash quietly now, Reed won't know we've done it."

Vega nodded. "Which might give us enough time to track him down." She turned to go out.

"Amanda," said Weir. "As soon as Nash is in custody, get in touch with Imogen and tell her it's safe to come back."

The tag trace on his phone placed Nash at his hotel along Pennsylvania Avenue, across from Pershing Park. Vega dispatched Davies ahead of the arrest team to establish for certain that Nash was in his room and hadn't simply left the phone in there.

Minutes later, Davies walked into the hotel's vast, Beaux-Arts lobby and asked to speak with the manager. He discreetly showed his FBI identification and asked for confirmation that Alec Nash was staying in Room 617.

The manager quickly looked over the roster. "Yes."

"Your key cards," said Davies, "are you able to register that someone is in the room?"

"I'm not sure I—"

"Do they have to be deployed in the wall slot for the electricity to come on?"

"Yes, it's an energy-saving device."

"Can you tell whether the power is on in 617?"

"Hang on," said the manager. He frowned as typed.

"Use the housekeeping screen," said the elegantly turned out young woman on the desk. Standing behind the manager, she pointed at something on the screen. "It's one way to check whether we can make up the room," she explained to Davies. She smiled pleasantly.

"And?" Davies asked the manager.

"The power appears to be on," said the manager.

"Can you supply me with a floor map showing the emergency exits please?"

The manager grabbed a laminated piece of paper and laid it on the desk ledge.

"Is this the sixth floor?" Davies asked absently as he looked over the floor plan.

"Floors four through eight are all identical in layout," said the manager. "May I ask—?"

Davies motioned him to step away from the desk. When he had him aside, Davies said: "We will be making an arrest within the next half hour. We—and I'm sure you—would like to do it quietly and efficiently."

"Yes," said the manager.

"Does this stairwell lead to the lobby?" asked Davies, pointing on the floor plan.

"It can," said the manager, "or you can go down one more flight to the loading bay area."

* * *

Trey Kelly had just received data on six possible matching cellphone numbers from Mike at NSA. He was sorting through the numbers, looking for parallels with Reed's known burner phone. The trace for the first two numbers he tried soon diverged from the known path of Reed's burner, and because Reed didn't leave it on all the time it meant Trey had to follow each trace for longer looking for overlap with Reed's burner.

As he watched the third such number diverge from Reed's known path, Trey wished he had called in for some help to run through the traces. He worried that Reed might also be changing the SIM on his personal phone, which would make searching for him that much more difficult and time-consuming. He sighed deeply, shook his head to clear his thoughts and moved on to the fourth number in the NSA batch. He looked up at the screen hopefully as it began to run.

Imogen had begun a whirlwind clean of the Catherine Street house when Amanda sent her a message saying it might soon be time for her to return to work. Having concluded that she would never get Calder's bloodstains out of the sheets, Imogen was at a home furnishings store on Mifflin Street paying for new sheets and towels when the message came. On her way back to the house she wondered what on earth she would tell her friends about what had gone on. Perhaps she couldn't tell them much of anything at all. Housework abandoned, she packed her bag, left it by the front door and waited for Amanda to call back.

Six agents in riot gear came through the hotel's delivery dock and stalked up the fire exit stairs. Vega brought up the rear.

On the sixth floor, they could see Davies standing at the far end of the hall blocking escape via the elevators or main stairs. Vega took out the key card the manager had handed her at the loading dock. Crouching by the door, she could hear a news program on the television inside the room, waffling away about some plot to rig the presidency. Poised at the door, Vega signaled to Davies down the hall, who dialed Nash's number.

Just outside the door, the agents heard the phone ring in the room. As they heard him answer, Vega pushed the key card into the slot and heard the mechanical rasp and click as the door unlocked. Crouched low, she turned the handle and put her shoulder hard into the door. The security bolt caught the door when it was only about four inches wide. She leaned away as another agent crashed through the latch with his battering ram.

Four other agents, with guns aimed high and low, poured through the open door. For a moment, Nash stood frozen at the foot of the bed. He looked quizzically at his phone.

"Lie on the floor! Arms and legs spread wide," commanded the agent holding the battering ram.

One agent kicked open the bathroom door, gun at the ready. He checked behind the shower curtain. All clear. Vega, still at the doorway, walked into room 617. "Alec Nash, you are under arrest," she said to the man lying face down on the floor, his hands cuffed behind his back.

"You have the right to remain silent."

Across the street from the hotel, Frank Reed was arriving to meet Nash. He needed to tell Nash that their efforts in the House had backfired and the Capitol Police had started an investigation. Deciding on their next steps couldn't wait until the next day.

As part of his routine precautions, he had surveyed the building as he walked past the front of the hotel on the Pershing Park side of the street. He had then turned down to walk along the "F" Street side of the building. Nothing looked amiss, and Reed was just about to cross the street toward the hotel's back entrance when he froze, his heart beating wildly. A large UPS truck stuck out across the sidewalk in one of the delivery bays. In the other bay, two black SUVs were parked at right angles.

Reed stepped into a passageway leading to a suite of shops and pretended to be fascinated by a display of watches, all the while keeping an eye on the delivery bays in the shop window's reflection. The SUVs could be security for any foreign dignitary or VIP, but he needed to know what was happening.

He didn't wait long. Four men in FBI armor walked quickly out to one of the SUVs. Reed turned to get a better look. Behind them, inside the bay, he made out three agents shoveling a hooded man into the back seat of the other SUV. Although his face was obscured, Reed could tell who it was from the trim build and the tailored cut of his blue striped shirt over fashionable slim-cut trousers. Nash was shoeless.

A moment later, agents Vega and Davies came jogging across the street to Davies's car. Reed turned away slowly and began walking the opposite way. He glanced at the reflection in another window to see if they had noticed him. They stepped into their car, made a U-turn and drove off.

"Got you, motherfucker!" Trey Kelly hissed triumphantly. The fourth trace had paid off. It was perfectly synched. He turned from the screen as it went on charting Reed's past movements and began setting up a second trace that would plot his current location and movement.

Before starting, though, he sent a text to Vega and Weir:"Found a match for Reed! Working on current location."

Vega texted back immediately: "Great. Heading to detention center with Nash. Guthrie on alert for you. He's looped in on this text. I called Gen. She's on her way back."

Trey smiled, glad that Imogen would soon be back. He resettled his chair and got down to work again.

Reed turned the corner on 14th Street and headed back toward Pennsylvania Avenue. There was a bus stop at the corner of 14th and Pennsylvania, in front of the Freedom Plaza. Reed stood off the curb and peered down 14th Street as though looking for his bus, then behind him and out along Pennsylvania Avenue, before scrutinizing the plaza behind the bus stop.

At that moment, Imogen was flying down Interstate 95, her sunny mood a sharp contrast with the dreary January skies. She allowed herself to dare to contemplate a future, for herself and Duncan.

Satisfied he was not being followed or watched, Reed sat down at the bus stop. He pulled out his burner phone and turned it on. As it cycled on, he reached for his billfold and rifled through.

On his screen, Trey could see that Reed had stopped at the corner of 14th Street Northwest and Pennsylvania Avenue. An alert sounded, telling him that Reed's burner had just come on. It sprang to life right next to the trace he had established for Reed's personal phone.

Reed had found the slip of paper he needed in his billfold and was dialing the number written on it.

Trey called Guthrie, thrilled that his trawling had paid off: "My map shows a bus stop right where he's located—14th Northwest and Pennsylvania Avenue," Trey was telling Guthrie.

"Christ! That's four blocks from here!" Guthrie was sprinting down the stairs at FBI Headquarters to his SUV.

"He's calling someone," said Trey, but Guthrie didn't hear him as he ran. With his free hand, Trey pressed record. The number Reed was calling, he noted, was new.

Guthrie had reached the garage and was sprinting toward the truck.

Listening in on the line, Trey heard the call being answered. "Yes?"

"This is Mr. Cooper. Mr. Fisher is now compromised."

"What about the others?"

"Unclear," said Reed.

"Abandon," said the voice.

"I've got one last thing to do."

"Follow protocol," the voice admonished and hung up.

At Bus Rentals, Trey stopped recording and immediately began tracing the new number.

At the bus stop, Reed pulled a handkerchief from his pocket and wiped his flip phone thoroughly. He stood up and threw it in the road, then crushed it under his heel as he stepped off the curb, breaking it in two.

Still on the phone with Guthrie, Trey told him he had just lost the burner signal. "It looks like he may be still on the move."

"Where?" Guthrie shouted as he weaved in an out of traffic. "I just crossed Eleventh."

Reed switched off his personal phone as well, and walked across the street into Pershing Park.

"It looks like he's—"

"Where?" panted Guthrie, who was fast approaching 13th Street.

"It's gone dark," Trey told Guthrie. "He must have switched off."

Reed walked purposefully to the far end of the park, where he trotted down the steps from the park to 15th Street. He hailed a Red Top taxi and climbed in, asking for Logan Circle. "Drop me anywhere between Rhode Island and Vermont Ave."

A block away on 14th, Guthrie screeched to a halt in front of the bus stop at the far end of Pershing Park on 14th. The plaza was deserted on this dreary January day, and none of the stray pedestrians matched Reed's description. The Red Top cab pulled away. Guthrie stood on the running board of the truck to get a better view into the park. Nothing.

"He's gone," said Guthrie into his phone. "Any idea which way he went?"

"It looked like he might have been heading toward the park when the signal went dark," said Trey. "I can't say a hundred percent."

Inside the taxi heading north along 15th, Reed pushed the end of a bent paperclip into his phone to pop out the SIM card. He rolled the window down an inch and tossed the SIM out. Once again, he took out a handkerchief, this time to wipe off his personal phone. As he put the handkerchief back in his pocket, his hand bumped the gun he had used to kill Hague. He stared broodingly at the butt end.

Guthrie, dejected, looked at the ground. Near the front left tire of his truck he saw the smashed burner. He reached into the cab for an evidence bag, pulled on a latex glove and put the remnants into the bag. He got back in and drove along Pershing Park toward the entrance to President's Park. He pulled over in front of a line of parked cars and got out, to scan Pershing Park again.

At the corner he stood for a moment, hands on hips. There were far too many DC and park police around for Reed to risk going into President's Park, he thought. And there would be cameras. If Reed came this way, he thought, he'd have probably gone north or south on 15th. He peered toward the gatehouse at the entrance to the park. He could just make out a small security camera sticking out over the entrance. He would need access to that feed.

Guthrie peered up and down 15th Street. He looked back in the direction of the bus stop. There! Directly above him, mounted on a traffic light was a camera. Guthrie ran across to the gatehouse and showed his FBI identification to the guard.

"Has this man passed by in the last ten minutes or so?" he asked, showing the guard a picture of Reed on his phone.

"No," the guard said, shaking his head. "I don't think so."

"This camera," said Guthrie, pointing above the entrance. "Does it play back here? Can we re-run the past fifteen minutes?"

"Sure," said the guard. "I need to notify my supervisor."

"Do it," said Guthrie. "Tell him it's an FBI priority." He paused as the guard picked up the phone. "Also: that camera over there," he said, pointing to the one standing sentry over the corner of 15th Northwest and Pennsylvania Avenue, "is it one of yours?"

"Yeah," said the guard. "It's useful—"

"—I need to see it, too. Now."

"Well, we've got a full house here," said Weir brightly as he and Dyer entered the interrogation room at the detention center, shaking hands with the prosecutors and with Vega. "Unlike the White House, if we don't hurry up," he said under his breath, in one of the sardonic asides with which he reminded himself just how big the stakes were. This was why he had dozens of people around the country chasing the flickering evanescences of phone signals.

In the shabby surroundings of the interrogation room, Nash sat up straight in his chair, his arms flat on the table, trying to convey some dignity. He was usually exquisitely groomed, but his appearance over the past hours had suffered. His salt-and-pepper hair was matted and twisted, and his carefully cultivated stubble looked more like what it was, a three-day beard. Without shoes or a jacket, he could easily have been a refugee from a bachelor party, being made to answer embarrassing questions about things he couldn't remember. "I have asked to speak with an attorney," he said, "and I refuse to answer any questions until my attorney is present."

Weir nodded and looked to Vega, leaning in the corner, arms crossed. "It's been almost two hours," she said twisting her left arm to glance at her watch. "Do you really think anyone's coming?"

Nash looked at the table top.

At Bus Rentals, the data for the new phone number came back immediately. Trey was trying to create a trace for the number Reed had called. It linked back to a phone outside Fairmont, Nebraska, fifty miles west of Lincoln. But it was moving. Trey had good contact for the 20 seconds during which Reed and his unknown contact had spoken, but trying to isolate the phone's movements after that was impossible as Reed's contact appeared to have switched it off.

As Trey worked quickly backwards on the new number, he found that the cell tower coverage was even worse in central Nebraska than it had been in central Pennsylvania, where Deptford, Kimball and Carpenter had operated. Little of the data on the new phone was serviceable. The traces relied on location points created by triangulation between towers, but the towers in rural Nebraska were so far apart that unless the phone was active, the triangulation often didn't work. Trace lines would flutter in and out of existence across his screen as he tried to plot them. Worse, the target phone had not made or received a single call the entire month. Like Reed's, it now seemed to be abandoned.

He texted Vega: *"Not much info on the call Reed made. Somewhere in Nebraska. Terrible cell tower coverage. Wont be able to track it using past methods. Sorry. Still trying to figure out an angle."*

At the sentry gate to President's Park, Guthrie had spotted Reed on the surveillance video: same camouflage coat, same unkempt hair. He saw him getting into a Red Top taxi, and noted its number. Would the Red Top dispatcher co-operate if he told him he was FBI? He could only try. "This is FBI agent Ron Guthrie", he said. "We need your help. Red Top taxi number 1-8-4 picked up a fare at Fifteenth Street Northwest and Pennsylvania Avenue. I need to know where he is now."

The dispatcher was compliant, didn't refer him to head office, didn't ask for a warrant, didn't insist on a personal letter from the DA. Thank God. A citizen believing his ears and willing to help law enforcement. He went off the line to call the driver. When he came back on, he said the cab was currently vacant, near Dupont Circle, and had dropped the fare at Logan Circle fifteen minutes earlier. The fare had paid in cash. Guthrie noted the names of the driver and the dispatcher for his report and ran out of the gatehouse.

As she approached the beltway north of the city, Imogen called Vega. "Hi, Amanda," she said, as Vega stepped out of the interrogation room to take the call. "I'm getting near the beltway, where should I go?"

"Come here first," said Vega. "Detention cells. We can debrief you. Reed's still at large, and I'd like to make sure you're not taking unnecessary risks."

"About twenty minutes," said Imogen.

Hugh Salter sat stone faced in the news director's office with two other equally abashed Capitol Hill beat reporters.

"Nothing?" the news director shouted at them. "You've got nothing? You think CBS has got nothing? NBC? The fucking Capitol Police and the Secret Service are working on something, and not one of you fucking idiots even has a clue what it is?"

"It's obvious it has to do with the contingent election in the House," Salter began.

"Obvious to whom? You've already said no one'll confirm or deny anything," the news director shrieked. "Fuck!" he screamed, looking at his watch.

Salter stared at him. The news director was younger than he by eight or ten years, but Salter felt certain he would outlive his boss. Even so, he hadn't thought this would be the day. There was a vein on his forehead standing out so far Salter half expected it to join in on the harangue. Foamy spittle glistened at the left corner of his mouth. Salter had lamented the pleasant, assured news director of a day or two before, but he now regretted ever wishing for the return of this histrionic toddler. As he looked at his colleagues, one looking toward the window, the other at the floor—professionals all— he wondered if yelling at adults ever succeeded in spurring results. At any rate, he had had enough.

"The FBI seems to have been left out of all this," he said, rising from his chair, "which strikes me as odd. Maybe someone there can give us a look in—or at least some context.

Anything else?" He walked out of the room to make some more calls.

In truth, no other news network had anything more than their own unsubstantiated hunches.

The taxi dispatcher had said that Reed was dropped off between Vermont and Rhode Island Avenue at Logan Circle, which is where Agent Guthrie met Vega's assistant Guy Davies. As Guthrie made a slow circuit in his car, Davies walked the sidewalk. When Guthrie returned, Davies was peering down a storm sewer.

"Bring me an evidence bag," he called over his shoulder to Guthrie, who took one from the box on the floor of his car and snapped on a latex glove.

"Right there," said Davies, pointing at a smart phone resting on a clump of leaves, suspended between the asphalt and falling into the sewer. Guthrie lay flat on his stomach and reached into the opening, being careful to hook his gloved hand underneath the phone so as not dislodge it and lose it to the storm drain.

A woman in her mid-fifties came out of the Victorian house opposite where Guthrie lay on the ground. Her small hands were crossed in front of her, holding close a man's heavy overcoat which she had grabbed as she hurried out.

"What is it?" she asked, stopping at the low wrought-iron gate leading into her front garden.

"Possible evidence, ma'am," said Davies.

"I saw a man throw something down there half an hour or so ago. People are always throwing things down there."

"Yes," said Davies absently, his attention divided between the woman and Guthrie, who was still on the ground, fishing for anything else that might be with the phone.

"It seemed too small to have been a bomb or anything," she said.

Guthrie drew back from the drain opening onto his knees, put the phone in the evidence bag and stood up, brushing dirt and leaves from his clothes. "Did you get a look at this guy?" he asked her. "Do you know which way he went?"

"He was in his forties," she said. "A little rough around the edges. Grey hair. Olive drab, army style jacket."

Davies and Guthrie exchanged a look.

"I didn't like the look of him," she said wrinkling her nose.

"He went back down Rhode Island."

"We'll take my car," said Guthrie whose car was parked at the curb.

"It wasn't a bomb, was it?" she asked.

"No, ma'am."

"It'll be flooding again if they keep using it for trash. So inconsiderate, just because they don't live on this street. I've spoken to the . . ."

She was in full spate as they jumped in Guthrie's car and sped away.

They made a quick circuit and headed back along Rhode Island Avenue. "Slow," Davies instructed Guthrie. "Maybe his car's along here. He drove a dark grey Buick Lacrosse. I'll watch this side, you watch yours." Systematically, they gazed at the irrelevant cars. "He probably ditched it after I chased him," Davies added, "but you never know."

12

Vega met Imogen at the detention center outside where Nash was being held. Imogen was momentarily overwhelmed as Amanda reached to hug her, but reciprocated gratefully. It had been a chilly few days.

Jezek conducted a sleekly dressed man to Nash's cell. Despite his expensive tailoring, perfect hair and power tie, his expression betrayed apprehension, possibly confusion.

Amanda snorted derisively as Jezek opened the door to let him in. "Oh, this just gets better and better," she said as Jezek closed it and walked away quietly, dispensable now he had played his part. "Nash's friends won't answer his calls," said Amanda. "That's not a criminal lawyer," she added, peeking into the room. "But he's the only one who'd come." She beamed gleefully at Imogen. "Whaddya think? Copyright lawyer? Pharmaceutical counsel? Lobbyist? His cousin?"

Imogen shrugged. "I'm way out of my depth there," she said.

Amanda's thumb jerked toward the room. "So's that guy!" She turned away from the window. "The prosecutors say the case is really strong. Nash's only hope is to cut a deal. They think they can get him to flip, maybe lead us farther up the food chain."

"Great!" said Imogen.

The door opened. Weir and the two prosecutors stepped out.

The prosecutors walked away down the corridor to confer.

"We're giving him a moment to confer with his client," said Weir. "Imogen, good to see you." He shook her hand warmly.

"Thanks. Things seem to be going well. Do you need anything from me immediately?" she asked. "I'd like to drop in on Trey."

"Sure, sure," said Weir.

"And I'd really like to see Duncan and Pollack. How are they?"

"Still in the hospital," he said.

"Is there any chance I can get in to see them?"

"Hmm." Weir frowned. "We'll see."

"I'd really like to go," she said to him.

He considered pros and cons. "You certainly can't discuss the case with either of them—particularly not the professor. They're both definitely out of the woods. You can be certain of that," he offered.

"The last I saw of them was almost a month ago, as I was rushed out to meet with the AG. Blood everywhere. I've dreamed about it."

"Yes," said Weir, nodding but not sounding convinced.

"That's why I'd like to see they're okay. And . . . and this is personal, too. I don't think this is known, but Duncan and I were . . . together," she said. "I've been frantic to know he's alright."

Weir exchanged a look with Vega, standing behind Imogen.

"Together?" Weir's question mark gave a different intonation to the word.

"Yes."

"You didn't think that was something we should know?" he asked, his voice edged with annoyance.

"It never quite seemed germane," she began.

Weir stared blankly at her. "Germane?"

"I never knew when or how it might be appropriate to bring up," she offered.

"Well, let's get it all out there, Agent Trager now that we're talking: Kurtz, Professor Calder . . . anyone else?" he asked with exasperation.

"Two men in six years?" she stated forcefully, her expression defiant, her green eyes staring right into him, seeming to dare him to make any more of it.

"Yes," Weir stated coldly. "And both men used for target practice by these guys," he hissed.

Her boldness evaporated. He had a point. Her private life was public now.

Weir stared for a moment at the floor. Finally he looked up, exchanged another glance with Vega. He sighed deeply. "Yeah. Alright," he said, scratching his head. "I'll get you into the hospital tomorrow." He stared at her for a moment.

"Do I need to send a chaperone with you?"

Vega stifled a laugh and looked away.

* * *

Davies and Guthrie hadn't seen any further trace of Reed. They had passed a hotel on Rhode Island Avenue, and on a hunch Davies suggested they check it out. They doubled back to it.

Guthrie offered his credentials to the young man at reception, and showed a picture of Reed. "Have you seen this man?"

"Yes. He checked out about half an hour ago." He rifled through some papers. "Here's his check out form."

Guthrie took it. "Peter Snyder. Do you take ID when they check in?"

"Yes. We make a photocopy. I haven't matched the paperwork yet, though."

"Do it now, please."

The photocopy was of a Pennsylvania driver's license for a Peter Snyder of Lancaster, PA.

Davies whispered, "I think that's the address for one of the guys we have in custody," and stepped aside to call Vega to confirm.

Guthrie continued to look over the reservation records.

"He paid cash?" he asked.

"Yes," said the young man.

"Did he say where he was going when he left?"

"No, just that he'd had a nice stay, and he looked forward to being back." He paused. "You know, he almost made a point of it. I asked, like I always do, whether he'd had a nice stay, and he said 'Yes, very nice.' I took his money and printed out his receipt, and before I could say 'thank you for choosing us and we hoped to see you again real soon,' he said 'I'm really looking forward to coming back'."

Trey Kelly was doing what passed for tidying up when Imogen arrived. This routine consisted mostly of walking around the office sweeping accumulated debris from the table and desktops into a wastebasket he carried.

"It's really coming together," he effused. "Nash is on ice, Deptford's cooperating—has been cooperating. The other two are on ice as well. We just got a lead on an alias for Reed: Peter Snyder. He was using Kimball's house in Lancaster as a drop. Also, I was able to check it against the personal phone trail I established. It checks out: Snyder's the name he used when he set up that phone. We've got the goods on all of them. And, the House looks set to vote tomorrow."

"Amanda says she thinks Nash'll roll over and give up names," Imogen added.

"I'm hoping we can get even more now that we've got Reed's alias," said Trey.

"What does that make, three aliases? Figgy, Mr. Cooper and now Peter Snyder," asked Imogen.

"Yeah," Trey grinned. "I guess we should double check that he's really Frank Reed. In any case, he was using both phones—the burner to communicate with his co-conspirators, and his personal Snyder phone to communicate with others. We've got some leads on calls he made with that personal phone. A couple of them went to a friend of yours—that reporter, Hugh Salter."

Imogen made a sour face.

"Well, maybe 'friend' isn't quite the word," Trey grinned.

"In any case, Vega or one of her crew will follow up with Salter to get him to cooperate."

"Can you get away?" Imogen asked. "I think we deserve a drink."

"Let's do it tomorrow. I'm waiting for results from a hunter program I've got running to see if I can find anything else registered by Mr. Peter Snyder. One of the prosecutors wanted to check in, too."

Vega arrived back at headquarters, heading straight to her office. Weir had asked her to look into what was happening with the Secret Service and the Capitol Police. He found the silent treatment the Bureau was getting disquieting, and he hoped she could work some back channels to get information about what was going on.

Guthrie knocked as she was sitting down at her desk. "Here's the write-up on the chase. We hunted Reed all across town, but always five or ten minutes behind." He shook his head sadly.

Vega took the files and laid them next to her keyboard. "Good, good," she said absently as she typed in her computer password. "The Peter Reed connection was key. That's great work."

"Thanks," said Guthrie. "Davies'll be by in a minute with that file."

Vega froze. "Davies is here?"

"Yeah, just down the hall." He pointed in the general direction of the office he and Davies shared.

"Who's shadowing Imogen?" she asked.

"She's at the detention center, isn't she?"

"No. She left almost an hour ago," said Vega. "Get Davies now," she said. A moment later, he appeared. "Get in the car," she ordered. "Start for Arlington. I'll call to confirm where she is and let you know. Go!"

Imogen sighed contentedly, just that little bit more at ease as she turned on to her street, North Filmore, a warm smile on her face. It was funny, she thought, to feel such relief about returning to a place she had never much liked, one she had chosen in haste years earlier and repented—when she had leisure to do so—ever since. Not this time. As she turned down the empty, narrow street the feeling of reprieve was real; the affection for the bland, sober brick façade genuine. She was looking forward to a shower, to her own bed. She couldn't wait to see Duncan tomorrow!

Had she been less engaged in her own thoughts she might have noticed someone sitting in the passenger seat of a car parked next to the driveway leading to the building's underground garage. Frank Reed sat low in the seat, twisted slightly so he could keep both the rearview and wing mirrors in view. A pistol sat on his lap, a small, deadly Smith & Wesson Shield, hidden under the front section of that day's Washington Times. When he spied Imogen's car turn onto the street, he confirmed it was her, checked forward that the street was clear, checked both mirrors again, and waited for her to drive past.

He'd been contemplating this murder for weeks during his stakeouts, entertaining himself through the tedium with various scenarios of how he would do it. This was the best option: he knew from watching other cars enter that she would have to wait at least 15 seconds for the garage door to rise enough for her to drive in. More time than he'd need. She'd be a sitting duck, stopped, waiting for the door to rise, the nose of her car angled steeply downward. A brick fence pillar at the side of the driveway would hide his approach. If he was careful, the pillar would also hide him from the security camera situated directly above the garage door. He smiled. The car was drawing nearer.

As she came near the driveway, Imogen leaned over and turned the latch on the glove box. It fell open hard with the weight of the pistol Amanda had made her take along. She pushed the butt of the gun out of the way in order to grab the garage door control. At that moment, the phone, sitting beside her on the passenger seat rang. She could see it was Amanda, but she couldn't pick up—one hand was on the wheel, about to turn, the other held the garage door control.

As she drove past Reed's car, about to turn into the driveway, she pressed "open" on the control, the phone still clamoring for attention. Reed threw his door open, crouched behind it for a brief moment, then rushed to the pillar as Imogen's car came to a stop in the driveway three feet from the slowly rising door. She tossed the remote back into the glove box. She was still leaning over the passenger seat reaching to answer the phone when Reed fired.

Her passenger window exploded. Glass flew everywhere. Reed fired again. The driver's window erupted.

Reed expected his first shot would only break her window. He had been counting on a second rapid shot to hit her. Then he would move closer and finish the job.

Inside the car, time seemed to stretch and stop. Her ears rang, her breath wouldn't come, her mouth tasted of iron. Imogen's only thought was: "it's happening again."

From his long planning, Reed knew everything that would happen, everything to expect. He knew that even if the second bullet hadn't hit her, she would be pinned down. As he moved closer, he expected shots three, four and five would do it.

Then, something he hadn't expected to happen: in the confusion, Imogen's foot came off the break and the car rolled forward three feet and rammed into the rising garage door, stopping its progress. Reed would be forced to move into an open position where the security camera could record him.

As he stepped quickly over the broken safety glass and down the driveway to get a clean shot, taking care not to lose his footing, a second unexpected thing happened: Imogen was armed.

As she lay across the passenger seat, her hand quickly closed around the gun. She heard his quick steps draw closer, saw the gun come into view through the shattered passenger window—and she fired. Reed recoiled, firing wildly. She fired again, this time through her back passenger window, covering Reed in glass. As it cleared, Imogen fired again, catching him in the bicep. He twisted with the force of the bullet and fell onto the glass strewn driveway. "Fucking *bitch*!" he roared as he hoisted himself up to a crouching position.

Imogen rose slightly and tried to sight him between the seatbacks. She reached across her body with her left hand and unhooked her seat belt. She heard him slipping in the broken glass as he moved up the steep incline of the driveway. Also: distant, but distinct, she heard police sirens.

She twisted in her seat, trying to figure out exactly where he was hiding. She was still trying to hear where he was when he stood fully up and fired three rapid shots through the rear window. With each shot, he took a step back, and by the time she was able to return fire he was at his car. As the car sped past, and Imogen got ready to open her door to shoot, he fired again through his open passenger window. And then he was gone.

Imogen sat for moment, drinking in the relative silence. Slowly, the normal world came back to her. She noticed for the first time that her bumper was caught on the garage door, trapping it in a four-inch cycle of closing, attempting to open and closing again. The sirens were drawing nearer. She opened the car door, scattering more glass on the ground and stood up. She trudged up the driveway, and before she sat down on a low part of the retaining wall she inspected herself dispassionately for wounds. Eleven shots exchanged at close range, and only one—hers—had found its mark.

The sirens drew closer. Seeing no more immediate danger, she placed the gun beside her. The police would probably insist upon her putting it down anyway.

Davies arrived some five minutes later, the frenzy of his dash across town giving way to slow rolling terror as he rounded the corner to Imogen's street and saw the mass of squad cars in the middle of the street, their lights flashing. He pulled over, jumped out of the truck, and began running towards the police line, holding his credentials in front of him. A patrolman raised a strip of yellow tape hanging across the road and waved him through. Davies sprinted for the next half block down the narrow street, coming to a full stop as he saw Imogen with a group of policemen. She was resting on the hood of a squad car, nodding at something the lead investigator was saying and picking bits of glass out of her thick red hair.

She was scuffed and disheveled but whole. Davies let out a deep sigh. At that moment, she looked away from the policeman she was talking with, saw him, and smiled. Davies smiled back weakly and started toward her.

"Thank God, you're all right," he said as he walked up to her.

Imogen gave a deep sigh of her own, like someone who's just run a great distance.

"That's two lives saved," he observed: "Yours. And mine. Though Hurricane Amanda may still do me in. I'm very sorry. I was supposed to be shadowing you. I thought you were still at the detention cells."

"It was Reed," she said. "I hit him with one, but I don't think he's badly wounded."

Vega arrived twenty minutes later, just as the car was being hoisted onto a flatbed and towed away. She stood trancelike in the road as it rolled past her, the windows still dropping shards of glass. Her gaze turned to Davies, who bravely walked toward her.

As he drew near and was about to speak, Amanda held up her hand. "I'll take Trager's report," she said, her dark eyes suddenly blazing. "You will go back to headquarters and write this whole thing up. You and I and Weir will discuss it all tomorrow morning. First thing." She walked away from him toward Imogen. Davies' execution not been stayed, but only postponed.

For her own safety, Imogen spent the night in the spare bedroom of Amanda's mother's small, post-war cottage in Takoma Park, a cheery pistachio-colored box with the winter remains of a rambling but well-tended front garden, set amidst staid, ascetic Craftsman homes and gaudy, out of scale suburban contemporaries. Mrs. Vega was gracious and seemed genuinely pleased to be cooking for more than just two.

Her small, wiry frame moved about the kitchen with energy and purpose. The house filled with lively, enticing aromas as she stirred and fried and tasted—all the while calling instructions to Amanda from the kitchen: "Mija, she should sit in the nice chair," and "Mija, get the table cloth from the drawer." Vega complied with each request, but she had the look of someone who feels she has made a grave error of judgment. Twice, she stepped outside onto the front slab to make a phone call.

For her part, Imogen was experiencing a kind of whiplash. Less than two hours earlier, she was hunted prey, pinned down in her car being shot at. She remembered shutting her eyes as glass exploded and rained down on her. She had mastered her fear in order to return fire; had listened intently for clues as to what would happen next.

It had all happened, it was real. Though she remembered it, she had no recollection of how it felt, only the silent, sickening, empty aftermath. And now dinner. Poised between abject fear and the warmly affecting normal wholesomeness of the Vegas' home, she felt weightless, like plunging over the hump on a rollercoaster, waiting terrifyingly for gravity to take her in again.

"Amanda," she said as Vega walked in from making a call, "are you two safe with me here?"

"We're all safe," said Amanda, gently. She sat down next to Imogen in the nice chair and laid a comforting hand on her arm. "I've got agents watching the house, and we weren't tailed here. I don't see him making a move. His trying to take you out was clearly not what his bosses wanted him to do. The wiretap has them telling him to roll it all up."

"Still," she said, "the thought of you—your mother . . ." She stared intently at the front window, expecting it to shatter in a blaze of bullets at any moment. Her breath came short.

Amanda patted her arm. "Think of your strength," she said. "I've been in two gun battles. The first time, I'd only

241

been on the job for a year or so: I was pinned down and I froze. It took me a full four or five seconds to find it in me to fire back."

Imogen stared at her blankly.

"But you," Amanda continued, "you didn't hesitate at all. A trained fucking hood fires seven or eight shots at you. And stuck inside your car you shoot back and hit him. Wing him at least. You're no shrinking wonk violet." She leaned in close, peering intently at Imogen. She reached out and plucked a bit of glass from a wisp of hair just above her ear. "After dinner, you're gonna want a shower, I think. Are you still planning to go to the hospital to see Calder and Pollack?"

"Yes," said Imogen.

Vega nodded. "I've talked with Weir. On Monday, you're going to have to meet with the shooting inquiry people. There'll be an FBIAA rep there with you. You'll also have to make an appointment with the shrink. It's all standard, nothing to worry about. Davies is going to bring a car around tomorrow morning. He can walk back to headquarters after that for all I care."

Next morning, Imogen rose when she heard Mrs. Vega in the kitchen. She had slept well—better than she had expected given how strange she felt. She ate ravenously—eggs, beans, rice and some leftover chicken—under the approving eye of Mrs. Vega. Amanda, for her part, ate daintily, a bit of coffee and some plain yogurt.

Now, she was anxious to get to the hospital in Fort Belvoir to see Duncan. She brushed out her hair and pulled it back in a single braid. She packed her clothes away and thanked Amanda and Mrs. Vega for taking her in. She hugged them both warmly.

As she drove south, putting distance between her and Washington, she also felt herself putting the events of the previous day behind her as she looked forward to seeing Duncan. She mused that it was almost exactly a month since she had sat at Dulles Airport waiting for Duncan's flight to arrive. A little month—yet it had been a different life, before

242

Faithless Electors were anything more than an arcane political science topic, before vote-rigging, plots and conspirators and murders. Sitting at Dulles that day, waiting behind a line of taxis, her coffee going cold, she had been forced to confess to herself that she had arrived early not because she had misread her watch, but because she was eager to see him.

Driving now, she realized she was eager again; once again she would be early and she would probably have to wait to be admitted; but this time, her quiet thrill didn't feel unseemly. What they had been through together—privately and publicly—was a bond they both felt: strong, true, and anything but ridiculous. The thrilling, prickly mix of anticipation and apprehension drove her on. She found herself pressing the accelerator ever closer to the floor. She sailed through the sparse, early morning Martin Luther King Day traffic, as the suburbs gave way to woods along the Richmond highway.

She arrived at the Army gate 25 minutes early.

The guard let her through, but the nurse at the visitor information desk told her she would have to wait for someone to come down and escort her up to the secure floor. The atrium lobby was empty except for herself and the nurse at the desk, who sat filling in forms that would later be keyed into a computer so that algorithms could turn them into officious letters. Imogen perched on the waiting room couch, scanning the open upper floors of the atrium every half a minute for anyone who might be her escort. She was relieved when a crisp army nurse walked out and asked Imogen to follow her, please.

It was a long walk through three separate security-controlled areas before they reached Duncan and Pollack's wing. The nurse stopped. "He's in the room at the end," she said. "Last door on your left. When you're ready to leave, let the duty nurse know, and someone will conduct you back. Have a good visit, ma'am." She turned and walked away, leaving Imogen momentarily unsure whether to salute.

She saw Duncan before he noticed her, through a window into his room. He sat at a table by the window, poring over his Washington Post, a small plastic coffee cup in hand. She paused at the open door and looked at him. He was a little paler, a little thinner. The scars and bruises on his face had largely healed. She wanted to run over to him, but sudden misgivings about what their time together really had meant made her hesitate.

Duncan looked up and smiled, full and bright. His "Imogen!" dispelled all doubts. He put down the cup, let fall the corner of the paper he was holding. He stood, now self-conscious in his hospital robe, smoothing away unseen wrinkles in the fabric as she walked in.

Just as she was about to close her arms across his back, he stiffened.

"Careful," he said with a tight, apologetic smile.

She folded her arms across his back, feeling bandages everywhere beneath his clothes. He pressed her tightly to him and kissed her. "My God, you're more beautiful than I remembered." She kissed him again, conscious of blushing happily.

"How are you?" he asked finally.

"How am I?" she asked with amusement. Had he heard about the gun battle? If he hadn't, she would leave it for later. "I'm fine." She paused, stroked his salt-and-pepper hair. "I spent three horrible days thinking you were dead. They wouldn't tell me anything. When they finally did, they wouldn't let me see you or call you. I kept asking how long, and the answer was always 'We'll see'."

He laughed in recognition. "I'm sorry. Sounds like you had trouble enough, though."

"Yes," she admitted. "But it may all have been worth it: we've got most of the bastards—or we hope so—and it looks like we're going to be able to get them to roll on their superiors."

"Fantastic," said Calder.

"Maybe I should've been a professor," said a voice from behind her. "I mean if this is how former grad students greet you."

She twisted, still in Duncan's arms, and looked toward the voice. Doug Pollack sat in his wheelchair, smiling but looking

244

very much like someone who had barely escaped death. He had glimpsed her red hair as she walked by his room, and had felt a surprised delight, as if spying a cardinal in the garden in the dead of winter.

Imogen leaned down and hugged Doug too. "Oh, Sharon's going to be so jealous of me," she said.

"I didn't mean to interrupt," said Pollack. "I—"

Imogen hugged him tighter. He smiled warmly.

The duty nurse appeared in the doorway. "Excuse me," she said, "Assistant Director Weir just called. He said you might like to see the House vote. It looks like it's going to happen." They moved quickly to the television room, Calder pushing Pollack's chair.

As the screen flickered on, a stunned anchor was summing up: ". . . really unprecedented," he was saying, "as, in fact, have been a great many of the events surrounding this election. You can see behind me that Congress will soon come to order in a joint session. Senators and representatives are still taking their places.

"This is to be the House vote for president. The Senate has already met and fulfilled its role in the contingent election, having decided upon Bob Moore as the vice-president elect. The senators have no vote this time. It may be that this full session has been convened to solemnize this final vote."

"We're hearing," said her co-host "that beyond the vote, there may be some further announcement. There has been a flurry of activity among the Secret Service and the Capitol Police, but there has been no official—or unofficial— statement about what's happening. Like our viewers, we can only speculate on what this all means."

The anchor and her co-host were about to begin their speculation when the Speaker of the House rose and gaveled the joint session to order.

"We are gathered here for the contingent election of the president of the United States. We are here to vote state by state, with each state having one vote. There has not been such a vote since the election of 1824." The Speaker paused to let that sink in. "Nearly 200 years ago. And such a vote has occurred only twice before in the history of this nation.

"There being few precedents, we have, by a vote of this House, and in a departure from our usual proceedings, asked our distinguished Senate colleagues to join us on this historic occasion. Senators, I thank you," he said, nodding toward them. "Before calling the roll of the states, I would like to recognize David Carr, of the Commonwealth of Pennsylvania, speaking as the Keystone State delegate."

"David Carr, Republican of Pennsylvania," the anchor intoned, practically whispering. "I don't believe he's even the majority leader in his own state. This is indeed unprecedented."

David Carr rose. "Thank you, Mr. Speaker," he began. "Mr. Speaker, I bring news to this House of a grave threat to its integrity. Six of my esteemed House colleagues here—as well as myself—have been threatened. Our families have been threatened as part of a covert, illegal effort to install James Christopher as president. I would ask that those six members please rise."

There was a gasp and rumble in the gallery as the six members rose. All were Republicans—from Ohio, Florida, Virginia, North Carolina, Michigan and Wisconsin. "We seven", Carr was saying, "and there may be others . . ." The Speaker gaveled for silence.

"Mr. Speaker, we seven members have met with our respective caucuses, with yourself, and with the Capitol Police, delivering evidence. That evidence has been shared with my Congressional colleagues. We seven stand here now before you and the House. We shall not be coerced. We shall not be threatened. We stand in defense of our democracy and the sanctity of this House." There was a smattering of applause that quickly began to grow.

Pacifying motions from the Speaker calmed the House, and Carr continued: "We stand in the face of threats. We stand in defiance of those who would undermine and twist our laws to their own illegal ends. Risking the lives of ourselves and our families, we stand." More applause and acclamation for the

Congressmen and women who had pushed back against the coercion.

"Mr. Speaker, for the ultimate sacrifice of seven others—seven dead Electors—murdered as part of what has become known as the Faithless Elector plot: we stand!"

At this, every representative and senator also stood, their clapping and cheering almost drowning out Carr's final words: "We stand that their sacrifices will not be forgotten or made in vain."

Imogen, Calder and Pollack sat in the sterile television room at the hospital, struck dumb.

The cheering in the House continued for some minutes. Finally, the Speaker gaveled for order. "Mr. Speaker," Carr continued in a quieter, somber tone, "we will not allow this abuse to stand." The Congress rose again to its feet, cheering.

When the applause had died down and the other members had taken their seats, Carr, still standing, concluded by saying, "Thank you, Mr. Speaker for the opportunity to present this information to the House," and took his seat.

"Thank you, Congressman Carr for your remarks. I have been in further contact with the Sergeant-at-Arms, and I can state that the Capitol Police, working through the Office of the President and the Secret Service have now assured me that all members and their families are currently safe and protected, and that the investigation leading to arrests is also under way. I now recognize the majority leader."

In Fort Belvoir, Duncan Calder, staring at the screen whispered "Holy shit."

"Secret Service?" said Pollack.

The House Republican majority leader rose. "I have been in communication with James Christopher earlier today in light of these allegations and evidence. He has authorized me to tell this assembly that if he had become president and found that any crime such as this plot had been done in his name, he would have resigned his office immediately."

There were rumblings again from the gallery, but not a sound from the senators and congressmen, who sat in resolute silence.

"I must stress," the majority leader went on, "that Governor Christopher had no knowledge of this plot. There is no evidence that he is in any way involved or implicated in it. He has stated that under the circumstances, with such information coming to light now, he would withdraw his name from further consideration in this assembly."

The gallery above erupted again, and it took two minutes for the Speaker to restore order. "At this stage," the majority leader added, "I have been advised by counsel, however, that he may not withdraw his name; and we must still vote. I yield to the minority leader."

"Thank you, Mr. Speaker. There is nothing now more important than proceeding with the vote."

The Speaker began: "I could begin by calling the roll, state by state and have it recorded, but before I do so, the House majority leader has asked for the opportunity to speak further."

"Thank you, Mr. Speaker," he began, "I have caucused my delegation, and I move that instead of calling the roll state by state, this vote be conducted by acclamation of unanimous consent."

The minority leader rose and was recognized. "I second the motion," he said.

The Speaker stood at the dais, looking out over the assembly. "Having heard the motion, and second, the motion before us is that Diane Redmond be selected by the House by acclamation as president elect of the United States of America. Is there any state or member of the House who objects to the procedure?" There was not a sound, not even in the gallery.

The Speaker began: "Hearing no objection, I will proceed directly to a vote by voice. What say you all?"

"Aye!" erupted as a chorus across the House of Representatives.

"Nays?" asked the Speaker.

Again, not a sound was uttered.

"Hearing all ayes and no nays, I declare that the House, exercising its proper constitutional responsibility, declares Diane Redmond president-elect for the United States!"

Once again, congress rose to its feet, as did members of the gallery, all cheering wildly. The Speaker called for order, and although the tumult had only slightly subsided, he called from the dais: "Sergeant-at-Arms, please open the main doors!"

The doors swung wide open.

"Members of Congress," the Speaker called, "people of the United States: we welcome the President-elect Diane Redmond, and the Vice-president-elect Robert Moore of the United States!"

Diane Redmond and Robert Moore walked in to more thunderous applause and deafening cheers. It took some minutes for them to make their way along the aisle as they stopped to shake hands or to embrace various House members. At the dais, they each shook the Speaker's hand. The Speaker stood to one side as Redmond and Moore turned to face the applause. They stood side-by-side, joined hands and raised them as the cheering grew louder.

"My God," said Imogen, watching it all on television.

"Secret service?" said Pollack again. "Well, that's a kick in the nuts for the FBI."

*   *   *

Less than an hour later, and seven miles due north of the capitol, in Silver Spring, Maryland, Frank Reed, his bandaged arm partially immobilized in a makeshift sling, asked the ticket agent how long his return bus ticket was good for.

"Six months," she said, and looked past him to the next person in line.

"Perfect," Reed said and walked out to a bus bound for Cincinnati, his first of many stops.

At the detention center, prosecutors were working on Alec Nash.

"We're the only friends you've got," said one of the prosecutors. "Your guy lost today. He left in disgrace."

"Did he?" asked Nash coyly.

"Talk to your client, counselor," said the lead prosecutor. "All his work was for nothing, and the guys who were calling the shots are walking away free. He's facing life in a federal penitentiary without possibility of parole. We can make it multiple life sentences. We have your whole network, Alec, and they're cooperating. If you don't cooperate, you're going down a hole. No one'll ever hear from you or see you again."

Nash's attorney leaned forward, his expression one of bland bewildered astonishment. He was about to speak when Nash held up a hand.

"My attorney was about to say, Fuck You!" said Nash.

* * *

That evening, Don Weir came to the hospital in expansive mood. He found Imogen, Calder and Pollack in good spirits, despite the antiseptic surroundings and a melancholy gray dinner in a segregated plastic tray.

"This is one for the history books!" he said cheerfully. He clapped Imogen on the shoulder as he shook her hand. "Professor, it all started with you."

"And Matthew," said Calder, awkwardly offering his left hand.

Weir pulled a bottle of champagne from deep inside his coat. He grinned mischievously at the unlikely celebratory group.

"And we've seen it through," Weir continued. He went into the bathroom and grabbed two plastic cups. "I was talking to Amanda Vega just a little while ago," he said, peeling the foil from the neck of the bottle. "She said that as hard and dark as this has all been, she thinks it'll make the Bureau stronger; that we'll be better for it."

"I think she's right," said Imogen.

"Definitely," Weir agreed, twisting the cork.

"Where are we now?" Pollack asked Weir.

"We began the depositions on the crooked election judges in Illinois yesterday, and they'll be arraigned tomorrow," said Weir as the cork popped out of the bottle. He began hurriedly pouring into the available cups. "We're arraigning Deptford, Kimball and Carpenter," he said as the champagne overflowed the shallow cups and gushed across the food trays. "Nash doesn't want to cooperate—so far—but I think once he sees what he's up against, he'll come around."

"Absolutely not!" declared a voice from the doorway. It was the night nurse.

Weir looked at her innocently, as though wondering what she could be talking about.

"These two patients are on serious pain-killers. They may not have alcohol." She stepped forward, extending a hand for the glasses and bottle.

Pollack was enjoying the scene.

She picked up the cups, and reached for the bottle. Weir held fast to it. "Fine," he said drawing it to his chest protectively, "just me and Imogen, then." There was a challenging look in his eyes.

The nurse stared back. After a moment, she drew a deep breath, looked at the two cups in her hand and withdrew. Weir winked at Pollack, who smiled and shook his head.

"I'm still trying to see a way forward to arrest Senator Eliot, but we may not win that one," said Weir, as he poured some of the champagne. He glanced over his shoulder for the nurse, and, seeing that she was engaged elsewhere handed Pollack a small cup.

Pollack nodded as he took it. "I suppose you could at least ask the senator some awkward, public questions about what he did and didn't know, couldn't you?"

Weir grinned. "That'd be fun," he admitted. "I'll leave it with the AG, though. Let her figure how best to do all that."

Imogen raised her little cup in salute, and drank it off. "And Reed?" she asked.

"Nothing," Weir said to her. "We'll get him, though. Your work—and Kelly's—broke this wide open, and now we know one of the aliases he's using. Your analysis made all the difference."

Imogen smiled, accepting the compliment.

"I guess we know what Option Three was now," he said, refilling her cup and gesturing for her to give it to Calder:

"blackmail and worse. And they failed," said Weir drawing up a chair to sit at the table with them.

"It'll never work," said Calder, taking a tiny sip.

"What do you mean?" asked Weir, looking at Calder, his expression a mixture of defiance and wounded pride.

"Like the VP and president being from different parties, you mean?" asked Pollack.

"Yeah," said Calder. "That, too." He took another micro sip from the cup and laid a hand absently on Imogen's arm. "We'll see."

"This is all good news!" Weir exclaimed trying to rekindle the triumphant mood. "We did it. We succeeded. We have a president to inaugurate . . . and the conspirators really are on the run now. We put this in the win column for the Bureau after we took a huge beating. There's a ton of work still to be done—sure—but essentially it's over!" He beamed at the table.

Imogen sat back in her chair just to the right of Weir, taking it all in. Pollack looked relieved, and content. Weir appeared lavishly happy. Calder smiled primly, despite himself, loathe to dilute the feeling.

Imogen rose and leaned in to Calder, kissing him. He embraced her gingerly, and as he did so, she whispered in his ear: "The hell it is."

REVIEWS are the lifeblood of authors and books. Consider letting James and others know what you think, on Amazon and/or Goodreads

James McCrone graduated in 1990 from the University of Washington in Seattle with a Master of Fine Arts in Creative Writing.

He lives in Philadelphia with his wife and family. Look for more in **the Imogen Trager series**, including *Consent of the Governed*, coming next!

If you'd like to keep up with James, you can follow him on Facebook and on Twitter '@jamesmccrone4'

FIVE STARS for *Faithless Elector*! the first book in the **Imogen Trager series**

You can find *Faithless Elector* on Amazon, at Barnes & Noble and your local independent bookstore. Watch for *Consent of the Governed*, coming next!

"A gripping and intelligently executed political drama."
-Kirkus Reviews

Publishers Weekly calls *Faithless Elector* "A fast-moving topical thriller." Its "surprising twists add up to a highly suspenseful read."

"The pleasure of *Faithless Elector* lies not just its smooth evocative prose, but in the author's justified confidence that good writing can make chases through recognizable locales sufficiently exciting without a Navy SEAL or a terrorist plot."
-Lauren Kiefer, **Plattsburgh Press-Republican**

Book Viral calls *Faithless Elector* "taut and well-paced, but for readers reading between the lines it also works on a moral level."

"Be prepared to read this book in a very short period of time—it's that intriguing There are mysterious deaths, romance, and a plot that will have you wondering who done it right up until the end...and maybe afterwards." Florence Osmund (author/reviewer)

"I could hardly put it down. The characters in this book were strong and believable...particularly Imogen Trager...The descriptions and imagery were fantastic. It reminded me so much of Tom Clancy's Jack Ryan novels... MarchaCox (author/reviewer)

CPSIA information can be obtained
at www.ICGtesting.com
Printed in the USA
LVHW01s1028181117
556805LV00011B/670/P